Praise for *Five Midnights*

"*Five Midnights* combines Puert... thrilling mystery. The members... trying to solve this one as they re..."
—*Bustle*

"You're in for a suspenseful ride through some very thrilling Puerto Rican lore." —*Locus*

"I looooove . . . Characters are indeed sassy AF and the narrator gets their attitudes, accents, and inflections so, so right." —*Book Riot*

"A thrilling spin on legendary source material as well as a study in identity, community, and connection. A story that lingers in sinister shadows." —*Kirkus Reviews*

"Wickedly thrilling." —William Alexander, *New York Times* bestselling author of *Goblin Secrets*

"Flat-out unputdownable." —Paul Tremblay, author of *The Cabin at the End of the World*

"Lupe and Javier are characters I rooted for, at every dark twist and chilling turn." —Julianna Baggott, Alex Award–winning author of *Pure*

BOOKS BY ANN DÁVILA CARDINAL

Five Midnights
Category Five

Five Midnights

Ann Dávila Cardinal

TOR TEEN

A TOM DOHERTY ASSOCIATES BOOK
New York

FIVE MIDNIGHTS

Copyright © 2019 by Ann Dávila Cardinal

A Tor Teen Book
Published by Tom Doherty Associates
120 Broadway
New York, NY 10271

www.tor-forge.com

Tor® is a registered trademark of Macmillan Publishing Group, LLC.

The Library of Congress has cataloged the hardcover edition as follows:

Cardinal, Ann Dávila, author.
   Five midnights / Ann Dávila Cardinal.—First edition.
      p. cm.
   "A Tom Doherty Associates book."
   ISBN 978-1-250-29607-8 (hardcover)
   ISBN 978-1-250-29608-5 (ebook)
   1. Teenagers—Crimes against—Juvenile fiction. 2. Murder—
Investigation—Juvenile fiction. 3. Monsters—Juvenile fiction.
4. Blessing and cursing—Juvenile fiction. 5. Mystery and
detective stories. I. Title.
   PZ7.1.C3903 Fi 2019
   [Fic]—dc23

                                                2019285380

ISBN 978-1-250-29609-2 (trade paperback)

Our books may be purchased in bulk for promotional, educational,
or business use. Please contact your local bookseller or the Macmillan
Corporate and Premium Sales Department at 1-800-221-7945, extension
5442, or by email at MacmillanSpecialMarkets@macmillan.com.

First Edition: June 2019
First Trade Paperback Edition: June 2020

Printed in the United States of America

0 9 8 7 6 5 4 3

For my real tío,
Stephen Dávila Altieri,
who has always made me feel protected
from monsters real and imagined

Five Midnights

July 4, 11:30 P.M.

Vico

💀

VICO WOKE UP with a start, his body bathed in sweat, his heart beating faster than it did when he was high. While he slept the darkness had returned, a feeling that had followed him like a shadow for years, disappearing whenever he whipped around to see what was there. He pulled on a shirt and his shoes, grabbed the backpack from under his bed, and headed out into the night.

A chill moved through his body as he drove down the dark, narrow cobblestone streets of Old San Juan, his SUV barely squeezing by the parked cars that lined either side. He looked over at the backpack in the passenger seat. To all appearances it was a worthless, beat-up school pack. No one would guess the fortune of cocaína it held inside. He patted it as if it were a dog. He had to clear his head. This deal was too important to blow. He drove up Calle Norzagaray, the street that ran along the edges of El Rubí, the barrio where the deal would go down. His car buzzed by the restored Spanish villas on the left, where wealthy young families tucked their children into bed, their homes snuggled among the sixteenth-century fortifications that surrounded the island's tip. On the right-hand side, over the waist-high wall, and down a fifty-foot drop lay El Rubí, where children went to bed with hand-me-down clothes and short futures.

He parked his car a few blocks away from the wall, his electronic lock beeping farewell at his back. His ride was too good to park close to El Rubí. He'd worked hard to build up his reputation *and* his bank account. He was the youngest player in the city, bought his first Cadillac Escalade at sixteen, his own condo in the Condado at seventeen. Now, on the eve of his eighteenth birthday, he was about to make the biggest deal of his life. His lieutenant, Keno, should have been with him, but at the last minute he got a call from Vico's sister, Marisol, Keno's on-and-off girlfriend, and backed out. Vico chuckled. Cabrón let himself be led around by his nose like a castrated bull.

He slung the backpack on one shoulder and lit a cigarette in front of the pink house that stood across from the entrance to El Rubí. The moon was rising high over the surf beyond El Morro as he crossed the street, the inky sky pushing it up over the buildings behind him. The dark night made it hard to see the crumbling stone steps, but he could've run them blindfolded. Vico had been going to El Rubí his whole life, since when he was little to visit his grandmother, but after he turned thirteen, to buy drogas with his friend Izzy, and now to sell them. Pana had to earn a living in the tanking economy.

He loved the way the decaying cement and wooden shacks were painted in bright colors. And the smell: salty ocean with notes of frying plantain, beer, garbage, and urine. Life. To him El Rubí was teeming with it, unlike his old neighborhood, where families stayed locked up in their gated homes, pretending everything was fine. Pretending fathers weren't laid off, mothers didn't die, and kids came right home to do their homework. In El Rubí everything was out in the open: fights, love, drugs . . . no worries about what the neighbors might think.

By the time he reached the bottom step, the moon was completely cut off by the buildings above, the only light the warm glow of his cigarette floating in front of him in the dark, and from the shadow under the stairs came a scraping sound. He turned around and peered through the dark. Nothing. He shrugged and threw what was left of his cigarette on the ground. *I'm just jumpy,* he assured himself. *Half a mil riding on this deal. That'd make any pana nervous, verdad?* He chuckled and turned back. With the money from this score he was going to throw one hell of an eighteenth birthday party tomorrow. Just then he heard a rumbling sound and a stone flew past his foot as if kicked. His chest filled with heat, his hand automatically reached in his pocket, the yellow skulls on his switchblade glowing even in the dark.

"¿Quién está ahí? Show yourself, pendejo, and maybe I won't cut your heart from your chest!" Vico's voice sounded more secure than he felt. Damn Keno! He should be here. Not that he couldn't handle himself, he'd proven that again and again, but there was something about the sound that made the hair on the back of his neck stand up. He squinted into the dark and saw the glow of two yellow eyes. Vico stumbled backward, his pulse pounding behind his face. But just as quick they were gone. He shuddered. He must have imagined them. They'd been so strange and yet . . . familiar. He forced himself to turn around and continue walking, blade out just in case.

He hadn't taken more than a step when a growl came from behind him. He wheeled around as a street dog with one ear and matted fur streaked out from the shadow beneath the stairs and took off down a side street, tail between his legs, ears pinned to his head. He let out a deep breath and chuckled. "A stupid sato. Scared of a mutt, ay Vico? I need a vacation, man," he said as he folded his blade closed and tucked it away. He grabbed another cigarette from his shirt pocket. Maybe he *would* take a vacation after this. Head to Miami for a few weeks, lay low.

His lighter flared to life just before something big hit him like a linebacker from behind, knocking the air from his lungs. The backpack with all those neatly wrapped bricks of white powder slipped from his shoulder. He tried to reach for it but he was pinned upright. His left hand held the still flaming lighter, and he ran his right over his chest. When he pulled it away it felt sticky, wet. He looked down and, in the glow of the flame, he saw red on his palm and watched his shirt grow dark. Another shove hit him from the back. A long serrated claw emerged from his chest, as if it had pushed through from his nightmare. He was numb, his eyes wide, his mouth open in a silent scream as he realized his feet were leaving the ground, his sneakers dangling as he hung as if mounted on the claw. The lights of El Rubí faded as he was dragged backward. Ludovico tried to scream as he heard the sound of jaws snapping behind him. Then everything went dark.

July 6, 12:50 P.M.

Lupe

💀

"BUT TÍO, I can take a cab. I'll go straight to your place, promise." First her father had waited until they were at the airport to tell her he wasn't going with her on their annual trip to Puerto Rico to see *his* family, and now that she'd landed, her uncle was suggesting further humiliation.

"Absolutamente no. I'm sending a squad car. It's not safe for a young woman to travel around the city by herself."

Lupe harrumphed. He'd made up his mind, so there was no arguing with him. The man hadn't become police chief by being a pushover. "Fine." She hit End and waited for the other passengers to move so she could exit the plane. At least without her father along she didn't need to hide a dozen tiny empty Bacardi bottles that he'd scatter around their seats like insect husks.

The clunk of her Doc Martens echoed in the airport's linoleum-lined artery, suitcase rolling obediently behind. She'd never come to Puerto Rico without her father, never walked to baggage claim without struggling to keep up with his long impatient stride. She smiled. This was her first trip *as an adult.* Okay, so sixteen wasn't adult, but she was off leash. She swallowed down a momentary feeling of panic as strangers rushed by her on either side. It wasn't like she was in a totally new place. She took a deep breath and felt the press of familiar ground against her feet. It was a teeter-totter feeling of familiarity and not belonging. But she was used to that. Lupe held her head a little straighter, walked a little taller.

She could handle this.

When she pushed open the glass doors to the loading area, the hot, humid air hit her. Year after year, she was shocked when she walked into the heat from the air-conditioned airport. Particularly compared to the still cool, early July morning breezes back in Vermont, the sultry temperatures held trouble in the moist air.

Waiting in the cabs-only section of the pick-up zone was a police officer in full midnight blue, handgun on his hip, dark sunglasses hiding his eyes, holding a sign that read SEÑORITA LUPE DÁVILA.

Oh. Right.

Lupe ducked her head. She considered walking by the policeman and calling Uber on her father's dime. Her father had given her the keys to her uncle's house; she could just let herself in. Yeah, it'd be rude and her uncle would be pissed but, as her father liked to say, it's easier to ask for forgiveness than permission. Instead she pulled on her own sunglasses, walked up to him, and whispered, "I'm Lupe Dávila."

"Bienvenidos, Señorita Dávila. I'm Officer Ramirez," he said in a way-too-loud voice. She followed him to the double-parked cruiser and felt the heat of stares from the other travelers.

So much for being off leash.

After popping the squad car's trunk, Ramirez tried to wrestle her suitcase from her.

She swung it into the carpeted trunk. "I'm pretty used to taking care of myself." He looked almost dejected that she hadn't let him help her. "So, my uncle dragged you away from some important police work to chauffeur me around, huh?"

He slammed the trunk, the midday sun glinting off the shiny black paint. "Your tío asked me to bring you to his house. He can't get away and your aunt is in Humacao today. And I hear your father couldn't get away from work either."

Lupe snorted. "Yeah, that's what he told me, too." He stood holding open the door to the backseat, but Lupe edged around him, opened the front passenger door, and slid in. No way she was riding in the back like some kind of perp. Though it was probably against the rules, this experience was already humiliating enough. In the side-view mirror she watched him pause for a moment, then close the door and walk around the car with a defeated look. She smiled. Lupe often reduced adults to this look of defeat. But humiliation or not, she was glad she wasn't driving. She couldn't wait to use her newly minted driver's license at home, but driving on the island was another story: it was beyond aggressive. Her father liked to joke that this was where they trained New York City cab drivers.

As they made their way along Highway 26 she was struck as she always was by the billboards. They were illegal in Vermont, so she was unaccustomed to the barrage of colors and pithy messages. Thirty-foot-high women in tight dresses begged her to drink Medalla beer with open crimson lips; handsome unshaven men held minuscule cell phones to their story-high ears.

"So where's tío that he couldn't pick me up?"

"He's at a crime scene in El Rubí."

She perked up at this. "You mean the drug dealer who was eviscerated on the fifth?"

Ramirez looked at her with one substantial eyebrow raised.

"I mean, I saw it on *El Nuevo Dia* online."

He nodded. "Yes, a terrible thing." He made a quick sign of the cross, kissing his thumb at the end.

Lupe had always wanted to see her uncle on the job. *And* to visit her uncle on the job. Her father had shipped her off to the island, so why shouldn't she finally do what *she* wanted to do? She usually dreaded coming down and being dragged from relative's house to relative's house, heat and clouds of mosquitoes surrounding her like a gang. Maybe this trip she'd have a chance to see the real Puerto Rico. As she watched the bright green palm trees file by, she formulated a plan.

"Oh, no!" She put her hand to her mouth in faux surprise.

"What's the matter, Señorita Dávila?"

"Lupe. Call me Lupe, please. It's just . . . the keys to Tío Esteban's house, my father was supposed to give them to me this morning, but I guess he forgot." She put on a concerned face as she lay her palm over the outside pocket of her backpack as if he could see the keys hidden in its depths.

Ramirez grimaced. "Ay, we'll have to call your uncle then. I'm not sure what he would have me do." He pulled over to the highway's shoulder and put on the flashing lights.

She had to admit. She loved the lights.

He pushed a speed-dial button and Lupe could hear her uncle's booming voice on the other end, barking in rapid Spanish. Ramirez listened, nodding as if the chief could see him. "Bueno. Sí, jefe."

Lupe watched him tuck the phone away in his shirt pocket. "Well? What'd he say?"

Ramirez pulled back into traffic and flipped off the lights. "He wants me to bring you to the crime scene. Your aunt is two hours away."

It worked! Lupe had to restrain herself from pumping her fist in victory. She'd seen thousands of crime scenes on television, had talked to her uncle about them since she was twelve, and now she was going to a real one? Not your typical tourist attraction and that was perfect. If her father didn't like it, too bad. If he'd been with her this never would've happened.

"So, m'ija—"

Lupe loved the way adults addressed her on the island: *m'ija*, as if she were this hardened police officer's daughter as well. Considering her challenged luck in the parental lottery she'd take any decent parental-type figures she could get.

"—are you excited to be back in Puerto Rico?"

She shrugged. "I guess." She thought about the crime scene they were about to visit. "I mean, Vermont's pretty boring."

They chatted about the difference in weather, driving conditions, usual small talk, then Lupe decided to see if she could get some information about the case, especially since now she was going to the scene of the murder.

"So this murder, it's interesting, huh?"

The smile bled off of Ramirez's face. "Interesting, yes."

Lupe glanced at him out of the corner of her eye as he drove, his fingers tightening around the steering wheel. But he didn't say anything more. She was going to have to work a bit harder.

"Do you have any leads as to who the murderer is?"

"No," he said, and made the sign of the cross again.

Lupe watched him through narrowing eyes. All the signs of the cross, avoiding the conversation, even the news article was spotty . . . something was up with this murder, and she was going to find out what.

Seemed like the summer wasn't going to be a total loss after all.

They drove the rest of the way in silence, passing her favorite fort, San Cristóbal, then uphill along the sea wall. It wasn't hard to find the spot; dozens of emergency vehicles crowded the narrow street, the red and blue lights flashing against the sides of the buildings like some kind of goth disco. The colonial stone buildings ran the gamut from abandoned and graffiti-covered to pristine and elegantly appointed, all in one city block. Ramirez parked in front of a pink house from the latter category and they made their way to the steps down to El Rubí.

Lupe was beyond excited: she'd always wanted to visit El Rubí. The neighborhood was famous and infamous. She read about it, watched videos of raids online and music videos that were shot on the neighborhood's streets.

Until today Lupe thought she would have to be satisfied with viewing its color-wheel buildings and gritty streets from the safety of the battlements or on Google Earth, but here she was, walking down the crumbling staircase. She followed Officer Ramirez down the last few steps and her uncle came into view. He stood among broken glass and what looked like brown paint but must have been dried blood.

Lupe swallowed.

"Lupe! Over here, sobrina."

She thanked Officer Ramirez and made her way to her uncle, skirting the police tape and picking her way around milling uniforms.

Her uncle kissed her on the cheek and gave her one of his typical bear hugs. Esteban held her at arm's length and smiled into her face, his dark mustache accentuating his wide grin. "Ay, m'ija, you're getting so grown-up."

Lupe smiled back into her uncle's face. New gray streaks had appeared at his temples. It seemed like he'd aged five years in the year since she'd last seen him. "You look tired, tío." She didn't like seeing him so worn-out. He was the Dávila rock, the human equivalent of a building's foundation. Her father seriously depended on him.

He sighed. "We have spent thirty-six hours here trying to figure out what happened to this young man."

She looked around and compared the crime scene to the ones she'd seen on *DOA Newark*. But this wasn't a television show. These were no perfectly made-up pretty actors in tight pants and high heels. No rule-breaking female lead. The police officers' faces were ordinary and tired, washed gray above the blue of their uniforms and contrasting with the electric blue of the cloudless sky and the brightly painted buildings that surrounded them. And there was trash heaped up against the walls; the salt air was heavy with the smell of urine. It didn't bother her though. It felt even more real. It was on her skin, in her nostrils, not trapped in a flat screen. She rubbed her hands together. "What do you have already? I mean, clue-wise?"

Someone appeared at his left elbow and asked a question in rapid-fire Spanish, and Esteban answered with a raised finger that bought them a minute. "Phone conversations about my cases when you're tucked away safe in Vermont are one thing, but this?" He gestured around to the hive of activity that surrounded them. "I'm sorry you have to see this, Lupe. I shouldn't be surprised that your father forgot to give you the keys, but he always disappoints me."

Welcome to the club, Lupe thought, but a feeling of guilt for the deception haunted her. Well, for a few seconds, anyway. She was at a real crime scene! It was worth the white lie.

"I'm afraid I still have about an hour of work left." The lines around his eyes seemed deeper as he glanced around.

She smiled at him while duplicates of herself smiled back in the lenses of his sunglasses. "It's okay. Anyway, you know I love this shi . . . stuff."

He looked at her reproachfully, then sighed. "Yes, well, I have to figure out how to tell your aunt about all this shi . . . stuff." He pulled out his phone.

Lupe paused. "Why would tía care?"

He dialed as he spoke. "The young man who was killed was her nephew Izzy's friend."

"Cousin Izzy?" Wait. "He isn't mixed up in the murder, is he?"

"I don't think so. But he and Vico, the boy who was killed . . . they were like brothers."

Lupe nodded solemnly. She didn't have a friendship like that, but she often wished for one. What must it be like to have it . . . then lose it? Her eyes fell on the bloodstain. And like this.

Esteban let out a breath. "Well, don't worry about that, niña." He held the phone to his ear, forced a smile, and put his large hand on her shoulder. "You're on vacation! Just sit over there and wait for me." He pointed to a brightly painted picnic table by the wall, the kind at which a child would eat out of their lunchbox. "I shouldn't be long."

Lupe made for the bench as expected and sat perched on the edge. Images of her wild cousin ran in her head like a digital slideshow. They had been inseparable when they were little and she used to count the days till summer when she would see him again. But even then he made her nervous. Izzy was the kind of kid who enjoyed taunting death. Skateboarding down Calle Santa Cruz while holding on to a car's bumper, leaping from concrete pillar to concrete pillar whenever the adults looked away. He was like a kite you could barely hold on to, the string vibrating with its need to break free. She loved him for that.

She'd get more details later.

The sun baked her from overhead and she wondered if eyeballs could boil in their sockets.

Just behind the police tape an old woman dressed in a long-sleeved black dress, her head covered in black lace, stood staring into the center of the police activity, at the bloodstain on the steaming pavement. She looked so out of place among the shorts-and-T-shirt-clad spectators.

The old woman made the sign of the cross and stepped back, the crowd filling the gap she'd left like the tide coming in.

Lupe got to her feet.

She glanced over at Esteban, who was absorbed in a phone conversation. If Izzy and his friends were in some kind of trouble, she was going to help. Which meant she had to listen to her instincts and at the moment they were telling her this old woman was connected.

When her uncle was out of sight, she stood up cool and calm-like and strolled down the street. As she walked and looked for the woman, Lupe took everything in: the colors, the sounds, the smells. There were people scurrying along the roads, not even paying attention to the police activity in their backyard. It made her think that this was a regular occurrence.

She sped up as she made her way down a main drag, looking for the black-clad figure. She couldn't have gotten far. Lupe felt like Detective Leah Carlson, the rule-breaker on *DOA Newark*.

A few people looked up as she rushed by as if she were some sort of oddity, her ridiculously pale Irish skin (literally the only thing her mother had given her before skipping town) standing out. Music spilled out of houses as she passed by, the sizzle of frying grease, and the sounds of babies crying carried on the hot afternoon air. There was no doubt in her mind that this place was a home. A real and true home.

Lupe reached the end of the main drag. No sight of the woman but she thought better of heading down the side alleys. She'd been so busy looking, she hadn't noticed the catcalls that trailed behind her from a group of men standing against the buildings. They wouldn't have dared do it if she'd been walking in her father's large shadow like normal. Blood rushed to her cheeks. Maybe she'd better get back to her uncle.

As she turned back she saw the old woman on a corner up ahead. Activity bustled around her but she was still as stone, her black dress moving only slightly with the torpid afternoon air, ruffling like the feathers of a raven. Lupe approached with caution. The woman was worrying a set of brown wooden rosary beads in her wrinkled hands, her lips moving in a constant trickle of prayer.

The woman looked right into Lupe's eyes and she froze. Well? What could she possibly say to this lady? *Sorry to stalk you, but you looked suspicious in your black lace and orthopedic shoes?* But as she turned to walk away, a tremulous voice called out to her.

"It was not our fault."

Lupe froze. "I'm sorry, Señora?"

The old woman's hazel eyes were covered with a hazy filter of age but were intense nonetheless. Lupe's skin tightened.

"Mi nieto, his death." She pointed back toward the stairs and the hive of police activity.

Nieto. Lupe sorted through her half-assed and rusty Spanish vocabulary. Then it clicked. "The boy who was killed, he was your grandson?"

The old woman nodded, her eyes never leaving Lupe's face. "My daughter. It was not her fault. They didn't know he would really come."

Lupe took a step closer, the old lady's scent of talcum and roses reaching for her with delicate fingers. "They didn't know *who* would come, Señora?" She spoke quietly, coaxing the woman to continue. A voice in her head told her to take off and run for the safety of her uncle. Another voice, the stronger one that sounded like Detective Carlson and usually won out, wanted to hear what the old woman had to say, to poke at the feeling with a stick and see what happened. "Señora, your grandson was friends with my cousin Isadore. Do you know Izzy?"

She pointed a crooked finger at Lupe. "Isadore is a good boy. A good boy. But he'd better andar con cuidado, be careful, or *he'll* come for him, too. He'll come for retribución."

Lupe's heart started banging against her ribs. "Retribution? For what? I'm sorry, Señora, but who exactly will come for Izzy?" This was getting real.

The woman just shook her head, her eyes shining with unshed tears. "May God forgive us." And with that, she turned and started back down the street, her shoulders hunched and appearing to age with each step.

Lupe stood frozen to the spot, watching the woman shuffle through the people on the sidewalk. Finally she willed herself loose, and ran after her.

"Señora? Wait, Señora!" she called, catching glimpses of her white hair weaving among the midday street traffic. She thought she saw her down one of the side streets, so she bolted toward the corner, her breath coming in shallow with the heat. Lupe came to an abrupt stop, chest heaving as her gaze swept the street. There was no one there. She spun around and searched the faces, but the grandmother was nowhere around.

She stood in the street, feeling alone, adrenaline cooling like when she sat in the tub and let the bath empty around her, sitting there as the cold air replaced warm water.

July 6, 4:15 P.M.

Javier

☠

STOPPING AT THE entrance to the church, Javier ran his hands across the curtain of black rubber strips that hung from the doorway. He and Vico used to compete to see who could make them fly higher as they ran through. Abuelo told him the strips were there so they could leave the doors open during mass but keep the birds out. Vico always said it looked like a carwash. With a heavy sigh Javier shoved the worn rubber aside and headed into the cool darkness of the church.

The crowd in the church was an odd combination of players and citizens from the neighborhood. He should have stayed in touch with Vico. Maybe he could have helped, made him talk to Padre Sebastian.

Maybe his friend would still be alive.

Javier found a seat at the end of a pew, in the shadow from the balcony above. He really wanted to avoid seeing any of his old "associates." Not that he wanted to use again, but they could be so damned persuasive and today he was feeling like an open wound. For two years he'd lived without the darkness trailing behind, and he wanted to keep it that way.

As if on cue, a wave of voices rose at the entrance to the church and he looked back to see a group of Vico's gang, Las Calaveras from El Norte, the drug-infested north end of Amapola, pushing toward the center aisle. They were puffing and preening like pigeons, shoving one another and spewing obscenities. Javier could feel the tension come off the people in the pews like static electricity. They cast disapproving looks out of the sides of their eyes, but no one seemed as if they were going to say anything. These were regular mothers, fathers, and grandparents who worked hard so their young would not end up like these boys. And Javier was damn sure they never expected to bury them first.

Padre Sebastian had taught Javier not to get involved, that other addicts' problems were not his own, but he was on his feet before he could talk himself out of it. The church was filled with viejitas, powder-scented ladies all around him, so no way in hell was he going to let something happen to them, in a church no less. He'd only taken a few steps when a tiny old woman dressed in black from head to toe made her way to the center of the aisle. It took him a minute, but Javier recognized Vico's grandmother. She lived in El Rubí and had refused to move when her family tried to get her out.

The guys pushed their way forward, their attention only on one another, when the lead kid noticed the old woman ahead of them. He stopped short, the others plowing into him from behind, their voices dying down in a wave. She lived among gangs like these, there was no fear in her stance. Good thing, since guys like that smelled fear like wild animals. She pointed her finger at them, the lace mantilla over her head shaking with the movement, her voice carrying across the church.

"You will show respect for the dead."

The guys froze for a minute, then nodded their heads and quietly made their way to the front of the church, giving her a wide berth as they passed by.

Javier smiled. Seven words from a tiny old woman could control a gang of thugs.

Only in Puerto Rico.

The organ music rose from behind the altar and Javier settled into that numb state that mass always brought. He welcomed it.

After the service he sat in the pew in the darkened nave until most of the mourners had filed out.

"Man, all this and Vico's body ain't even here!"

"Yeah, the police got what's left of him."

"I heard there were claw marks—"

"I heard that he was sliced in two!"

Javier caught pieces of conversations from the players as they shuffled out. He knew that stories were passed from one of these guys to another like a game of telephone until they reached supernatural proportions, but the talk still made his skull feel heavy. It was like something from his childhood nightmares reaching forward to pull him back. But the way Javier figured it, it was just Vico's time to pay the check for years of peddling the hard shit on las calles. After that much darkness, no one gets away clean.

He just hoped it wasn't too late for him.

Javier decided he might as well head out. To where, he didn't know. He had the day off from work and the idea of going home to his small, empty apartment wasn't very appealing, but the air was getting thin in the church, so he stood and walked quickly to the front. Someone coming from the center aisle brushed by him, knocking against his shoulder. In the old days this would've earned the other guy a right hook, even in a church, but on this day he had no fight left.

"Sorry, man. I didn't see— Javi? Is that you?"

Javier squinted in the semidarkness and recognized Memo from the neighborhood. His face looked the same, all bones and sharp angles, and he hadn't gotten much taller than he'd been at thirteen. But even if he'd looked totally different, Javier would've recognized him anyway from the twitching and shifting from foot to foot. Memo was always strung a bit tight. Javier offered his forearm for a shake and couldn't help smiling at the familiar face. "Damn, Memo. I haven't seen you in ages."

"I know, right? It's good to see you, Javi. You clean up nice."

Javier laughed. Even though Memo was a few days older than he was, he always felt like a little brother. Memo was a follower, like a puppy that stays at your heels no matter how you treat him or where you're heading. "Thanks, man. You doing okay? You still living in the neighborhood?"

"Yeah, pana. It's home, you know. I look in on your mom from time to time. Make sure she's taken care of." His eyes were far away. "She always been good to me. Never criticizes or judges me."

Javier was always surprised to hear what other people thought of his mother. They didn't know her like he did. But it was good to hear that she helped Memo. The poor guy's own mother put everything he did under a microscope and passed judgment like it was a matter of life and death. Or an excuse for a new therapist or medication. No wonder he was nervous all the time. Memo brightened up. "What about that Carlos, hey Javi?"

He smiled. "You mean Papi Gringo?"

"Yeah, man. He's doing good for himself. Traveling around the world, all those hot mamis throwing themselves at him. He's a star. Pana has it made."

Javier was always shocked when he saw their childhood friend on television or heard his voice booming from a car driving by. It was surreal. "That he does, hermano. That he does."

Memo was shifting back and forth, even more than usual.

"Something bothering you? I mean, other than the obvious?" He pointed back toward the altar, where an empty box stood in for their friend.

Memo's eyes darted back and forth, never landing on Javi's face. "I don't know, man. It's just with Izzy missing after what happened with Vico—"

Javier's breath caught. "Wait, Izzy's missing?"

Memo started talking fast, really fast, something he always did when he was scared. "Yeah, I mean, I heard he was trying to kick the junk, you feel me? Go straight? But no one's seen him for, like, weeks, and with all the talk about what happened to Vico . . ."

Javier waited, willing Memo to say what he needed to say. Or to not say it, because truth was, he wasn't sure if he really wanted to know. What he did know was that it was hotter than hell in his suit. "I'm sure Izzy's just laying low." Hell, Javier had to withdraw completely from his life in order to get clean. Memo leaned in close, and Javier could smell the alcohol-like scent of his friend's asthma spray.

"Javi, aren't you . . . worried about all this?"

"Worried about what? It was only a matter of time with Vico. We all knew that."

Memo's eyes darted toward the crucifix hanging at the back of the church, whispering as if God himself was trying to overhear their conversation. "I been getting that feeling, you know? That dark feeling we used to get?"

Javier shuddered. He stared at Memo, a memory scritching at the back of his mind. Like a craving for smack, he knew it was something he couldn't allow in. He pulled back from Memo and straightened his tie and jacket. "You on something? You're talking some weird shit."

"No! I'm not! Not when I'm in church." He did a fast sign of the cross. "You know what I'm talking about, I know you do. Remember—"

A shout from just outside the door interrupted their conversation. "Damn, Memo! You comin' or what? We gotta roll,
pendejo." Javier took a deep breath as the spell broke.

A group of guys were on the steps and, even in their Sunday-
best funeral wear, Javier could tell they were gang members.
Anger rose in his chest. "Tell me you're not still hanging with
those guys from El Norte. Didn't you listen to anything Padre
Sebastian told you?"

Memo shuffled his feet on the marble tiles as if doing some
intricate, anxiety-fueled dance. "I know, but they're my friends."

Javier wanted to take him by the shoulders and shake some
sense into him. "They're not your friends, man. Anyone who
encourages you to do bad shit is not your friend." He felt the
anger leak out, pity rushing in to take its place. "Why don't you
come to the parish with me now? It'll give us some time to catch
up, you know, talk, like old times." Even as he was saying the
words, Javier knew it was a waste of breath. Sometimes you can't
even teach a *young* dog new tricks. And part of him was hoping Memo would say no. This whole conversation was like a
dark cloud he wanted to outrun.

"Nah, man. I mean, thanks, and all, but I gotta go." He was
already moving sideways toward the door, as if the scumbags
outside were tugging on some kind of leash. "It was good to
see you, Javi!" Memo took off in a run toward the group who
had already turned and started walking into the park, shoving
one another, cigarettes hanging out of their mouths.

Javier stared after Memo for some time, rooted in the church
aisle, as he felt darkness seep through the soles of his feet. He
should have insisted. Would Memo end up like Vico? Padre Sebastian warned him that you were lucky if you saved one out
of every hundred; at the end of the day, at least you had saved
one. But this one hurt more than most: this one he felt in his
chest like a blow. Memo was like a brother, one of los cangrejos. This *and* Vico? It was like losing a part of himself.

He was mustering the energy to go out into the afternoon heat when he realized someone was saying his name.

"Javier Andres Utierre?"

His full name, which was never good.

Javier looked up to see a large man silhouetted in the doorway, removing mirrored aviator sunglasses as he walked into the church. He could spot a cop a mile away, but as the man came closer Javier recognized him. Not just *a* cop, but *the* cop: Esteban Dávila, the chief of police. Javier could feel his feet pulling beneath him, as if his old skills, his old life, still ran through his veins telling him that cops were people you ran from. But that was then. He was clean now. "That's me."

The policeman stood in front of him and though Javier was almost six feet tall, Dávila towered over him. Jefe was big, in more ways than one.

"Esteban Dávila." He flashed his badge, the gold glinting in the low church lights, as if Javier didn't know who he was. "You're a friend of my wife's nephew, Isadore, verdad?"

Javier nodded.

"And Ludovico Belasco?"

Another nod.

"Mind if I ask you some questions about him?"

Javier looked back up at the shrouded altar as if Vico were there, watching them from the shadows, reminding him of the code: never talk to cops. But that wasn't his code anymore, and it certainly hadn't served Vico well. "Yeah, I suppose." He looked longingly at the doorway, wishing he'd left when he'd had the chance.

Chief Dávila pulled out a small, leather-covered notebook from his jacket pocket without taking his gaze from Javier's. Javier had only met Izzy's tío a few times, but he was always surprised by the warmth in the man's eyes, by the thin lines that punctuated his expression, as if a lifetime of smiling had etched them there. Izzy always had respect for him, and fear, Javier remembered that.

"Ludovico was a childhood friend of yours, right?"

"Yes. We lived on the same block."

"I'm sorry for your loss." Javier was certain Dávila said that line all the time with his job, but it didn't sound insincere. "When was the last time you talked to him, son?"

"At his mother's funeral. Right here. A year ago April, I guess."

Chief Dávila just stared at him. "A lot of loss for a young man." Javier wasn't sure if he meant Vico, Izzy, or Javier. Didn't matter, he supposed. They'd all seen more death than someone five times their age. His throat tightened and he just nodded.

"So you and Señor Belasco were members of a gang called—" He consulted his notebook. "Los cangrejos?"

Javier snorted. "Gang? No, man. Our mothers gave us that name when we were little kids."

Dávila smiled, just a bit. "The crabs? Why?"

"There were five of us born in the same two weeks in July." The big man just stared at him. "You know, Cancer? The crab? Our mothers met at a birthing class before we were born, or some shi—something like that." Javier felt his temper slipping. The whole thing was giving him a headache. "Look, I have to go."

The smile was gone: the policeman was suddenly down to business. "Javier, do you have any idea who could have done this? Did Ludovico have any enemies?"

Javier chortled; it was an angry sound, stones spitting away from tires. "All drug dealers have enemies. You know that as well as I do."

Dávila nodded. Then he just stared. Javier started to feel like the man was looking through him, into his soul and seeing all the things Vico and he and Izzy had done together when they were younger, seeing the weakness Javier fought on a daily basis. He looked away, trying to break free from the cop's stare.

"Padre Sebastian tells me you're clean, is that right?"

Javier raised his head higher. "Yes."

Chief Dávila snapped his book closed. "Good. That's no life for a young man. And he says you have a job at the church?"

Javier nodded.

"Excellent." Then he handed Javier his card. "Call me if you think of anything, tu sabes?"

Javier nodded.

"Oh, and son, have you seen Isadore around lately?"

Javier swallowed. So even Izzy's family didn't know where he was. "No." They just stared at each other, the moment frozen between them, that shadow he felt pressing down on them.

The moment broke when they both noticed raised voices coming from the church steps.

The two of them started toward the door, their footfalls echoing among the buttresses of the now empty church.

When they arrived in the doorway they found a girl blocking the entrance, her thin arms spread wide, her high heels far apart on the black and white tiles. "I told you, blanquita, you're not coming in this church. You will not dishonor my brother's memory with your white-girl presence."

When he arrived at the edge of the crowd, Javier recognized Vico's sister, Marisol, blocking the door. She was surrounded by a crowd of teenagers; from the way they were dressed they had just come from the service. Half of them looked horrified, the other half hoping for a fight. Javier couldn't say he was surprised—Marisol had had a screw loose since she was eleven, she had even done some time in a psych ward after their mother died—but when he noticed the other girl time seemed to slow.

She was standing tall, her hands on her hips, the sun catching her honey-colored hair as she faced Marisol. She wore black jeans, a T-shirt, and a beat-up pair of laced boots. She was completely surrounded by onlookers, but she didn't look scared at all, just pissed. Javier wasn't about to pick a fight with Marisol and find out, but he thought if he was facing off with her, he might be scared.

"What's going on here?" Esteban Dávila boomed and everyone froze, except the blond girl.

She put her hand up to him like *she* was the cop. "Nothing, tío. I got this handled."

Tío? The girl was Chief Dávila's niece? Izzy's cousin? That made no sense. Javier couldn't take his eyes off her. There was something about her eyes, like they were lit from inside.

Even when she talked to her uncle, she never took those eyes off Marisol. "Look, this is a public place and I have a right to go into any church I damn well please."

Javier smiled. Gotta love a girl who used a curse word at the entrance to a church.

"I don't think so, little white girl. Why not skip on off in your combat boots and run to Starbucks or something. You don't belong here."

There was a chorus coming from the onlookers, varying from "Leave the girl alone" to "That's right, girl, you tell her!"

Dávila's niece took a deep breath and said, "Look, I'm sorry about your brother. I know you must be—"

"Oh no! Don't you patronize me, blondie!"

Marisol was not street like her brother, but Javier knew she was dangerous nonetheless. From his viewpoint he could see the muscles across her back tense like a lioness about to pounce. This blanquita didn't know who she was dealing with. Before he knew it, Javier was ignoring Padre Sebastian's noninterference advice yet again by slipping underneath Marisol's arm and placing himself between them, putting the blond girl at his back.

"Think you better cool down, Mari."

At the sound of her nickname, Marisol finally pulled her eyes from the girl and a crooked smile snaked across her lips. "Well, well, if it isn't Ja-vee-air. You come back to the old neighborhood to slum it? You get clean and think you're better than us, huh?"

"I don't think I'm better than anyone, I just—"

Javier felt the niece shove him from behind, pushing him into Marisol. "Hey, I don't need you to fight for me!"

Before he could turn around, Marisol poked her bony finger into Javier's chest. "So much for los cangrejos. You get out and never look back, just leave Vico behind like garbage, you self-righteous pendejo!"

Javier felt like he'd been punched. He began to stammer. "It—it wasn't my fault—I mean, Vico could have—"

The flames behind Marisol's eyes caught higher, like he'd thrown gasoline on them. He supposed he had.

"Okay, enough of this." Dávila literally lifted Marisol and placed her to the side. Marisol's eyes shot up at him when her feet hit the floor again, but Javier could see her recognize the chief and hold back her retaliation. Javier could still feel her rage as if it were heat.

Some of the girls were pulling her away, but she strained to look back at Javier. "Somebody's gotta pay. Somebody. It's people like you and this gringa here"—she threw her arm in the direction of Dávila's niece—"who killed Vico. Monsters don't come unless someone calls them!"

Javier thought he knew what angry was until he looked into Marisol's eyes. But that wasn't new: she'd changed sometime when los cangrejos were still together. One day Vico's little sister was gone for good, replaced by an enraged and dangerous person. He made the sign of the cross. The girl gave off dark energy. Suddenly he was pulled around by his jacket sleeve, and found himself staring into the ocean blue of the niece's eyes.

With all the pain from Marisol's words, he was glad he had at least protected the girl—

"What the hell was that?" Her hands were back on her hips again.

"Lupe . . ." A warning from her uncle.

Lupe. The blanquita's name was Lupe. "I— Look, you don't know that girl like I do. I was only—"

"And you don't know *me* at all." She poked her finger into the same spot that Marisol had. Javier wondered if there would be a bruise. "I don't need anyone to fight my fights for me, comprendes?"

Javier couldn't say anything. He just stared at her and—God help him—he smiled. That really seemed to piss her off, her glowing eyes becoming stormy. Her uncle was guiding her away before she could yell at him some more, but Javier wished she would stay and yell at him all she wanted.

"Lupe, I think that's enough excitement for your first afternoon, don't you?" As he walked her down the steps, Dávila looked back over his shoulder and flashed a sympathetic grin at Javier.

Javier gave a half-wave and stepped outside so he could watch them walk to the car. Even as they were pulling away from the curb, he scanned the silhouettes inside to try to catch another glimpse of Lupe until all he saw were the red brake lights like eyes, peering around the far corner of the square.

It was then that he was grabbed once more, this time from behind. Would this never end? He was pulled around 180 degrees and left staring into the face of Keno, the guy from Vico's gang who'd been calling Memo earlier. Javier yanked himself from Keno's grip.

"Hands off, asshole." He straightened his tie and jacket. Thugs like this didn't scare him. "You run out of old ladies and little kids to bully?"

An oily grin spread across Keno's face, lifting the admittedly fierce scar next to his left eye. "You always did have a smart-ass comment for everything, didn't you, Javi?"

Javier matched the grin. "I try." He looked around at the gaggle of thugs that surrounded them. Just before he looked back to his opponent, he noticed Memo hiding behind one overly tattooed guy in the back. "Was there something you wanted?"

"Oh, I see. You're all 'I'm a good citizen' and shit now, huh?" Keno leaned in until his face was right in front of Javier's, the smell of drugstore aftershave overpowering. "I remember when you were a strung out mother-f-er. You weren't so good then, jefe."

Javier felt his hands instinctively tightening into fists. He tried to breathe slow and steady. "What. Do. You. Want."

"You bring that cop to Vico's funeral? You disrespecting my homeboy's memory before he's even in the ground, pana. What kind of friend are you?" He shoved his finger into Javier's chest. Now there was definitely going to be a bruise.

He poked Keno back. "I didn't bring him, he was asking about Vico, trying to find his killer. You don't want to know who killed Vico? What kind of friend does that make *you*? Or does that make you something worse? I mean, Vico's not even in the ground yet and already you're taking over Las Calaveras? Now that's friendship right there."

There were mumblings among the posse. Javier could see the color rise in Keno's face. Once again his smile betrayed him. This seemed to really piss off Keno, too.

"I'm watching you, Utierre! I find out you turned narc, and you'll wish for a death like Vico's."

"I heard he was killed by someone with claws . . . a relative of yours maybe?"

Keno lurched toward Vico, his right fist making a wide arc,

but before it connected with Javier's face, Memo leapt from the back and grabbed Keno's fist until he was hanging off of Keno's arm. It was almost comical when Keno noticed Memo hanging there and tried to shake him off. But Javier realized that laughing again probably wasn't a good idea.

"Damn, Memo, what's the matter with you?" He finally shook him off, but the mood was broken. Keno rolled his shoulders and looked back at Javier. "You're in my crosshairs, Prince Javi. Remember that." Then he turned and strutted away with his ape gang.

Javier sighed and relaxed his own shoulders.

It truly had been the day from hell.

July 6, 4:45 P.M.

Marisol

MARISOL YANKED OFF her spike-heeled pumps and kept walking. The cracked and uneven concrete of downtown Amapola dug into the soles of her feet, but she didn't care. In fact, she welcomed the pain. Her mother was dead. Their family home repossessed. Now her brother was dead, too. *Vico is a drug addict and idiota, but he's family.*

Was.

Past tense.

The scene with the gringa outside the church had been the topper on the worst day of her life. Who the hell did that girl think she was?

Marisol stopped, closed her eyes, and took a deep but shaky breath. The thumping had started inside her skull, like something was trying to get out. Last time it had gotten this bad she'd woken up in the psych ward after a two-day blackout. She'd woken up to find out that her brother was dead.

The afternoon was cooling off a bit, and she could feel a slight breeze moving through her hair. She felt her heartbeat settle a bit, and opened her eyes.

A car drove by and honked, a female voice yelling, "Mari!"
She waved at the receding lights and smiled. Damn, she missed
her neighborhood. People knew her here, accepted her, freak-
outs and all. Sure, her cousin's condo was fancy and he and his
wife were nice to her, but she felt like some kind of pathetic
orphan there. Besides, she didn't fit in in Isla Verde. Too fancy
and beachfront for her tastes. She liked the real Borinquen. The
island beneath the one the tourists saw.

Speaking of which, the smell of frying plantain and garlic
suddenly reached for her like a carnival barker. In response her
stomach growled and her smile widened. Chachu's! She could
identify the smell of the restaurant's delicious tostones from
miles away. Deep-fried goodness from right here in Amapola:
that would make her feel better. She walked to the next block,
slipped on her shoes, and waved to the men sitting at the outside tables sipping their cafecitos. The minute she stepped
through the open doorway, Chachu's sister Nivea called to
Marisol and came out from behind the counter.

Nivea gathered her up and locked her in a tight hug. Marisol started to pull away, but the woman just held her tighter,
and eventually she let her body melt into the cushion of Nivea's
ample bosom and lost herself in the smell of flour, oil, and a hint
of bleach. She reminded herself she wasn't going to cry. Not
today.

Nivea released Marisol and held her at arm's length. "M'ija,
I'm so sorry about Ludovico. But he's reunited with your mother
now, descansen en paz." She let go of Marisol just long enough
to make the sign of the cross. "How are you, niña?" She looked
her up and down with that discerning Puerto-Rican-mother
eye. "You look too skinny, verdad, Chachu?"

Nivea's brother's graying handsome head appeared in the
pass-through window to the kitchen. "Leave the girl alone,
Nivea! You can't make the whole world as gorda as you!" He

flashed the dazzling smile that broke many a heart in his day, and said, "You let us know if you need anything, Mari. You hear?" And then he was gone.

Marisol's throat tightened as she looked into Nivea's big brown eyes. "I'm okay, thank you for asking, Señora."

Nivea dropped her grip. "Bueno. Good. Now what can I get you?" She scooched behind the counter, moving sidewise so her wide hips could fit through the narrow entry.

Marisol ran her eyes over everything in the glass case: golden fried plantain and yuca, pieces of moist chicken peeking out from a sauce of fresh tomatoes, onions, and garlic, and crispy chunks of pork stacked on a bamboo skewer. Her mouth watered at all the options. "Do you have bacalaítos today?"

Nivea's face lit up. Like so many islanders she loved feeding people. "For you? Of course!" And in seconds she was handing over a golden salt-cod fritter cradled in a white napkin.

Marisol brought the delicacy to her mouth, blew gently on the edge of the oily pancake, and took a careful bite. The crispy breading gave way, releasing a puff of steam, and the taste of the mild white fish filled her mouth, followed by a citrusy hint of cilantro. She closed her eyes and allowed herself to be lulled by the sound of plates clattering, oil sizzling, and conversation around her. She opened her eyes and smiled at Nivea. "Delicioso, Señora. Just what I needed." She flipped open her purse, but the older woman reached across the counter and stopped her hand.

"No! Your money isn't good here, cariño." She looked at Marisol with the liquid eyes of pity that the girl was getting way too much of lately.

Marisol let her hand drop and took another bite. "Gracias, Señora." Her abuela had taught her not to talk with her mouth full, but she figured Nivea didn't mind. "I miss your food so much! I have to ask my cousin to bring me here next weekend for dinner."

Nivea sighed. "I'm afraid we won't be open."

Marisol stopped chewing. "What? What do you mean?" But in the pit of her stomach, she already knew.

"The building has been sold—the whole block, actually. We can't afford the new rents." The older woman was looking off in the distance as if to a bleak future.

Marisol's throat closed.

"Monday is our last day. The Americano investor who bought—"

Marisol didn't wait to hear the rest of the sentence. She stormed out the front door, throwing her shoes and the rest of the cod fritter into a garbage can on the corner, the concerned yells of the restaurant owner trailing behind her on the heavy dusk air. She took off in a march, her body leaning forward with determination, her fists tight by her sides.

The food fought to come back up as her bare feet hit the pavement with teeth-rattling thuds. The tears she fought so hard to keep down were also threatening, the image of the purple evening streets mottled behind her water-filled eyes. With each step she felt the familiar heat of rage igniting her limbs, running through her veins, filling her lungs. She strode faster and more determined, weaving through traffic, turning corners with race-car precision.

She didn't realize where she was heading until she stood in front of 60 Calle Santa Cruz.

Her childhood home.

Marisol weaved her fingers through the chain-link fence that surrounded the partially destroyed building, the edge of the metal sign that pronounced that it was the future home of an American fast-food restaurant cut into the side of her hand. Grasses had overgrown the path of stones where she had taken her first steps. A sleeping backhoe sat dug into the side of the building, invading her mother's bedroom with its metal claws.

The fading yellow front of the stone building was covered with spray-painted names and its windows were dark and empty eyes staring out onto the crumbling street.

No.

She was not going to let this happen.

She'd lost her family and her home, and now her neighborhood was being stolen piece by piece, by people like Lupe.

Sold by complicit Puerto Ricans like Esteban Dávila.

The "cangrejos" who wasted their energy on drugs, money, and music while their island was being destroyed beneath them by invaders. Even her idiot "boyfriend" Keno, who was more concerned with the labels of his clothing than the fact that their home was being yanked out from beneath his two-hundred-dollar sneakers.

No.

She was done.

Tears flowed freely now, salty and cool on her overheated cheeks. She tightened her fingers on the fence, welcoming the sharp pain of the metal edges cutting into her palm, her fingers, as if it were something earned, until her blood dripped down the silver links.

They were going to have to pay.

The thumping filled her skull, but this time she welcomed its familiar rhythm, reveled in the blackness, the numbness it brought with it.

July 6, 6:36 P.M.

Lupe

♦

LUPE WAS STILL buzzing from the confrontation in front of the church as she and her uncle sat on the patio outside his low concrete house, watching the sun inch lower. It brought relief from the 100-degree heat of the day. She reminded herself to be aware of the deepening orange light dancing along the surface of the pool, to listen to the tiny coquís begin their evening serenade. She knew she should be appreciating it, but all she could see was that girl's twisted face.

And how was Izzy messed up in all this? She pulled out her phone and typed another message.

Primo! It's Lupe . . . again. Where r u?

She put her phone away and looked over at her uncle. He seemed almost relieved by the silence. Lupe bet his job didn't allow for much quiet. When he finally spoke it was as if he'd read her mind.

"That incident at the church this afternoon, Lupe, that had nothing to do with you."

Her head shot up. "What? Of course it did! That girl—"

"I looked into her background: that girl isn't well to begin with, and then her brother was just brutally murdered."

"Yeah, I know." Lupe felt chastised. She hated feeling chastised. "But I didn't do anything to her and she got in my face."

Esteban nodded. "That's true."

"What was all that about white people ruining her life?"

Esteban shook his head. "I don't know. I didn't find out anything about that, but I'm going to look into it further."

Lupe sat up straight. "Wait, is Marisol a suspect now? She wouldn't kill her own brother . . . would she?"

"It's very unlikely, but you know we have to consider all options."

"And that guy, who the h—who did he think he was, stepping in like I can't defend myself?"

Her uncle chuckled at this. "Yes, that wasn't wise on his part. But many boys here are raised to protect girls, though I think that tradition is starting to fade away."

Lupe folded her arms across her chest and stared at the ground. Yet another thing she didn't understand. It didn't help that she couldn't stop seeing the boy's face, the deep brown of his eyes. That only made her angrier at herself. "Clearly he's never met a feminist."

Her uncle chuckled. "Clearly he had no idea with whom he was messing."

A smile tugged at the edges of her lips despite her best efforts to stay angry. Unlike her father, her uncle seemed almost proud of the fight in her. She took a deep breath of Guaynabo's cooling evening air, heavy with the scent of night-blooming flowers, and the buzzing quieted a bit. The sounds of water running, the metal clang of pots, and the sizzle of oil coming from the open kitchen window were so comforting. Being with her aunt and uncle, well, it was almost like she was part of a normal family.

Speaking of family.

"Tío, I want to see Izzy, but he's not answering my texts."

Esteban paused, took a sip of his soda, then looked at the surface of the pool. At the setting sun. Anywhere but at her. "Just keep trying, sobrina." Still no eye contact.

Hmmm. Something was up. Maybe she could get something out of her aunt Maria. She started to stand. "I should go help tía in the kitchen."

Esteban took her hand and stopped her. "I'm sure she can manage, m'ija. Besides, you do the cooking at home, yes?"

She snorted. "If you can call it that. I eat a lot of dinners by myself in front of the television."

He tugged her back to sitting. "Still, this is your vacation. I'm learning that you have too many responsibilities for a young woman."

"Yeah, you could say that."

He cleared his throat. "There's something your aunt and I want to discuss with you. But she felt it was best if you and I spoke alone first."

Lupe swallowed hard. She hated when adults started conversations like this. It always meant something serious was to follow. Like, "About your C in algebra, we feel you're not working up to your full potential," or "We know you were the one who crossed out Columbus Day on all the calendars and wrote in 'Celebrate the Oppressor Day,'" or "I'm afraid your mother left us." It's never good news.

"Okay?"

"We don't talk about it much, but even though we're far away, we know things haven't been easy since your mother left. It seems that Jorge isn't meeting his responsibilities."

She could see the anger build behind Esteban's eyes.

Whenever they were down there, tío was always lecturing her father about responsibility and family. It was nice to have someone get mad on her behalf.

"You know we have no children of our own."

Now Lupe really started to squirm. She always wondered why they'd never had kids, but it's not like it was any of her business. She concentrated to will him through so they could get whatever this was over with, like when her father stepped on an imaginary brake whenever she was driving.

"This solo summer visit is the perfect opportunity to try things out."

"Try what out?" What was going on?

"Your aunt and I would like to invite you to come live with us."

Huh? Her mouth hung open as she stared at her uncle. Live there? In Puerto Rico? Her entire body went numb. *This* she hadn't seen coming. Was he serious? Probably *You've got to be freaking kidding me* was not an appropriate response. Her mind was skittering around like a dog on ice.

"You would have your own room and go to a private school nearby. You would want for nothing. We haven't discussed this with your father yet; we wanted to see how you felt about it first." He cleared his throat and regained his Police Chief posture. "Lupe, this isn't the way I would normally handle such things. Traditionally, with someone of your age, I would have talked to your father and if he agreed, everything would be arranged without consulting you at all, you understand?"

Lupe felt her back go up like a cat about to hiss. A flood of choice words for this *option* rose up from her gut. Before any made it to her tongue, she noticed her uncle was laughing.

Now she was just confused.

"That look, I know that look of yours. You've had that look since you were two years old and didn't want your diaper changed." His eyes twinkled at her in the dusk light. "I like this side of you. That's why we're talking to you about it first. You're excessively . . . independent."

She relaxed in her chair and smiled back. What would it be like to live with people who actually cared about her? Who knew where she was at all times and asked her how her day had been? It was that *knew where she was at all times* piece that made her feel like her skin was too tight. People telling her what to do made her want nothing more than to do the opposite.

Esteban cleared his throat again and she realized she had to say something. What was the proper response to such things? She didn't have a clue. "Tío, I'm just so . . . that's so kind of you. It's just, I've always taken care of myself."

"Yes, and you shouldn't have to. You should be going to movies and dating boys." He put his hand on his sidearm. "Nice boys, that is."

She laughed out loud then. The idea that he wanted to physically protect her was so alien, yet still so comforting. And a slight bit claustrophobic. Yeah, she was in a tailspin.

"In some ways it's selfish." His look softened. "You're the closest thing I've had to a daughter."

Lupe's throat tightened. It was the kindest thing anyone had ever said to her. Her uncle coughed and Lupe looked off at the horizon.

"Just think about it, niña. I know this is a big decision. You have your life and friends in Vermont."

If only he knew. A bunch of "acquaintances" who thought her bizarre, a father who had checked out, and a school that hadn't challenged her since the second grade. Would she hurt him if she said no? Did she even *want* to say no? It wasn't like the house in Elmore felt any more like home than her tío's house. What about her father? Would he drink himself to death without her around?

This would take some serious thinking. She was tired just *thinking* about that much thinking. Silence fell over them again, but it weighed heavier this time. The question was a huge-ass elephant sitting on the wicker coffee table in front of them. She could almost see it mocking her with its trunk and massive waggling ears.

Lupe's uncle sighed and slipped deeper into his patio chair. "Ay, sobrina. An old man gets tired."

Though Esteban was a few years older than her father, he was the one her massive father deferred to. He was impossibly tall and strong.

"You're not old."

"Ah, but this drug dealer's murder is going to age me, I'm sure of it." He took another sip of his soda, his thoughts pulling him away from her again.

Lupe was at a loss. When on the phone, the talk about his work had always energized him, made him more, well, him. Her father didn't have anything to give him that sense of purpose. He dragged himself to his state job every day as if it were simply a step toward the real goal of returning home in the evening to the couch, with *NCIS* on the tube and a bottle of rum.

"Do you have any leads?" Talking to him was the only time she got to try out the language she learned from *DOA Newark*. He never laughed or made fun of her and she learned a lot. Besides, this conversation took them away from the massive question of his offer.

He shook his head. "I don't know. This body is not your typical murder, if there's such a thing."

"What about the body?"

"That boy, he was wounded by some unusual weapon, something my coroner has never seen before. And so close to El Rubí, all those children sleeping two blocks away." He smacked a mosquito on his arm, leaving behind a bright red smear of blood.

At those words, Lupe remembered the old woman in El Rubí, the victim's grandmother. She felt that electric feeling bumping across her skin, like a tiny wave making its way over rocks and shells. She shook it off.

Her uncle stood up to his full height and adjusted his belt. "Okay, sobrina. We're going to work on a self-defense move"—his voice dropped to a whisper—"especially if you're going to wander around El Rubí all alone."

Lupe swallowed. Of course he knew. He knew everything.

"Stand here. No, there. Good. So, if someone comes at you from behind, I want you to stay calm. Try not to struggle."

"Oh yeah, right!" She held on to her uncle's hairy arm, which he held loosely around her neck, and made to bite it. He bent his tall frame into a crouch in order to hold her.

"No, really. You need to relax your elbow, pull it back, then yank it back into your assailant's nose." He pulled her arm up in the proper movement. "See?" He let her arm go.

"Like this?" And her arm yanked back as if it were on a spring, nailing her uncle so hard in the nose, she heard a crunch. He dropped to the ground with a groan, taking two lawn chairs with him.

Lupe put her hands to her face. "Oh my God! Tío! I'm so sorry!" She went to help him to his feet, but he was so heavy he pulled her down to the ground. "You did that on purpose!" she yelled and jumped on his back, and he reared around like a horse with a gnat. By the time her aunt came out they were laughing and covered in grass stains.

"I'm so glad that your uncle is helping to raise you as an elegant young lady, Lupe," her aunt said from the doorway with a sly smile. "Now wash up for dinner, you two."

They made their way inside, washed up, and settled down at the table.

Lupe looked down at the piping dish in front of her. It looked like a square of lasagna, but instead of noodles there were long slices of what looked like bananas on top. The smell was caramel sweet with a spicy edge. "What is this, tía?"

It was her uncle who answered. "Ah, you're in for a treat, sobrina. This is Maria's specialty, pastelón."

Maria chuckled. "Lupe, he's kidding. He knows my specialty is takeout."

He took his wife's hand and kissed it. "Well, that's what you prefer, but when you do cook, it's a delicacy."

Lupe loved watching them together. They were so kind to each other, full of respect. #relationshipgoals. She took a forkful and closed her eyes. The contrast of the sweet plantain with the salty, spiced beef danced on her tongue. She loved the starchy goodness of the plantain, caramelized and crispy on the edges, soft and rich in the middle. Yeah, this would be a good part to living on the island. She'd have to take up running.

"So, Lupe, what would you like to do while you're in Puerto Rico this trip?" This was the kind of thing adults always asked, but Maria was really interested. The woman listened like no one else Lupe knew.

She thought about her visit to El Rubí that afternoon. "I'd like to see parts of Puerto Rico I've never seen before."

Maria perked up. "Oh! Like the Camuy caves! We can go on a boat tour this weekend, perhaps."

She was so enthusiastic, Lupe hated to disagree. "Actually, not really the typical touristy things. I just want to get a better understanding of the *real* Puerto Rico." Did she even have an idea of what that was? Both her aunt and uncle were staring at her. Maybe they didn't either. "It's just, I don't even know what part of me is Dávila."

Her aunt smiled and pointed to Lupe's now empty plate. "Well, your appetite is totally Dávila." She put her fork down and put her hands together in front of her like she probably did in the hospital boardroom. "I like that you're interested in this, Lupe. How about we drive around Amapola and we can show you where your great-grandfather was born? Did you know he was mayor of Amapola at one time?"

Lupe perked up. "What?"

"Yes! Esteban, you've never told her about your family?"

Her uncle wiped his mouth with a napkin, his plate just as clean as hers. "No, but she knows more about the history of policing methods on the island than most of my staff."

Maria threw her hands up. "Great. Such an appropriate and interesting subject for a fifteen—"

"Sixteen!"

"—a sixteen-year-old young woman."

"No, he's right, tía! I love that sh—stuff! In fact, when we were in El Rubí today—"

Her uncle was reaching for seconds when his hand froze, and her aunt slowly put down her fork.

Esteban recovered quickly, serving out another helping of rice and beans to his plate. The air was slightly electrified, the silence crackling.

Uh-oh.

Her aunt glared at her husband. "You took Lupe to El Rubí?"

Esteban put his hand over his wife's and patted. "It's okay, mi amor. She was surrounded by my officers."

Lupe had no desire to upset her aunt, but this was important. "When I was there, I met this old woman who turned out to be Vico's grandmother. Maybe she knows something about what really happened?"

Esteban put his hand up in his stop-it's-the-police gesture and said, "Now Lupe, how could a seventy-year-old woman help with this case?"

"But maybe she can help with Izzy."

Her aunt's gaze shot up from her food. Maria was paying attention now.

Esteban seemed to notice that, so he gave his wife the condescending stop gesture, too. "Sobrina, I think it's best you leave this to the professionals. We—"

"She said something about how if Izzy didn't behave, '*he'll* come for him, too.'"

Her aunt stood up as if her seat were electrified, the chair legs scraping against the tile floor with a screech. Her eyes stayed focused on Esteban as she fingered the gold cross that hung from her long neck. Then, with shaking hands, she gathered her half-filled plate and scurried away to the kitchen without a word.

Lupe felt her food stick in her throat, her appetite leaving with a whoosh. She had a habit of speaking before thinking. Her uncle was still sitting there, probably deciding whether to go after his wife.

"Tío, I'm so sorry. I didn't mean—"

He waved his hand at her. "No, no. This isn't your fault. Maria is very worried about Isadore."

"But what's wrong with Izzy?"

Her uncle pushed the food around on his plate. "Nothing you should worry about, sobrina." He stood up and picked up his plate. "Are you finished?"

Lupe nodded and handed him her plate, wondering what the hell was going on that they weren't telling her about.

July 6, 11:36 P.M.

Memo

💀

"MEMO, MAN, YOU'RE shuffling again."

Memo smiled sheepishly and whispered, "Sorry, Ángel." Truth was, this casually-walking-around-the-store-while-preparing-to-rob-it thing was a stretch for him. When did Memo "casually walk" anywhere? But Ángel just smacked him on the back and nodded. His faith in Memo was infectious.

As they walked down the snack aisle, Memo concentrated on staying cool and calm, breathing in through his nose and out through his mouth like his therapist had taught him. He could sense the pressing of the familiar out-of-body feeling that usually preceded an anxiety attack, the sensation that he was being dragged into a gaping, dark hole in the ground, scraping his nails into the floor as he went. He counted his breaths, pushing the fear back, and swallowed an Ativan. He couldn't freak out now; he couldn't let the guys down. He just had to keep it together until they finished the job; it wouldn't be much longer.

After Memo defended Javi outside the church, Keno was pretty pissed at him. And home was no better. A few weeks earlier he'd been thrown out of yet another private school and his mother was on his back 24/7. If she only knew that he spent his weekends robbing stores he would be sent to military school faster than you could say "delincuente." She wouldn't get it. It wasn't about the money; she bought him whatever he wanted. It was for the way it made him feel. Like he meant something, like he mattered. Better than the high from any drug.

Memo took his position at the back of the store while Ángel walked toward the register as planned, casually striding with the six-pack of beer dangling from his forefinger. How did he stay that cool?

Yeah, Memo was afraid. And he'd thought about saying no, but it was actually running into Javier that had sealed the deal for him. Ever since they were kids Javi was always the smart one, the cool one, the leader. Memo had looked up to him like a brother. He'd tried to be happy for him when he cleaned up, he really had, but then Javi was just gone, los cangrejos had scattered, and Memo had been left in the neighborhood like an outgrown pair of kicks. But these guys from El Norte? They made him feel like he was somebody, like he was family.

Memo hid behind the stand of snacks, his stomach pressed against the cellophane-wrapped guava cakes with their bright red jelly leaking out of yellow cake like blood. Over the top he could just see Ángel's hoodie-covered head as he arrived at the register, the bored clerk hunched on a stool as he punched at his cell phone with his thick fingers.

It was happening.

It was really happening.

Memo straightened up, his head barely topping the rack as he tried to concentrate on what was going down in the next few minutes. He ran through the plan in his head. Ángel would point the gun at the clerk, who would hand over the cash from the register, and they'd hoof it the hell out of there and celebrate with the stolen beer.

There was an old man in front of Ángel in line, with a gray hat like the ones Memo's grandfather used to wear. Memo rocked back and forth while he watched the man fishing for change. Ángel was jiggling his hand in his pocket and Memo could picture his finger on the trigger of the revolver hidden in his sweatshirt. *Hurry up, viejo!* Memo silently urged the old man. He was gonna get himself killed in a minute. No one had an itchier trigger finger than Ángel.

Finally the old man took his brown paper bag and turned to leave, but just before he stepped away from the counter, he looked back toward where Memo was standing and stared directly into his eyes. All the air got sucked out of the store, and just for a second, Memo considered running, going straight home, apologizing to his mom, and leaving El Norte behind. But before Memo could move, Ángel glared at him and Ángel's voice returned to his head. *Sac-up, pana!* When Memo looked over at the old man again, he saw his back as he pushed through the store's glass door.

Across the length of worn linoleum flooring he could see Ángel waving the gun at the clerk, hear the clerk yelling back. What the hell was he arguing for? Didn't he see the gun in his face? They'd chosen this store because it was one of the few in the area where the person behind the register wasn't sitting in a bulletproof plastic box and the night staff seemed like they didn't give a shit. But this clerk was new and something wasn't right. Memo lurched out from behind the rack, knocking boxes of meringue cookies to the floor as he rushed to the front, with knife drawn, to back up Ángel. That's what he was there for, right?

When Memo was only a few feet away, the store clerk stood up. He was bigger than he seemed; his head reached the cigarette rack above. He lurched over the counter and grabbed Ángel by the front of his shirt. Surprised, Ángel's arms flailed and the gun dropped to the floor, skittering to a stop in front of Memo.

Time stopped, like in the movies. Memo stared at the gun silhouetted on the worn, gray floor while the other men stared at him. It must have only been a second, but to Memo it felt like a lifetime. There was no sound, only the rapid thumping of Memo's heart pulsing in his ears. Fear tightened around his chest like a rope until he felt as if his breathing would stop. He pictured Javier in the church lecturing him about his choices as if Memo were a kid or something, as if he couldn't control his own life. As he watched his friend's panicked eyes dart back and forth, Memo thought of how Ángel suggested him for this job, how he'd believed in him.

In one swift movement Memo bent over, picked up the gun, pointed it at the surprised clerk, and squeezed the trigger. The *bang* pressed on him like a weight, the whole store shuddering from the noise. He stared down the barrel of the gun and watched the clerk's mouth open in shock as he dropped Ángel and stumbled over the stool behind the counter, dragging it to the ground as he fell. The blood spread across his white T-shirt like the prize hibiscus flowers in Memo's mother's garden.

Ángel lurched behind the counter and was pulling cash from the register. Memo just stared at the empty space where the clerk had stood. The acrid smell of gunpowder snaked into his nostrils. His mind was blank and racing at the same time as fear rushed back in like tumbling surf.

"Memo! We got to get outta here!" Ángel was pulling at him, money spilling from inside his zippered sweatshirt. Ángel reached back to grab the six-pack of Medalla beer from the counter and lurched for the exit.

Memo pulled himself from his daze and followed his friend out the door, the bell above tingling happily as it swung back as if elated by their departure. As if they were just two more happy customers.

As if everything in Memo's life hadn't just changed.

Then they were running. He looked down and saw his Nikes flashing, felt the cracked pavement smacking against his soles. But it was as though he wasn't in control of his legs. Thankfully they were just going on their own. They had better survival instincts than the rest of him. As he ran he realized he was holding something. Something heavy. The gun.

Oh shit.

He'd killed someone.

He'd never killed anyone before. Never even come close. Memo was the kind of guy who hung back, let other, stronger guys like Javier or Ángel take the lead. Guys whose mothers didn't still buy their underwear.

Ángel scuttled around a corner, down the shadowed side street to the abandoned building that they'd found last week when they were scoping out the job. There were so many to choose from these days: businesses were dropping like flies. Memo saw his friend climb through the broken plywood that covered the mouth of where the front door had been and he followed close behind, his jeans almost catching on the jagged, wooden edge. He landed on the concrete floor with a thud, and ran through the dark, abandoned storefront toward Ángel in the back. Empty cans skittered away from his feet like rats, their aluminum clanks way too loud in the cavernous space.

Ángel was sitting in the corner, his chest rising up and down with each ragged breath. Memo leaned his back against the graffiti-covered store wall and stared at the shafts of light that sneaked their way through the broken windows.

He was numb.

Totally numb.

He'd fucked this one up big. He was sure he would be thrown out of the gang, and his mother. . . . damn, it would kill her if she were to find out. He bent down and put the gun carefully on the floor, pushing it away as if it might bite. He squeezed his eyes shut and braced himself for the sound of sirens. Ángel's voice in the dark made him jump.

"Man, that was some serious shit, Memo!" Ángel gasped, his breath slowing.

Here it came. The reprimand. The rash of shit. Memo steeled himself as he had for seventeen—shit, in a few minutes it would be eighteen—years. His mother had been dressing him down since he'd been old enough to walk. When he was a kid los cangrejos constantly teased him, criticized the way he threw a ball, talked to a girl. And now the Calaveras called him a pussy about twenty times a day; he walked wrong, talked wrong, hell, he couldn't take a piss right. Well, it probably made sense he'd get thrown out of the gang for an eighteenth birthday present. Memo braced himself and looked down at his friend. If he still *was* his friend.

Ángel was smiling back at him, his white teeth glowing in the dark like a beacon. "Memo's a man now, bro! I knew you could do it!" Ángel reached up and grasped Memo's forearm for a shake.

The second their arms touched, Memo felt a tingling rush through his body. Could it be true? He hadn't fucked up? Realization slowly muscled its way into his spinning brain.

He'd made it.

He wasn't a candy-assed rich boy anymore.

He was a badass, murdering man.

The laugh started deep in his belly, glee sparking like static all over his skin. To think he had almost run, had considered leaving la vida. Ángel was right. He was finally a man. He could feel it in every cell in his body, like he'd started the day as a boy and was ending it as a man. In a few minutes he would be eighteen. He *would* be a man. Next time he saw Javier he was going to be the one talking down. Memo slid his back down against the wall and smiled at Ángel in the dark.

Life had never been better than this.

Ángel started laughing, and then they both couldn't stop, gulping breaths side by side on the concrete floor of an empty building, not caring that their voices were echoing off the high ceilings. Ángel reached into his sweatshirt and tossed fistfuls of bills into the air like confetti. It was the best high in the world.

Until Memo heard a scraping sound from the blackness of the corner.

Ángel must have heard it, too, and their laughter turned off like a light switch.

They sat and listened to the silence.

A minute.

Two.

Nothing.

"What the hell was that?" Ángel's whisper sounded tight.

"I don't know, man." Was it the cops? Nah, they were just fired up. "Probably just a rat." He lifted his hand for Ángel to slap. Memo chuckled at his nervousness, but he felt the dark shadow he'd been talking to Javier about spreading like an oil spill, just beyond his line of sight.

Ángel cracked open a beer bottle and handed it to Memo. He held his own up to clink. "Here's to you, man. Welcome to the dark side . . . and happy birthday." The clink of the bottles sounded loud in the cavernous room, but it was such a normal sound that it comforted Memo. He was stupid to worry. They were on top of the world and no one could knock them off.

Memo looked at his phone: 11:59, almost midnight. "I'll be eighteen in one minute." Finally. Memo smiled big as he lifted the bottle but froze as it touched his lips. Next to him Ángel's eyes lit up, huge and round like twin moons, his bottle shattering on the concrete below.

"What's up, Áng—" Memo started to turn around, but something like a rope covered with skin had wrapped itself around his chest and he couldn't take a full breath. Was he having an anxiety attack? A heart attack? The pressure was almost beyond pain, past terror. Memo stared at Ángel, wishing he could lift his arms to reach toward his friend, but they were pinned down, pressing into his sides.

Memo felt a lurch, the bottle flying from his hand, the sour smell of beer filling the room. Then he was moving backward, his body dragging along the concrete floor, his jeans scraping over discarded nails, empty cans. He was frozen, fear turned his limbs to ice despite the antianxiety medications and hundreds of hours of therapy. He wanted to crane his neck to see what had him, to see what was pulling him like a ragdoll toward the shadowed store corner, but somewhere in his dark mind he knew. He knew that anything he'd ever feared before was meaningless. There was also a kind of relief, a theory proven.

Somehow he always knew this was how it would end.

Memo watched as Ángel got smaller and smaller and the shadow spread into his vision, blacking out all but a pinhole view in the center of emptiness. The pressure around his chest was tightening until his ribs cracked one by one like twigs underfoot on a forest walk. His body stopped fighting and his bladder gave way. For the first time in his life, he was resigned. He wished he could call his mother and say, "See? See, old woman? I *did* have reason to be afraid!"

Then there was nothing beneath him and his legs scraped on the ragged edge of the sudden hole in the floor, following his head and torso into total darkness.

July 7, 2:04 A.M.

Lupe

💀

SOMETHING WAS HAPPENING downstairs. Lupe wasn't awake enough to know much more than that, but her body was up and moving before her brain could even react. Growing up as she had, she could sense trouble in the night like a change in the temperature, even when asleep. She walked quietly to the door of her bedroom and listened. Her uncle was talking on the phone downstairs. Calls at this hour were never good news.

"Sí . . . sí . . . where?"

Then her aunt's voice, Lupe couldn't hear what she was saying. She headed downstairs.

Her uncle was strapping on his bulletproof vest over his shirt, while Maria watched him with haunted eyes.

Esteban noticed Lupe standing in the stairwell. "Bueno, I have to go. They found another body in San Juan."

Her aunt gasped, but Esteban was there in a split second holding her arms and looking into her brimming eyes. "It isn't Izzy."

Her aunt nodded. She looked relieved but still worried.

Lupe had to ask. "Izzy? Why the hell would it be Izzy?"

"Language, Lupe! I can't talk about this now. At least this time there was a witness. God willing that will help us find the killer." He kissed Maria gently on the lips. "Lo siento, mi amor. Go back to sleep."

"I'll try, papi." She smiled at him, but Lupe could see the tightness tug the edges of her mouth.

He kissed Lupe on the forehead, the spicy scent of his after-shave surrounding her like a hug.

As they watched Esteban walk out the door, it was Maria's turn to sigh. "Ay, Lupe. I never like to see him leave at this hour, but I *really* don't like this case. There's something evil about it. There will be no going back to sleep for me."

Lupe thought she should do something, like put her arm around her aunt's shoulders, comfort her, tell her it's not evil, just senseless. That everything will be all right. Isn't that what a normal niece would do? But she was frozen in place. She was actually kind of pissed that they were keeping whatever was going on with Izzy from her. Finally she offered, "I'm sure he'll be okay." But even she didn't believe it.

July 7, 3:40 A.M.

Javier

> damn! u hear 'bout Memo?

> Javi, pana, sorry about Memo.

> Memo? WTF!!!

The texts arrived in a burst like machine gun fire. Javier jolted up in bed and grabbed his phone. For a minute he thought he was still asleep, that he was dreaming. His hands were shaking as he responded to the last one that had come in, he didn't even know from who.

> ¿Que pasó?

> He dead, man. Fell after robbing a store w/ Ángel. Sucks.

> Fell?

> Yeah. Ángel's messed up. Keeps talking about something dragging Memo off. Like his mind is gone.

Javier sat staring, buzzing phone forgotten in his hand, his body so numb it was like it wasn't there, like he was just a mind floating above his bed. He jumped when the phone started to ring, switched it to Off, and put his head in his hands.

It felt as if a wave was building inside his skull, higher and higher, and soon it would break and his mind would be dashed against the side of his skull.

But now there was nothing to take away the pain, to cushion the impact.

Damn, he wanted to get high.

Why did his mind have to go there? After two whole years?

And why hadn't he dragged Memo's scrawny ass to Padre Sebastian's after the funeral? He might have been alive to see the sun rise.

Javier couldn't sit still, couldn't concentrate. Why had he agreed to take the week off from his work at the church? Sebastian was worried about him. Truth was, he was worried about himself. The last conversation with Memo kept running over and over again in his mind. What was going on with los cangrejos? Memo had said he felt a darkness, a shadow or something. Ángel said he was "dragged off"? Maybe Memo had been lying and he was off his meds.

Why hadn't Javier pushed harder? If his sobriety couldn't survive one uncomfortable conversation he didn't stand a chance.

Maybe Marisol was right. Maybe he'd turned his back on them.

If he'd been honest with Memo he would've admitted that since Vico died, he kept looking over his shoulder as if there were someone right behind him. It was a scritching at the back of his mind that he'd thought he'd finally silenced.

He jumped up, grabbed his keys, and left his apartment just as the sky began to lighten.

He drove around for hours thinking, just driving randomly for once and not worrying about wasting gas. In the old days he would always end up in front of his dealer Omar's building, no matter where he'd originally been heading, like he was caught in a loop.

This time his car found its way to the church rec center where he worked, just after nine thirty. He pulled into a space in the church parking lot and let go of a breath he'd been holding since the text had come in about Memo. He'd beaten the temptation "just for today" as they said in his Narcotics Anonymous meetings.

There was a group of some of the smaller kids he mentored shooting hoops in the pockmarked basketball court. Shreds of rope basket hung from the rusted metal hoop like entrails. He made a mental note to try to get a local sports store to donate a new one. His kids deserved better.

After a flurry of fist bumping and "What up, Javi?" Javier made his way through the side door and into the dark, cool bowels of the church basement.

Padre Sebastian was filling up file boxes in his office, the sleeves of his black shirt rolled up, the white of his collar stark against the walnut brown of his skin. He'd been in the middle of a huge office reorganization for weeks now. Months, actually. Javier suspected the man was just moving files from one spot to another. He never threw anything away.

The priest seemed to be ignoring him, so Javier coughed into his hand.

"What's the matter, Javier? Coquí in your throat?" The priest asked in his melodious Jamaican accent as he fit the cover on the now-filled box. When he finally turned to Javier, his locs swung like palm fronds, the long coils eventually resting over his wide shoulders.

Padre Sebastian was pretty young, like thirty-five, and he was about the coolest priest Javier had ever met. Actually, he was the *only* cool priest Javier had ever met. It was probably why the local players were so willing to listen to him, why Javier listened to him.

"Hey, Padre."

"Javier. I heard about Memo. I thought I might see you this morning." His voice was gentle, his accent adding soft music to his words.

Javier swallowed hard, hoping to hold back the tears that had been building all morning.

"I'm sorry, Javier. I truly am. Memo made some very bad choices for a smart boy, but he didn't deserve this fate."

"No, he didn't. It's just, Vico, now him. Padre, I'm . . ."

Sebastian walked over and put his hands on Javier's shoulders, looking deep into the boy's eyes. "Scared?"

Javier looked away.

"Not only is it okay to be scared, I don't blame you one bit. I'm scared."

Javier's head shot up at that.

Padre Sebastian walked over to the cracked window that looked out over the parking lot and pointed to the kids outside. "I'm scared for every one of those children out there. The older they get, the less likely we can lure them away from the temptation of the streets. Not many people are strong enough to face their demons like you have."

Javier wasn't sure facing his demon had been enough. In fact, he wasn't sure the demon was gone at all. "I don't feel very strong." He thought of how much he'd wanted to use that very morning. He didn't want to disappoint Padre. He didn't want him to know that he was still battling.

As if reading his mind, the priest said, "You're strong, m'ijo. I have faith in you."

Javier smiled sadly. Padre Sebastian always made him feel better, but there was still a pressing against his chest. "There's something about the deaths, Padre. Memo even tried to tell me he thought something weird was going on. There's a connection between them, but I can't figure out what it is."

The priest crossed his arms. "What kind of connection?"

"I don't know. Something . . . old." Javier shuffled from one foot to another, unconsciously picking up Memo's habit, wishing for some kind of relief from the storm that was building in his chest. He knew this feeling and it never ended well. "I think they were killed by the same person. Or something."

"Memo fell, Javier. The building was under construction and he fell through a hole into the basement."

"I know. I know I'm not making sense. It's just . . ."

The padre watched Javier fidget for a while. This was one of the things that Javier loved most about him. He listened. Really listened. "Javier, both those boys were on dangerous tracks."

Javier held his head in his hands. "I know, I know. But Padre, do you remember when I told you about the darkness I felt following me?"

"Yes, the feeling that started when you were a teen and stopped after you started going to meetings."

Javier nodded. "Yeah."

"What about it?"

Javier swallowed. "It's back."

Sebastian eyes widened. "You're not using again, are you?"

Javier shook his head so hard he felt his eyes rattle. "No! Nothing like that. It's like it's following me again. Like, right around the corner behind me, and when I whip around, it's gone. Know what I mean?"

"I do, m'ijo. I do. But couldn't it be that two of your old friends just died? That would be devastating to anyone."

"Maybe. I just wish I could shake it. I did it once, thanks to you."

He pointed at Javier and smiled. "Ah no, you did that yourself! Hmm. When I don't know what to do, I look back, see where I've come from to try to understand where I've ended up. Why don't you go back to where it all started? The time and place of your life when the shadow first appeared?"

Going back. Just the thought of it made his skull feel tight, but he wouldn't talk to Memo about the past and look what happened. He owed it to him to explore. He should go back to where things had started to change, go dark. "You mean go back to Amapola?"

"If that's what that means for you, then yes." The old-style black phone started to ring and he made his way around the desk. "And while you're there, give my regards to your mother, will you?"

Javier narrowed his eyes at his mentor.

"Ah c'mon, give her a break. She'll come around." He picked up the phone, lowered his body into the office chair, and nodded goodbye to Javier.

Javier turned the corner at the old Sanchez house with its overgrown front lawn and crumbling graffiti-covered walls. Back in the day it had looked nice, like someone cared. All the houses did. Until the neighborhood started to change. The island's economy tanked, middle-class families took off for the States, abandoning their homes, and the drug dealers spread out from El Norte and moved in to the better neighborhoods to fill the void. Javier remembered when his mother told him he couldn't play ball in the street anymore, tilting her head toward the most recent arrivals, a group of slick-haired guys with cigarettes dangling from their mouths.

Javier drove by a row of run-down houses with ratty laundry strung in front like forgotten garlands of a holiday long past and parked in front of his mother's house. He could see the edge of the flamboyán tree in the backyard. It was in full bloom, the dark orange blossoms impossibly bright in the morning sun. As he looked toward the backyard, Javier remembered the annual birthday parties they used to have, all of them together, the cangrejos, their mothers and siblings. Creamy tres leches cake and guava cookies, games in the backyard, balloons. He smiled as the years of festivities ran through his memory. When had they stopped having those parties? He had some faint memory of los cangrejos hidden in the shadows of the tree under the Amapola moon while their mothers chattered in the house. When was that? The flamboyán blooms looked like blood in the darkness, that he remembered. They had gotten in trouble for something that night. It was weird, like the memory was shrouded in black gauze. Now two of los cangrejos were dead, their blood splattered in two different corners of San Juan. Maybe his mother remembered something more. He had to try; it was too important.

Within her front gate everything was immaculate, as always. Neat rows of flowers surrounded by the perfect-length grass. Everything in its place, that's the way his mother liked it. Javier stopped and stared at the recent addition to the garden, a smiling frog holding a sign that said WELCOME. He considered kicking it across the yard.

Javier rang the bell and ran his hands through his hair. He thought about getting back in the car before she could answer. What the hell was he doing here anyway? A wild theory about going back to figure things out was not enough to justify putting up with his mother's shit that early in the morning. Christ, he hadn't even had a coffee yet.

Before he could move, the door whipped open and his mother appeared behind the gate in her bright designer clothes. "Mi hijo querido, what a wonderful surprise!" She unlocked the gate with her ring of keys, pulled him in, and kissed his cheeks, bringing with her a cloud of gardenia perfume. "Come in, come in. I was just about to have my morning café con leche. Please join me."

Javier stepped into the pristine living room and saw that she had set out her best china, sugar in perfect square cubes filled a delicate glass bowl, and a single Maria biscuit sat on a thin, white plate. Where the hell did she even *buy* sugar cubes? Did they make them anymore? The world could be falling down around her, zombies from the apocalypse knocking at the door, and she would continue to set up her little coffee service. Hell, she'd invite the zombies in for biscuits and cafecitos.

"Let me get you some coffee, mi amor," she said, already rustling in her linen toward the kitchen.

"No, Mamá, nothing for me. I just want to—" But she was gone.

"Nonsense. You have to have some coffee and galletas with your mother. I can only imagine how little you're eating, living on your own . . . and so young!" she called from the kitchen.

Javier just stood near the coffee table in silence. Silence was pretty much the only option around his mother. There was no oxygen in the room left for anyone else. It used to work to his advantage when he was getting high; no matter how stoned he was when he stumbled in she didn't seem to notice. She was too busy playing house, pretending Dad hadn't left, that her son wasn't snorting, shooting, or swallowing any drug he came across. That their home wasn't broken. There was a constant stream of cheery words accented by the clinking of silverware and china.

"Sit, sit, mi amor." Javier jumped as his mother reappeared carrying a tray in her perfectly manicured hands, the large golden citrine ring his father had given her when they were first married glinting on her finger. His father used to say the golden stone looked gorgeous against her Spanish olive skin. Dad was so proud of how European she looked. God forbid she have darker Caribbean skin. Bigot. Why did she still wear that ring?

"Tell me how you are. Did I tell you about Marianna's new

grandchild? You know, the woman who lives on Calle Martínez near your cousin Eudice? The baby was two weeks late, can you imagine? Two weeks in this heat. Well, Marianna—"

Javier put his hands up, hoping to stop the barrage. "Mamá. I really need to talk to you about something important."

His mother stopped abruptly and gathered the fabric at her neckline in her bony fingers. "I see. Important." She started re-arranging the pale blue and white Lladró figures on her end table, placing the Madonna and child just a bit closer to the dancing Spanish lady. "I suppose you don't really want to hear about the minutiae of an old lady's life, what with you being all grown up and living in the city. I mean, I'm *only* your mother."

Javier sighed. There was no talking when she got like this, no talking about real life when she was too busy focusing with her rose-colored gafas. "I'm sorry. I just have something important I need to talk about, and you're the only one I thought to turn to." There, that would do it.

She sat up straighter, releasing the linen at her neck. "Why didn't you say so, mi amor?" She reached over and put her hands over his. "You know I'm always there for you. Dime, tell me."

"Do you remember the birthday parties you used to throw when I was a kid? When we used to get together with our friends from the neighborhood? The other mothers and all my friends?"

Her face lit up. "Of course. Oh, what wonderful parties we had. The games in the backyard, trips to the park and the beach. Remember that year when you and Ludovico dressed up like Don Quixote and—"

He cut her off. "It's Vico I want to talk about. I'm trying to figure out what happened to him and Memo."

Her hands stopped moving and the smile bled from her face. "Yes, well, I don't really want to discuss that." She made the sign of the cross. "God rest their souls."

"Why did we stop having those birthday parties? What happened the night of the last party? I think we were turning . . . thirteen?"

His mother jerked to her feet and started to clear away the full cup of coffee in front of her.

Javier grabbed her wrist and coaxed her back to the couch. "Mamá, it's important. There's something weird going on. I feel like someone or something is stalking us."

"I don't have time to talk about such fantasies." She started to stand up again, but he wouldn't release her wrist. Her eyes darted to the door to the kitchen, the front door, any way to escape.

"I need to figure out what's going on."

She stared in his eyes now, her shoulders square with growing anger. "You're hurting me, Javier. Let. Go."

The quiet power in her voice made him shudder a bit and Javier released her. It was weird how she could do that. One minute she was a crazy old woman living in some kind of *Mary Poppins* stage set, and the next she was stormy and fierce. He wished she had been this way more often when he was growing up, particularly with his father.

His mother stood up, pulled the bottom of her jacket down to straighten it, and tossed her head. "I'm not going to sit here and be interrogated by you. It's unfortunate that your friends passed on so young, but nothing we did at that last party had anything to do with it."

Javier paused. "I never said you did— Wait, who's *we*? What happened?" But she ignored him and kept going.

"It was a long time ago and all of us mothers were doing the best we could with what we had. That's all you need to know."

Javier sat there, confused, as his mother pulled the untouched coffee cup out from underneath him.

She piled the plates and their uneaten galletas on top of one another. "¡Basta ya! I have things to do. You can show yourself out."

Javier watched her march out to the kitchen. He wondered if he should feel bad for getting her upset, but he quickly dismissed it. His mother had two modes, righteous fury and totally oblivious. Both were in full force that morning.

He was no closer to understanding what was going on with his friends, or what the darkness was that followed him.

July 7, 4:00 A.M.

Lupe

💀

LUPE COULDN'T SLEEP. Her uncle still hadn't come home and she could hear her aunt puttering in the kitchen. Clearly nobody was sleeping this morning.

As she lay in bed, she decided to do some research on Izzy. She didn't expect to find much since he wasn't on any social networking site, but while doing an image search, she froze. There was Izzy, looking out at her with a smirk as if he'd been waiting. He was wearing a baseball cap and a denim vest that showed an arm of intricate black tattoos and six-pack abs.

When had he gotten those?

And when did Izzy become such a badass? Dare she say it? He was hot. Weird.

Speaking of hot, who was that guy he was with? The caption read *Reggaeton star Papi Gringo and friend Isadore Rivera at the Nuyorican Café in Old San Juan.*

Lupe searched Papi Gringo. "Whoa," she said as she scrolled through the results. His real name was Carlos Colón, and he was from Amapola. Wasn't that where her father was from? Made sense.

She dug deeper. He was a Cancer, liked to surf, and had become a vegan when he was fourteen. "Blah, blah, blah."

Wait.

In an article about a lawsuit regarding some lyrics or something, there was a quote from his lawyer.

Tere Dávila.

Lupe's cousin.

"No, seriously?" She laughed. "How small *is* this island?"

There was a link to his latest music video. A song called "El Cuco." As the video loaded she felt like someone was watching her and her head snapped toward the window.

Idiot, you're on the second floor. She chuckled, but it sounded false to her own ears.

The video began, the setting a dark street, shadows following Papi Gringo as he walked toward the camera. Lupe soon found herself hypnotized by the throbbing pulse of the reggae-style beat, by the percussive rap lyrics.

Retribution, El Cuco will find you
Retribution, it begins inside you
Retribution, he sees all you do
Retribution

Every night I pray for you
El Cuco doesn't prey on you
Your fate is under your control
Don't let him find and bind your soul

Conscience is growing evil
Life's pumping through a needle
Your mother's words fade to black
El Cuco's cure will conjure that
It's retribution that rules the night
La madre's fateful words were right

Retribution.

Retribución.

She jolted up in bed. The old woman in El Rubí. She'd said something about retribución, and how "*he'll* come for" Izzy.

What the hell?

She opened her contacts and was about to call her uncle when she stopped.

What was she doing? She's going to tell him about some song lyrics about a monster, and what a grief-stricken old woman told her in El Rubí, an area she wasn't supposed to be walking through.

No way. That would be a disaster. He'd lock her in her room for the rest of the summer or send her to a shrink.

But there were too many connections, she just couldn't string them together. She looked back at the images of Papi Gringo. Maybe if she talked to him. He wrote the song; there must be more to it. Yes.

She pulled up Tere's contact.

Hey prima! I'm in PR! Any chance you can meet for coffee today?

Too late Lupe realized it wasn't even five A.M. yet. But the answer came right away.

Lupe! Hey chica! I heard u were coming! I have a break at 11:00.

Cafeteria Mallorca in OSJ?

What or who is OSJ?

LOL! Old San Juan. U need a ride?

Nah I can get tía to drop me. C U soon!

Lupe lay back down and smiled. Now she just needed some kind of excuse.

Lupe sat across from Tere for breakfast later that morning sipping dark, rich coffee. Tere was a second cousin, really, but it was hard to follow the complicated tree of her Puerto Rican family, since the branches seemed to go on forever. They were ten years apart in age and totally different in pretty much every aspect. Lupe was always spilling food on her clothes and forgetting to run a brush through her hair before leaving the house, while Tere looked put-together from the minute she stepped out the door in her vintage kitten heels. Lupe's skin color was like something that lived in a cave, while her cousin's coloring was rich and warm and filled with sun. Tere was full-blooded Puerto Rican with almost the same figure as Lupe, but on her it looked fabulous. She wore fifties-style dresses that emphasized her tiny waist and curvy hips and when she walked, everything swayed back and forth as if there were music playing only for her.

Lupe had to keep herself from babbling too fast since the strong, dark coffee and powdered sugar mallorcas were making the blood buzz in her skull like a hive of bees.

"So, what have you been doing since you got in?" Tere asked, her lipstick miraculously unmarred by the powdery pastry.

Oh, visiting the scene of a murder, which freaked out Aunt Maria, waiting for our uncle to get back from a second crime scene, you know, typical teen stuff. On second thought, best not to fill in *all* the details. "Tío has been pretty busy with these murders going on—"

"¡Ay! So horrible! I can't believe this is happening. Poor Esteban having to do such dangerous work. This is why I chose entertainment law, Lupe. No dead bodies."

Lupe laughed. Then she realized that was a perfect segue. "The two boys who were killed were friends, did you know that?" Did Tere know that cousin Izzy was friends with them? Damned if she was going to be the one to tell her if she didn't know already. "I read in the paper today that even that singer Papi Gringo ran with them."

Tere looked up at that. "Yes, but he doesn't really travel in those circles anymore. Those boys took a different path. Carlos lives pretty clean. He's a vegan, for heaven's sake."

"I get the sense he's a big star down here."

Tere laughed. "Not just down here, pretty much everywhere, chica. Where have you been?"

"Vermont. Trust me, no one's heard of reggaeton there."

"He's a good kid. I represent him, you know."

Lupe feigned surprise. "You know him?"

"Seguro. It's a small island."

Lupe tried to keep her voice even. "Do you think you could, maybe, arrange for me to talk to him?"

"Papi Gringo? Why do you want to talk to him?"

Lupe pulled up the excuse she'd made up earlier that morning. "I sometimes write for *Seven Days,* a statewide newspaper in Vermont, and an article on Papi Gringo would be cool." She made sure her voice sounded conversational, light. "You know, exposing New England to our musica?" Yeah, it was thin, but it was the best she could come up with. Did she feel good that she'd lied to two of her relatives in twenty-four hours? No. But that didn't stop her. It was all for the greater good.

She watched as Tere fished in her handbag. "If you want to talk to him, I can arrange it. Papi Gringo's in town this week. He's having a big block party in his old neighborhood on Saturday. It's a big deal, bringing some attention to Amapola. Lord knows they need it. Poor place is going downhill like it's being shoved."

Mission accomplished. "Oh!" She put her hand on Tere's arm. "Don't mention the Papi Gringo thing to Esteban, okay?"

"Are you kidding? Who do you think he'd be more angry with? The person who did it, or the older, 'more responsible' cousin who arranged it?" She winked at Lupe and opened her lip gloss wand.

One more question she had to ask. "Hey, how's cousin Izzy?"

Tere froze for a second, lip gloss in mid-swipe. Then she started moving again as if someone had flicked a switch. "You know Izzy. He's got his own life. I haven't seen him since Juan's wedding last year." And more to herself than to Lupe: "And he wasn't in very good shape then."

"Not in good shape. In what way?"

Tere closed her vintage straw handbag with a sharp snap. "Nothing for you to worry about." She motioned to the ancient waiter for the check.

As the car entered the old city the next morning her uncle gave her a lecture about staying on the main streets and not talking to strangers—as if she were five—but she just nodded and didn't say a word. Since Lupe couldn't tell him where she was *really* going she knew she'd better play it cool. If he found out, he'd ship her butt back to Vermont, and she'd never figure out what everything meant. Though they had often discussed his cases, this took it to an entirely different level. But with her cousin Izzy involved in some way no one was willing to explain, this case was personal. Family business. She knew Esteban wouldn't buy that so she figured out the bus route to where the reggaeton singer lived. After all, she was sixteen, almost an adult. She could manage to travel a few towns over all by herself.

That was her story and she was sticking with it.

The bus to Isla Verde was waiting for her when she arrived at the station, belching exhaust into the open concrete building. It took her a few tries to understand the bus fare. Seventy-five cents? That couldn't be right. Seventy-five cents didn't buy you anything these days. She shrugged, put her three quarters in the till, and made her way back through the bus. It was an odd hour, so most of the seats were empty. She fell into one in the next-to-last row, scooching over so she could look out the window. As they pulled out, they passed by the huge luxury liner ships that were spewing red-faced, hungover tourists onto the wooden slats of the pier. The tourists shielded their eyes from the sun as if it were attacking them. Lupe supposed it was.

The buildings began to change as the bus wove through traffic. They were gradually getting less cared for and there were more and more abandoned buildings, green vines pushing from their hollow insides like giant Chia Pets. Her heart started to speed up with the movement of the bus as the old city was left behind. Lupe had never done anything like this before. When she came to the island she was always in arm's reach of her father, never alone. And she'd certainly never lied to her uncle or her cousin. She swallowed hard, pushing the guilt further down into her belly.

The neighborhoods changed rapidly once they left the tourist area, the problems with the economy taking their toll on the island.

As the bus waited for a line of people to board on Calle Loíza, Lupe noticed the poster on the bus stop shelter. It was a huge ad for Papi Gringo's new album. His neck was draped with gold chains as thick as ropes, his eyes covered with black sunglasses, "El Cuco" in ornate script below. The ad was riddled with what appeared to be bullet holes. She shivered, a bad feeling crawling across her skin.

Was this a good idea?

Gradually the scenery changed again, becoming more colorful, with more people milling about the streets. Finally, she saw the first high-rise out of the windows on the other side, the winking turquoise ocean beyond. She remembered the Amigos supermarket up ahead from seeing it from the highway. Isla Verde. She rang the bell and made her way to the exit.

This was crazy. Here she was in a town she'd only seen from

a distance, and she was going to saunter through and meet with
a recording star?

Whose life was this, anyway?

The bus pulled away, leaving Lupe in a cloud of gray exhaust
that contrasted with the electric blue of the sky. Across the avenue was a long line of high-end apartment buildings. When the
light changed, she made her way across. Papi Gringo's condo
building was right across the street and she took deep breaths
as she made her way up the driveway, smoothing her dress
against her legs.

"You've got this," she said just before opening the glass front
door. The guard had her name already, so he escorted her into
the elevator, turned a key on the console, pressed the PH button,
tipped his uniform hat at her, and left. And there she was, riding
up in the mirrored elevator to the penthouse. She avoided looking at the seemingly hundred reflections that surrounded her.
She had struggled with what to wear but finally settled on a
simple blue sundress, thinking it was classier than her usual
choices. Now here she was, riding up in an elevator to a star's
apartment, and she felt prissy.

As she watched the lighted floor numbers shift, she could
almost hear her heartbeat, it was going so fast. It wasn't every
day that she talked to a celebrity. Who was she kidding? She'd
never talked to a celebrity. She flipped her hair back, the mul-
tiple reflections mimicking the movement.

Papi Gringo's song was playing in Lupe's mind as the elevator opened directly into the apartment. So *that* was why you
needed a key to press the button in the elevator. She found herself facing a wall of glass with an unobstructed view of the ocean,
the progressing shades of turquoise glittering with reflected
sunlight. It was decorated sparsely but super-elegantly, with all-
white furniture, a grand piano, and splashes of color on can-
vassed art that hung around the room. She could see a sliver of

a large, white and stainless kitchen that looked like the display model in an expensive appliance store. Papi Gringo wasn't much older than she was, but this looked like an adult apartment. She'd read he bought it when he was just sixteen, plus the entire floor beneath it for his parents to live in.

Lupe pulled out her cell phone to take a selfie. As she touched the button a smiling face appeared above her shoulder.

"I see you found your way up, Señorita Dávila."

Lupe's cheeks turned red as she shoved the phone in her bag and whirled around. She found herself looking up into the face of a tall, hot . . . man. Seventeen or no, this was a man. "Z'at okay?" she stammered.

She hoped she took the photo in time so that he was in it.

"Of course, would you like to sit down?" he asked, gesturing to the white leather couches. Passing him, she caught the scent of limes and some kind of spice. Boy, he smelled good.

As she walked toward the living area, Lupe assessed him out of the corner of her eye. His skin was pale olive, impossibly smooth, his hair shiny black and cut tight to his head, and his lips were full and the color of ripe guavas. He was dressed in dark jeans, and a tight black T-shirt hugged his muscular chest and flat stomach. Just like Izzy, his forearms were covered with intricate black tattoos. As he sat down across from her she noticed the lack of expected bling around his neck. The rope chains must be just for performance. Instead, in the center of his chest lay a simple gold cross on a chain. She adjusted the fabric of her dress as she sat down like some prim Catholic middle schooler. *Don't be such a loser,* she thought as she glanced up to find him looking her up and down, a small smile playing across his lips. She was embarrassed to feel warmth growing in her chest and spreading down to her stomach.

"Well, Lupe—may I call you Lupe?"

She nodded, numb. Her name sounded like silk on his lips. Smooth, sexy silk. The heat was spreading to her limbs.

"Lupe, what can I do for you?"

She coughed into her fist. "Papi Gringo—"

"Carlos."

"Huh? I mean, excuse me?"

He looked up at her, his eyes softer and tired. "My real name is Carlos."

"I know." She smiled at him then. It was as if she were speaking to another person entirely, someone who really *was* her age. Well, if she was going to make this ruse work she'd better make with the interview. She consulted her phone for the filler questions she'd come up with that morning. She was going to tread carefully, though. Starting out with asking about his murdered friends was sure to make him call security.

"So, how did you get into the business? Were you always into music?"

"Ah, well that was one good thing that came out of living in my old neighborhood."

She pretended to consult her notes. "Amapola?"

"Yes, exactly. You do your research." And he smiled that smile. The one that was higher on one side, topped by a small dimple on his left cheek like an accent. The smile that gave her that tingly feeling.

"In the Amapola of my childhood, music was everywhere."

"Of your childhood? What do you mean? How has Amapola changed?" Damn! She was good at this reporter thing.

He sighed. "Let's just say it's suffering in the way much of the island is. But as I was saying, my parents love classic Puerto Rican music: danza, plena, salsa." He paused. "You know this music, yes?"

Lupe felt the heat rush to her face. It felt like the *How Puerto*

Rican are you? test she sometimes got down here. She hated tests. But salsa she knew, and from the word "danza" she assumed they were dances and a form of music. She could usually fake her way through. "Of course. However, I've never had the pleasure of dancing them."

He smiled in that way again. "I hope to have the opportunity to dance them with you one day."

Boy, it was getting hot in there.

"Reggaeton was all around me, at school, on the calle. I loved the traditional music, but this was part of our generation, tu sabes? I followed it even after we moved to the mainland."

She stammered out a few more of the classic interview questions: whose music inspires you (Daddy Yankee, Don Omar, and Wisin y Yandel); what was it like being a star so young (great, but he still had the same responsibilities as other guys his age: college applications, helping his mother with grocery shopping . . . she didn't buy a word of this); and what was he working on (a crossover album in English). When she thought she'd done enough fake interviewing, Lupe got down to the real reason for her visit. But she had to fish carefully.

"Can you tell me about your new song 'El Cuco'?"

He paused and looked at her. After a minute he said, "Okay. What about it?"

The temperature in the room dropped. Lupe recited a stanza from the song. "'It's retribution that rules the night.'"

Carlos stared at her, his arms draped over the back of the couch. "It's just something my mom used to tell me when I was little to scare me into behaving. I think every boy in PR has heard the story of El Cuco."

"Well, it's a metaphorical monster, right? I mean, there's no such thing."

"Oh Lupe, of course there is. I think some people have their own personal monsters."

"I think real life is weird enough without believing in monsters."

"Well, down here it's everywhere. In every leaf, every stone. You just have to be open to it."

Okay, that's enough of that. "Yeah, okay. But I was wondering, retribution for what?"

"Señorita Dávila, it's just a song."

So he was suddenly formal. "Just a song," she repeated. Her cover story suddenly left her as she stared at the man with his legs casually crossed, his whole demeanor cool, calm, and collected. Then she pictured him as he was on the poster, holes spread across his chest, blood splattered all over the white of the pristine apartment like some scene from *DOA Newark*. Suddenly she was tired of cover stories and flirting. She believed that he could be in danger. "I'm sure you're aware that two of your childhood friends have been killed over the last few days?" She heard her voice, confident and strong, as if it were coming from a real detective.

He sat up straighter, his sultry look shifting to something more serious. "Yes, God rest their souls." He absently fingered the cross on his chest.

"Don't you think it's odd that two guys from your old neighborhood died in such a short period of time?"

He uncrossed his legs then, all pretense of the sexy star act gone. "Yes, well, Amapola isn't what it used to be. It's turning into a dangerous place and those two got into some sketchy things over the last few years."

He started to get to his feet, and Lupe got the sense she was about to be dismissed. Lupe the conversation killer. She rushed to speak. "I was thinking there might be some connection? I mean, these deaths seem like retribution for something, don't you think? Just like your song."

He sat back down, leaned forward, and looked her in the eye.

He said nothing for a full minute. Lupe shifted uncomfortably under his gaze. "Señorita Dávila, I got away from that life when I was a kid. If you're trying to say that I did something to get those guys—"

Crap. She was screwing this all up. Her heartbeat started pushing against the cotton front of her sundress. "No, no, not at all! That isn't what I meant. It's just that, what if someone is targeting your old friends from Amapola?" She had to get him to understand, she knew she was just a girl from Vermont, not a journalist or Detective Leah Carlson, but there was something about this case.

He relaxed a bit back into the cushions. "My mom would say that we reap what we sow. Luckily, we got out of there right after my thirteenth birthday. My parents moved us to Nueva York. I only saw those guys when I came down for vacaciones from then on."

"Oh." Lupe was disappointed.

"You going to get changed, Papi?"

Lupe looked up to see a gorgeous girl standing in the doorway. Though she couldn't have been much older than Lupe, her curvy body, skintight dress, and long shining locks made her look like she'd stepped out of a music video.

Papi hadn't moved. He was still looking at Lupe. Finally, he slowly stood. "Sí, mi amor. Well, Señorita Dávila, duty calls. I hope you will join us at my block party on Saturday?"

"What's the occasion?"

"My birthday, and more importantly, raising money for my old barrio."

"Sure," she threw out casually, though she had no intention of going. She didn't go to parties in Vermont; she certainly wouldn't go to one here.

Besides, she had work to do.

July 7, 1:00 P.M.

Javier

💀

JAVIER PRESSED THE elevator call button again and again as the doorman looked at him with an amused grin. Padre Sebastian sometimes teased him about his type-A personality. He could imagine Sebastian's voice: *You only need to press it once. Doing that won't make it come any faster.*

Javier smiled at the thought and forced his hand down by his side. The priest kept him sane, made him feel safe. When they had met two years ago, it was the first time an adult had actually listened to him, cared about what he thought and felt. It was easy to give up the drugs then. Well, not easy, but to have someone actually believe in him gave him a reason to change.

Finally the bell dinged, the doors started to open, and he pushed his large frame through the opening as soon as he could fit, his focus on the conversation he planned to have with Carlos. He ran headlong into someone coming out of the elevator.

"Ay, perdón, I didn't see—" He stopped as he looked into the face of the girl from Parque Central, the one who had been with the police chief, the one who'd faced off with Marisol. The girl who was lit from inside.

What was she doing here?

He saw a flash of anger in her blue eyes as she shifted out of the way. "Yeah, buddy. Next time—" She looked into his face and he thought she recognized him, too. They stood there staring at each other until Javier coughed. *She must think I'm an idiot,* he thought. *Say something!* "It was my fault. Please excuse me." *That's it? That's all you have to say?*

A small smile teased up the ends of her full, pink lips and she hesitated for a moment. Javier could feel his pulse behind his face. Did the AC in the lobby just go out or something?

"Yeah, well, you and I seem to always meet in doorways." With that, she pulled her arms in and slipped past him. He jumped aside too late when he realized he was still blocking the door, though he had to admit he was glad he hadn't gotten *all* the way out of the way when he felt the gentle brush of her dress against his hand as she passed.

He just caught a glimpse of her back as she stepped through the door, the sun making her hair shine like quartz. The security guard keyed the penthouse, and just before the metal doors clambered shut, he saw her look back at him over her shoulder.

Damn.

He stood there and almost lost his balance as the car jerked and began to move. He braced himself on the wall. He hated elevators. All small spaces really. They felt like the end of a bad high. The metal walls closing in on him as that feeling of being trapped and moved against your will rose from your gut. He thought of the girl, of her half smile and the freckles sprinkled across her nose like cinnamon, and his breathing started coming in slower, though another part of his anatomy stood at attention.

The elevator doors opened and Javier stepped into Carlos's apartment. He heard voices in the next room and then Carlos stepped through the door in full Papi Gringo gear—big black sunglasses, oversize baseball cap placed just so, and massive diamond studs glinting from his ears. He stopped mid-sentence when he saw Javier and a smile spread across his face. Suddenly the reggaeton star was gone and the guy he knew from the neighborhood appeared. Javier couldn't help smiling back.

"Javi, hermano, I was just about to head out when the guard called up and said you were here. I couldn't believe it. What the hell you doin' in my neck of the woods?" They hugged warmly, the scent of expensive cologne rising off Carlos's jacket.

"Looking for you, hombre." He stepped back, held Carlos at arm's length. "Damn! You're looking good. Fame agrees with you, Papi Gringo."

Carlos brushed off the compliment. "Ay, it pays the bills, right? It's amazing what money can buy."

"Man, I wouldn't know." He smiled. "Look, I didn't realize you got somewhere to go. I don't want to keep you."

Carlos waved the comment away and led Javier over to the couch. "Sit, man. Mi casa es tu casa."

Javier looked around at the swank penthouse, glimpsed a dark-haired, curvy girl walking on sky-high heels in the next room. "No, man. My casa ain't nothing like this." The leather of the couch sighed with him as he sat back.

"So, how you doin', hombre?" Carlos asked as he took a seat across from his friend.

Javier shrugged. "Bad freaking week."

Carlos crossed himself. "No shit. I mean, Vico and now Memo? That's messed up."

Javier sat up again and leaned forward. "That's why I'm here. I wanted to talk to you about los cangrejos."

"And then there were three."

"It just feels like too much to be a coincidence, tu sabes? That's why I wanted to talk to you. You're the most together. Besides, I don't have a clue where to find Izzy these days."

"Yeah, I heard he's MIA. I'm sure he's okay, brother is just trying to get clean."

"True." Javier disappeared himself when he got clean. Isn't that what Marisol was trying to tell him? "I thought you might be able to help me figure things out."

Carlos sighed. "I don't know how I can help, man, I wish I did, but Vico and Memo? They were into some bad shit."

"True, true. My mother said some weird shit about how the mothers 'had nothing to do with it.' I've been racking my brains about what 'it' could be. And something about the last cangrejo birthday party is nagging at me."

Carlos smiled. "Man, remember those? We had some fun, for real."

Javier smiled, too, visions of cake-fueled bike races and laughing until their sides ached. "Yeah, they were fun. Why did they stop?"

"I don't know. Probably 'cause I moved and Memo's mother thought we were"—he did air quotes—"'bad influences' on her son. He was afraid of the rain that fell. We only toughened him up."

Javier pictured Memo shuffling from foot to foot at the church. "Well, kind of."

They laughed, but it diminished like air from a balloon as thoughts of Memo's death invaded.

"I'm glad your parents took you out of the neighborhood. I wish my mother had gotten me out. Hell, *she* still isn't out."

Carlos leaned forward. "You want me to help her? I could give you some money and you could get her an apartment here in Isla Verde, or something."

Javier looked at his friend and felt a pressing on his chest. Since becoming famous everybody wanted something from Carlos: money, for him to listen to their mixtape, women wanted to date him. So for him to make that offer . . . well, Javi knew how much that meant. He coughed to hide the catch in his throat. "Carlos, bro, that's so generous—"

"Don't say another word. That's what we do for each other."

Javier thought of seeing Vico's sister at the church. "Maybe if you helped Vico's family. I saw Marisol at the church and she said something about losing the house?"

Carlos threw his hands up. "I could have killed Vico." When he realized what he'd said he made a quick sign of the cross. "May he rest in peace, of course, but when his mom was sick I gave him enough to buy the house outright and he just used it to buy product to sell. Left Marisol and their dying mother to fend for themselves."

Javier shook his head. Vico always did seem determined to dig an even bigger hole to bury his life in. "You're too good to us, hermano."

Carlos waved the words away again. "We're brothers, man."

Javier thought about that for a minute. "Carlos, do you remember anything about that last party?"

"I've had to go to about a thousand parties this year alone for work. I can't remember what happened at the one from last night. Why?"

"I don't know. I feel like after that night . . . my life went off the rails." He didn't want to talk about the shadows, as if just talking about it would call them back. "I remember my mom getting mad at us for something . . . I guess what I'm asking is, do you? Did we do this somehow? What happened to Vico and Memo?"

"Nah, man. Are you kidding? We couldn't even take a shit without our mothers finding out. We were powerless, hombre, totally powerless."

"Yeah, you're right. It's not like our little kid gang meant anything, right?"

"It meant something. But something good, you feel me?" He

paused. "You never answered my question. Can I help get your mom out of the barrio?"

"You don't know how badly I want that. But there's no way she'd move. She's totally sunk her roots in, no matter how bad the neighborhood gets. She pretends she's Susie Homemaker."

"I hear you." Carlos stood up. "If she changes her mind, you call me." He pointed his finger at Javier.

Javier stood. "Promise." They fell into a hug. "Thank you, man," he whispered in Carlos's ear.

"For you, anything." Carlos slapped him on the back, straightened his jacket and suddenly he was Papi Gringo again.

How the hell did he do that? He slipped the star persona on and off like a jacket. "Well, I better let you get back to your business," Javier said, pointing to the doorway where the hot girl waited.

"Like I said, it's a living." He smiled and walked with Javier to the elevator. "You'll let me know if Izzy turns up, yes?"

Javier nodded. "You, too."

"It's weird, you're the second person in the last fifteen minutes to bring up all this shit."

Javier stopped. "What? Who was the other?"

Carlos pressed the elevator button. "Some reporter chick. Though, if you ask me, she looked too young to be a reporter. Hot though, in a natural, gringa kinda way. She did have a decent-sized culo."

Javier tried to sound calm. "What was her name?"

"Lupe Dávila."

Javier's heart started to pound, hard. He wondered if Carlos could hear it. "She's the police chief's niece, Izzy's cousin. Did you know that?"

"Man, I don't know. I did the interview as a favor to my lawyer."

A phone started buzzing in Carlos's jacket pocket. He pulled it out and looked at the screen. "I gotta go, man. Great seeing you, though." The elevator doors rattled open. Carlos made a gesture that echoed the cell phone at his ear. "Call me anytime, Javi. I mean it."

Javier smiled and stepped into the elevator. With all they'd talked about, he couldn't stop thinking about Lupe. The gringa with the Latin name.

As the doors closed on Carlos's apartment, Javier could see smiling images of himself multiplied in the mirrors around him.

The lights flickered on and off as the elevator lurched downward. Javier was just thinking it was like a disco when they clicked off and stayed off. His breathing started coming in faster every second he stood in the elevator's blackness. When he heard the insect-like buzz of the fluorescent lights start to come to life again, he let out a long breath.

In the first flicker of the lights, Javier glanced over his left shoulder, and a dark shape loomed behind him, its edges ragged like it had been torn from the fabric of his nightmares.

The lights clicked off again and he sank back into darkness. A scream rose in his throat, the back of his neck twitching.

The lights came back on and stayed on.

Javier spun around, searching the mirrors' reflection for the shadow behind him.

There was nothing there.

He was alone.

When the door clattered open on the first floor, he pushed his body through the narrow opening as soon as he could fit, and tore through the lobby. Outside, he drew in gulps of the heavy, salted sea air, and looked around him at the busy Isla Verde Avenue.

People walked dogs along the sidewalk.

Cars buzzed by on the expressway a block away.

How could it look so normal?

Why did it feel like he'd just shared the elevator with a small piece of hell?

July 7, 1:50 P.M.

Lupe

💀

LUPE CHECKED THE time on her cell phone again. "Twenty-five minutes? How long does a freakin' bus take in this country, anyway?" She was the only person sitting at the bus stop waiting for the A-5 to Old San Juan and it was about three degrees hotter than Hades. She began to wonder if everyone else knew something she didn't. Maybe the entire bus service had been canceled and no one had told her. How much money could they make with a seventy-five cent bus fare, anyway?

She had to admit, though; she was doing something right. Not only had she talked to Papi "call me Carlos" Gringo in complete sentences, but he seemed to accept her as a real journalist. Then she remembered the selfie she took in the apartment. She pulled up the photo app and opened the most recent shot. There she was, the big white apartment with the ocean out the window . . . with Papi Gringo over her shoulder! She actually squealed as she posted it with the caption *Just hanging with Papi Gringo. No big thing.* At least she hadn't lied to her cousin Tere about one thing; she really was introducing northern New England to his music.

The sun was blazing above, baking her bare shoulders in her sundress, and she regretted not using some of the shopping cash her uncle had given her to take a cab. It was still early in the summer, though, and she figured she would take the bus again instead and save the cash. Her uncle would absolutely kill her if he knew she was traveling around the island on the bus . . . and if he knew where she'd been . . . and who she'd talked to . . . alone. But if she hadn't come she wouldn't have gotten to meet an actual celebrity.

"Damn, it's hot out here." Her voice sounded loud despite the constant thrum of traffic on the street in front of her. She leaned out and looked to the left again, wondering if miraculously the bus had appeared and was making its way toward her. She heard a car idling to her right, in the driveway to Papi Gringo's apartment building, the engine revving. She sat up straighter and felt a bristling along her hairline. Ugh. She was just waiting for the catcalls. She kept her eyes locked in the other direction as if she could make the bus appear. One more minute of revving and she was going to turn around and rip this guy a new one.

"Perdóname, Señorita Dávila?"

What? Her head whipped over to the right and she saw *him*, smiling out the window of a beat-up sedan.

He was calling her.

By name.

That damn heat rose up behind her face again.

"What?" Not the answer one normally gives a handsome guy who politely calls you by name, but this was not a situation that was natural to her.

"I just came from my friend Carlos's place."

Lupe just stared at him. Jeezum, he was handsome.

"You know, Papi Gringo."

She shook her head awake. "I just met him."

"Since we keep running into each other, sometimes literally, I wanted to at least let you know my name." He smiled again. His teeth were impossibly white. "I'm Javier, Javier Utierre."

Javier. She said it over and over in her head. "I'm Lupe Dáv— guess you knew that already."

He just looked at her as the traffic buzzed by and she looked at the sidewalk, the road signs, anywhere but at him.

"Buses are slow here."

She smiled. "You think?" His eyes were squinting from the sun, his lashes dark and thick, but there was a paleness in his skin that wasn't there earlier, like he'd aged in the last half an hour.

"May I give you a ride somewhere, Señorita Dávila?"

"Lupe." She said it as if her mouth wasn't under her control anymore.

"Lupe, can I give you a ride somewhere?"

She shook her head again. Did she think that would clear it like an Etch A Sketch or something? And why did this guy think she needed his help *again*? "No. I'm just going to Old San Juan. I can get there myself."

"I'd be happy to drive you there."

Lupe couldn't help herself, for a second she wondered what it would be like to sit next to him, what he smelled like, what his thigh felt like pressed against hers. . . .

"I can't." She felt like she had to say something to explain herself. That was a first. "My tío taught me never to take rides with strangers." Great, now she sounded like she was ten and her tío told her what to do. Well, her tío told *everybody* what to do.

"He's a wise man. You're lucky to have him."

"I am."

"How about I ride the bus with you?"

"What? Why? You have a car." This guy really made no sense to her.

"Well, *my* tío taught me not to let ladies ride the bus alone."

She felt that angry heat rise behind her face again. "Well, I guess you and your tío have never heard of feminism. I can handle myself. " Lupe turned to look down the street again. Part of her was afraid the bus *was* coming and that only pissed her off more.

"Good. Then *you* can protect *me*," Javier said, and then he was backing the car up the driveway, leaving Lupe to sit at the bus stop, her mouth hanging open.

What the hell? What was with this guy? She was horrified to find herself primping her hair. What was wrong with her?

She heard shouting coming from Papi Gringo's building and looked up to see Javier running down the driveway. "¡Espera, por favor!"

Lupe looked back toward the road and was shocked to see the bus door open in front of her. When had that happened? Probably when she was busy trying to figure out what this guy's story was. Javier was standing by the side of the door, gesturing for her to go in first.

"Yeah, no. No 'ladies-first' crap with me." Besides, no force on earth was going to make her go first so this guy could get the hi-def view of her ample ass.

"Ah, right. Feminist." He smiled and took the stairs two at a time. And the view of his butt wasn't bad at all.

As Lupe lifted her leg to the first step, she noticed a small blue car idling behind the large ad for Bacardi on the bus stop. Lupe paused. That car hadn't been there a minute ago, had it? She shook her head and pulled herself the rest of the way up the stairs.

July 7, 2:05 P.M.

Marisol

💀

SO HOLIER-THAN-THOU JAVIER was hanging with the gringa. Marisol saw them get on the bus together. It made total sense. She swore her blood reached a rolling boil as she got out of the car and walked down the underground parking lot ramp.

She'd seen the limousine making its way down the same ramp a few minutes earlier. If he wouldn't answer her calls she would find another way to talk to him.

The basement door to the building's elevator opened with a ding and released a flock of people who headed toward the idling black limo. And there, at their center like the eye of a hurricane, was Carlos Colón.

Big man and his entourage. They didn't know him like she did.

Marisol walked to intercept him before he got into the car.

"Don't take calls from old girlfriends now that you're a big shot?"

He jumped at the unexpected voice, like he was afraid of something. When he realized who it was, he regained his star attitude and smiled. "I wouldn't exactly call you a girlfriend,

Marisol. We went to the movies when you were, what? Twelve? We hung out for a week, maybe two."

"Yeah, you should have some respect. From what I hear it's the longest relationship you ever had."

The leggy girl in a micro dress next to him chuckled. Marisol turned her attention to her. "What are you laughing about, Barbie? Better get him to buy you some more plastic surgery before he dumps you, too."

The girl lurched toward Marisol. "Oh yeah, bitch? I'm gonna take off my earrings and you're the one who's gonna need some plastic surgery!" Carlos held the woman back as she stepped forward and, to Marisol's amusement, literally took off her earrings.

Marisol laughed and pointed. "Oh look! It's Gangsta Barbie!"

The entire entourage laughed but stopped as soon as Carlos turned around and gave them a look.

"What do you want, Mari?" Carlos asked with a tired and way-too-old voice.

"I want to know what killed my brother."

His face got serious then. Even he knew this was not a joking matter. "What? Or who? I loved Vico, you know that, but—"

"Did you? Did you love him, *Papi Gringo*? Or were you so busy buying Lamborghinis and jewels for your cheap girlfriends"—Marisol continued to speak as the Gangsta Barbie strained against Carlos trying to get to her—"to notice that your old friends, los cangrejos, were dying?"

Carlos's face fell. "Look, no one's more sorry than I am—"

Marisol started to yell then. "No one? Really, Carlos? Vico was *my brother*! Don't you think that makes me more sorry than you? Huh?"

Carlos said in a tired voice, "Mari, why are you here? Really?"

"Why? Because I know there's more to why your cangrejo

'brothers' are dying, one by one, and I think you know more than you're letting on."

"If I knew something, I would tell you. What would I have to gain?"

Marisol put her hands on her hips. "I don't know, maybe another hit song? That's all that matters to you anyway. Not people. Not *your* people."

There was the thunder of feet coming down the driveway, and three men in security uniforms, hands on the guns at their belts, appeared at the mouth of the garage entrance behind her.

Carlos put up his hand and they stopped. Marisol hated how his badly written rhymes gave him the power to control people like that. Leadership shouldn't be about popularity.

She *really* hated it.

"Don't worry, I'm going. All dangerous five-feet-nothing of me." She turned back to Carlos. "I'm going to figure out why my brother died, and if I find out you had something to do with it, you'll be wishing you were next!"

The entourage broke out in a chorus then.

"She just threatened you, man!"

"I heard it!"

"I got a photo of it!"

She stormed through the security guards and up the driveway, the thumping in her head returning like her very own soundtrack.

Her phone buzzed with a text. Keno. At least *he* didn't forget where he came from, didn't pretend to be something he wasn't.

Meet me in OSJ.

July 7, 2:15 P.M.

Lupe

💀

JAVIER'S JEAN-CLAD THIGH was pressing against hers, just as she had imagined. She felt like she should move her leg, but that would make it seem like she cared that his leg was touching hers. She realized he was smiling at her again. "What?"

"So, Lupe Dávila. You're not from Puerto Rico, verdad?"

"You figure that out yourself?" She could tone down the sarcasm a bit. He didn't seem to care, though. He was just smiling at her still, waiting. "I'm from Vermont."

"Ah, Vermont. Lots of skiing there, yes? And maple syrup?" He smiled, and she hated herself for it, but she couldn't help smiling back. She loved the way he pronounced "syrup," not to mention "maple."

"Yes, and armies of cows."

"We have those here, too. But your name is Spanish?"

"Yeah, my father's from here." Why was she telling him all this? The bus slowly made its way toward Old San Juan. Small talk really wasn't her thing and she needed to know what this guy Javier had to do with her uncle. She baited him. "And his brother, my uncle Esteban, works for the police department here."

"Sí, I know. I was there when you got into the . . . discussion, with Marisol."

She let out a laugh. "'Discussion,' that's what you call it."

"Well, with Marisol, that's how most discussions go."

"What a bitch."

Javier paused, and Lupe wondered if she'd stepped over some ill-behaved gringa line. So what if she did?

Finally, he spoke. "She's very . . . troubled."

"You can say that again."

"I don't think I need to."

Lupe stared at him. Was that a joke? She got an answer when he smiled that smile that went all the way up to his eyes, crinkling the skin at the edges like fireworks.

Lupe's heart surged like she'd just plugged it into a charger. There was something wrong with her. This guy had something to do with the two murders, and might know what was going on with her cousin Izzy. They weren't on a date. It was time to get serious. "What did my uncle want from you at the church?"

Javier looked out at the buildings buzzing by the bus windows. "The funeral was for a friend of mine, from when we were children." He paused. "Vico was into some bad things."

"What kind of things?"

"Selling drugs. Doing drugs. But he wasn't always like that."

Yep, so his friends were drug dealers. "And that guy Guillermo? Was he one of your friends too?"

"Yes. Vico, Memo, we were all close. Carlos, too." He paused, like he was wondering whether to say something. "And your cousin Izzy. The five of us were like brothers."

Lupe's heart was tight. Hearing her cousin's name in that crew scared the hell out of her. Especially since two of them were dead. "Is Izzy into drugs?" Was that the mystery? She braced herself, though she was certain she already knew the answer. Even though she hadn't seen him in a few years, it just seemed to fit.

"He was. To be honest, I haven't seen him in a while. Nobody has."

Her chest tightened. "What? He's missing?" That was what they were keeping from her? Trying to "protect" her as usual? They obviously didn't know her at all.

"Yes." He rushed to add, "But he's trying to get clean. When I stopped using, I had to disappear from much of my life."

So he was clean. But she'd heard that before. Her father "stopped drinking" several times a year. "How long since you've used?"

"Two years."

Not bad. Longer than her father ever made it.

A woman bustled by toward the exit with handfuls of Amigo grocery bags. Javier jumped up and held the door open for her as she smiled and made her way down the stairs.

This guy had the knight complex bad. Lupe noticed that they had already reached the Condado. In contrast to the ride out, this trip was going by quickly.

He sat down next to her. "My apologies."

This guy was too much.

"I'm trying to find your cousin Izzy."

She one-upped him. "Me, too, but I'm *also* trying to find out who's killing the others."

"The others? You mean Vico, right? Memo fell in an abandoned building."

He said that, but she could tell from the way he covered his mouth when he said it that he was lying. He didn't think Memo fell on his own. Another skill learned on *DOA Newark*. She shrugged. "If you say so. I'm not convinced it was an accident."

"Don't you think that's best left to your uncle? To the professionals?"

She turned her body to face him. "Yeah, well, sometimes the 'professionals' don't see what's right in front of their faces."

For the first time, she saw the smile settle out of his eyes. "And you think you can find something we can't?"

"Look, I don't know who 'we' represents in that sentence, but if you think you're somehow better than me—"

"That seems to be what *you* think. You come down to the island once a year and assume you know more than your uncle? Than me?" He stood, his lean body taut. "I'm surprised. This seems to be more of a typical gringa attitude than I would've expected from you."

"First of all, you don't know me so how can you 'expect' anything? And second—" She stood and faced him, boring her eyes into his. "I. Am. Not. A. Gringa."

The bus lurched to a stop and she was knocked off-balance and into Javier. For one second he grabbed her by her upper arms and righted her on her feet, and she yanked her body away from him. "Hands off!"

"Fine. Next time I'll just let you fall."

She noticed that everyone seemed to be exiting, and she looked up and saw the Old San Juan bus depot.

She turned and stormed down the stairs, ignoring the wet towel slap of the hot afternoon air, and marched toward the terminal exit. Lupe was certain the footfalls behind her were Javier's, but she would work on losing him in the press of tourists in the old city. She yelled back over her shoulder. "I don't need an escort."

She got to the corner, looked down, and stepped off the curb.

The next thing she felt was Javier's hands grabbing her arms, pulling her up and back onto the sidewalk.

"What—"

In that same moment there was a blast of wind in front of her, blowing her dress back against her legs as a beat-up blue hatch-back blew by them, plowing through the exact spot she had just vacated. She watched the hem of her skirt brush the car's dusty side in slow motion. Lupe stared vacantly as it careened around the corner in a rattling cloud of exhaust and disappeared. For one long second she froze, heart pounding. Then she stumbled and turned toward him.

Javier looked into her eyes like he could see into her. "Are you all right?"

She was so confused, so distracted. She had to consciously look elsewhere in order to speak. "Fine." Lupe's legs started to shake as her body caught up with what had just happened. "I could have . . ." *What? Handled it? Not likely. Died? More likely.* But Javier wasn't listening anyway. He was staring in the direction of the vehicle that almost hit her. "That car. It looked familiar."

"It did? Yeah, it did. I saw one like that near the bus stop outside Carlos's building."

"Really?" He was staring as if he could still see it. "I wish I could remember where I'd seen it before."

They resumed walking in the direction of the café, each lost in their own thoughts.

"Lupe, I don't want to argue with you. I'm not sure why I was."

'Cause I seem to have that effect on people. She kept that thought to herself. Let him think it's his fault.

He stopped and held out his hand for her to shake, and did that smiling thing with his eyes. "Truce?"

She stopped, looked at his hand, and just nodded.

He dropped his hand and continued to smile at her, but in a tired way. "It seems we both have the same goals."

She crossed her arms. The shakiness was beginning to pass, though she still felt a bit out of body. "And what are those?"

"To find Izzy. And with him, figure out who's killing the other cangrejos."

"The can-who-hos?"

"Cangrejos, the crabs. That's what our group was called. We were all born in July—"

Lupe nodded. "Got it, July, Cancer the crab. But what was that about 'killing'? I thought you said Guillermo had an accident?"

"Let's just say you made me think."

Lupe felt particularly smug at that. They continued walking. The setting sun was painting the city orange, the bright colors of the buildings changing with the light.

"Where are you meeting your uncle?"

Lupe pointed ahead to Café Poético on the Plaza de Armas. "At the café." She looked at her phone. "In fifteen minutes."

Javier stopped walking. "As I was saying, seems we both want the same things. Maybe we could work together?"

Lupe examined this boy across from her, wondering why he was so insistent on spending time with her. What did he want? She shook her head. "Not a good idea."

He gave her a sad kind of smile. "Can I at least give you my number? In case you need someone to ride the bus with you again?"

Lupe was staring at him. His number? His brown eyes were twinkling, actually *twinkling,* in the afternoon sun. What was this guy's deal?

He stepped closer to her, so close she could smell the clean floral scent of detergent from his clothing, could feel the heat coming off his body. She went to hand him her phone so he could enter his number, but instead he produced a pen from his pocket, took her hand, and she watched as he wrote his number on the back, the black ink bold against her pale skin, his warm fingers cradling her palm.

Javier stepped backward and smiled. "Miss Dávila. I hope I hear from you someday."

He turned around and she was staring at his back. She liked the way his legs bowed slightly at the knee as if flexed to spring, and the way his wide shoulders alternately lifted as he walked. And his manner was positively old-school. It infuriated and fascinated her all at once.

Then he turned the corner and was gone.

She headed up toward the café, occasionally looking at the number written on her hand, each seven crossed with a line in the middle like her father did. As if to spite her, her heart was beating a rhumba on the inside of her ribs. Plaza de Armas was bustling with after-work traffic. Hundreds of pigeons pecked, rose, and settled again in one mass like a scarf. The rushing of the water in the fountain provided background to the hum of conversation from the people walking through the park.

She stepped into the café and saw her uncle was already inside, sipping a dark cafecito as he spoke into his cell phone. He waved Lupe over to the table, not breaking from the conversation. Her favorites, an iced vanilla latte and a slice of guava pastry, sat waiting for her. How did he remember that from the year before? She started to feel bad for deceiving him about where she'd been all day. And spending the afternoon with a musician and then a recovering drug addict who might be tied to his case. Oh, and then there was the issue of almost getting run over. She almost laughed out loud at the ridiculousness of it all. She put the hand with the number written on it under the table and shoved half the guava cake in her mouth.

Her phone buzzed and she looked at the screen. It was a message from a girl she knew from her high school, Jessica. Lupe smiled. She was sure the kids from her school were abuzz from the photo of her and Carlos.

Isn't this the same guy?

The message included a link to a news site. The image was dark, but it was a photo of Carlos surrounded by a group of people, including the girl she'd seen at his apartment. They were facing a girl with a bunch of police officers or guards behind her. Lupe almost choked on her cake. She enlarged the image so she could see the girl clearer.

It was Marisol from the church.

It was posted a half hour ago, right after Lupe left.

What the hell?

Just then her uncle's conversation came into focus. "Yes. Isadore Rivera and Javier Utierre. We need to talk to Isadore by midnight of the ninth, Utierre by the eleventh. Uh-huh, right, see you then."

Lupe just stared as he pressed the End button with his big forefinger. She tried not to appear too eager. "What was that about?"

"Nothing, m'ija. You done with your cake?" He took what was left of her piece, shoved it in his mouth, and stood. "We have to head out to Guaynabo soon to meet your aunt. I'm taking us all out to dinner since I left in the middle of the night last night."

"Um, Izzy and Javier Utierre . . . are they suspects?" Why hadn't she thought of that? Were Vico and Memo really Javier's friends? Or his victims?

Had she spent the afternoon with a murderer? And her cousin . . .

"I know we usually talk about my cases, sobrina. But this one . . . I don't want you to know anything about it."

She scurried to catch up with him. "Why the hell not?"

His eyelids lowered.

"I know, I know. Language, but what is it with this case,

tío? You always tell me about your work. Is it because Izzy's missing?"

He squinted at her for a moment. "Where did you get that idea?"

She noticed he didn't deny it.

"We just need to talk to them as soon as possible. Come on, we're going to be late."

Lupe stopped short. "But why the ninth at midnight?" But her tío was already halfway down the block. "Tío! What does that mean?"

He wasn't having it. "Keep up, sobrina."

July 7, 4:15 P.M.

Javier

AS JAVIER BOARDED the crowded bus heading back to Isla Verde and his car, the events of the afternoon played over in his head. He'd probably never see Lupe again, and damn, she was a pain in the ass, but she made him smile. The way her nose crinkled when she laughed. How her voice got slightly breathy when she was talking, like she couldn't get the words out fast enough. Even the way she had a snarky comeback ready and waiting at all times like rows of shark teeth. Then there was the long cut of muscle on the sides of her legs that reached beneath the hem of her skirt.

Yeah, he had to stop that line of thought.

A group of boys tumbled onto the bus at the next stop, like a litter of puppies chasing and teasing one another in the crowded aisle. Javier watched them in their plaid school uniforms, white shirts, and ties and tried to remember what it was like to be that young, when your biggest problem was how to talk your mother into buying you the newest pair of Nikes or getting the attention of Camille Carrion in science class.

Then Javier noticed the little girl trailing behind, watching the boys with a sad type of hunger. One of the boys imitated a monkey, swinging from the metal straps as if they were vines, and the young girl's laugh was a beat too late, trailing after the others until it was the only sound.

One of the boys glared at her. "Damn, Rosita. What's the matter with you?" The others kept going toward the back of the bus, while the boy whispered to her. "Don't think you're sitting with us, midget. And once we get off the bus you go on home. We got important shit to do and we don't need no shrimp trailing after us."

The girl's chin wobbled but her eyes were fiery. Javier already liked this kid. "Mami doesn't like it when you use bad words around me."

"Yeah, well, Mami's not here, is she?" He resumed his strut toward his friends while the girl slumped into a nearby seat.

Javier's heart tightened for the girl, and another slice of memory opened up to him about the last birthday party of los cangrejos.

He was back at his mother's in Amapola, making his way with his four friends around the low cement house, ducking under the lit windows as if all their mothers were parked behind each one, ten eyes like searchlights scanning the dark. He sat with them in a circle beneath the flamboyán tree in the backyard; he could almost smell the moist dirt, see the glow of the moonlight.

They could hear their mothers talking and laughing in the kitchen, the clank of birthday party dishes being cleaned, dried, and stored away in cabinets. Occasionally their voices became low and serious when the boys assumed they were talking about them.

Javier felt better in the shadows beneath the tree, he felt stronger in the dark. "Well, panas, this year we're teenagers, not little boys, verdad?" The others crowed agreement like roosters, giving one another high fives in the dark. "Los cangrejos are men!"

Izzy started to hoot, but covered his mouth when the rest all shushed him.

"So this year me and Vico decided we should do something a real gang would do, something to make this stupid group birthday party mean something to us instead of just our mothers."

Memo started rocking back and forth. "Wattya got in mind, Javi?"

Vico pulled out a black switchblade with yellow skulls glowing on its handle. He waited until all the boys were looking at him and pressed the button, everyone but Javier gasping as the shiny silver blade popped out with a clean swish, the edge catching the light from the kitchen window. Even though he knew it was coming, Javier was pleased at just how badass the knife looked, at how the other guys were quiet with respect.

Carlos nervously glanced at the back door. "Vico, man! Where did you get that blade?"

Vico beamed, his head held high. "Keno gave it to us. That's not all he gave us, ay Javi?"

Javier waved at Vico. "Damn, pana. This is important."

The back door slammed open and all five boys lurched, Vico shoving the knife beneath his folded leg.

A small person peeked from behind the door, haloed by the light from the kitchen, and they all groaned, their bodies relaxing as they recognized Vico's little sister.

"God, it's just Marisol," Memo exclaimed. "Vico, can't you control your little sister?"

"Why you buggin' us, Mari!" Vico made his voice overly breathy like he was really impatient.

Marisol's voice was small in the quiet yard. "Can I join your club, too?"

Everyone but Javier and Vico started laughing, loud, exaggerated guffaws. Memo and Izzy fell backward in the dirt, holding their bellies.

Javier cringed, remembering how the poor kid's face fell.

Vico's eyes looked glossy and angry in the dark. "It's not a club. We're a gang and it's serious."

The laughing of the others stopped abruptly at Vico's last words.

"I can be serious," Marisol said as she ironed her face of expression in an attempt to appear somber.

Vico jumped to his feet and lurched toward his sister, the hand gripping the knife extended out as if to strike her. "Go back inside before I kick your ass!"

Izzy, always the diplomat, stood between them and put his hand on Vico's arm. "What are you doing?"

"What? I wasn't going to stick her or nothin'. She's just always following us around like a shadow. I'm tired of her shit!"

"What's in your hand?" Marisol asked, staring at the switchblade, the skulls glowing from between Vico's fingers.

Vico lurched toward her again, but she didn't even flinch. Javier remembered being surprised by that. Instead she stared back at him, her voice low and steady. "I'm telling Mama." Only then did she turn around and head back into the house, the door snapping shut behind her.

"Go ahead, snitch!" Vico yelled as Javier pulled him back to the circle, afraid that if Vico's mother came outside they might get caught with the knife. Or worse.

All five of them stood frozen for a moment, expecting Vico's mother to burst through the door, yelling. Nothing. One by one they sat back down in their circle in the dirt, but Javier quietly moved a bit farther away from Vico.

Thinking back and watching the sad little sister on the bus, he felt bad for being so mean to Marisol. He'd been the undisputed leader of their little group. He should have told Vico to throw away that knife. Padre Sebastian always reminded him that he wasn't responsible for other people's actions, yet he couldn't help wondering if he had something to do with how Vico turned out, how Marisol turned out.

But there was more about that night he couldn't remember. It was like he was reaching in the dark for something he couldn't quite see.

His cell phone buzzed in his pocket and pulled him back to the present. Javier pulled it out and looked at the screen. He didn't recognize the number, but the text was unmistakable.

Javier smiled.

July 7, 4:28 P.M.

Lupe

💀

AS HER TÍO drove them to the restaurant, Lupe waited for a respectable amount of time before pulling out her phone. She feigned nonchalance as she snuck peeks at the number on her hand and texted Javier.

OK things r getting really weird.

Yeah, so she had said she wasn't going to contact him, but this whole thing was getting out of control. And the Marisol photo? What in the holy hell was that about? All Lupe was sure of was that it was all somehow connected and Javier was a piece of that puzzle. She still wasn't sure where he fit, but if she was going to find Izzy and figure out what the entire picture was, she'd need him. Besides, it wasn't like she had a vehicle and it would help to have someone who knew the island and all the players in this drama.

Lupe I presume?

The beep was loud in Esteban's sedan. She switched the phone to silent. No it's Jennifer Lopez.

JLo I told you it's not going to work out between us.

Lupe snorted and covered it up with a cough.

Why the hell is my uncle trying 2 find Izzy by the ninth and u the eleventh?

Silence.
Dots indicating typing on the other end.
Nothing.
Lupe was about to text again, when a message came through.

Oh shit

?

Just realized Vico n Memo were killed on their 18th birthdays.

That roiling started in her stomach.

What?? Wait. What does that have 2 do w u & Izzy?

Silence.

Javier?!

The ninth and the eleventh are Izzy n my birthdays.

She put the phone down on her thigh and stared out the window.
Jesus.
It was like someone had just chucked another puzzle piece at her, told her the clock was ticking, and she had no idea where it fit. She was right on the edge of figuring out something big about

these murders, she knew it. Like all those years of talk with her tío were dress rehearsals. This was the real thing. The stakes were high for her uncle, for Izzy, and yes, even for Javier.

She picked the phone up again.

We need 2 come up with a plan for what we're going 2 do.

We?

YES! We!

I like we.

Lupe's face flushed.

"Who are you texting, sobrina?" She jolted at her uncle's voice, hiding the hand with the number under her leg.

"No one! I mean . . . Jessica. Uh, a friend. In Vermont." *Shut up, Lupe!* She winced. He didn't seem to notice, just continued to smile as he drove. He probably thought she was chatting with some boy back home. Little did he know. Now that she had committed to finding Izzy and figuring this all out, she had to see if she could pull something out of her uncle about the murders, anything that might help.

"So, tío, what were you saying back there about having to find Izzy by midnight on the ninth?"

Her uncle's fingers tightened around the steering wheel as he stared forward. "This isn't a case I can talk to you about, Lupe."

"But Izzy—"

He hit the steering wheel with his palm.

She jumped and stared at him with her mouth open.

Her uncle seemed to gather himself. "I'm sorry, Lupe. But it's precisely because this might involve Izzy that I can't talk to you about the case. You're too close to this."

"But what if Memo's death wasn't an accident and Izzy and the other two boys are in danger? What if—"

He was glaring at her now. "How did you know there were two other boys?"

Uh-oh. "I kind of . . . overheard you when you were on the phone." Yes, that's it. Overheard. Would he buy it?

He harumphed and kept his eyes on the traffic.

There was no way in hell she was going to tell him she'd met Carlos, in his apartment alone, no less, or even mention Javier. He wouldn't understand at all and she wouldn't learn anything about the murders after the top of his head blew off. "Tío, I—"

"Basta."

They sat in silence, her uncle's shoulders near his ears with tension. Lupe was getting pissed. It was precisely *because* Izzy was involved that she needed to help solve this case, to find the real murderer. And her uncle didn't know about Marisol showing up at Carlos's right after they were there.

She got back on her phone and typed furiously.

K. We need 2 figure out if the deaths are connected and for that we need Izzy. The police r looking 4 him, he must know something.

She sent him a link to the photo of Marisol at Carlos's.

And then there's Marisol.

A pause. Then:

I really don't think Marisol is involved.

We'll see.

July 8, 10:00 A.M.

Javier

💀

JAVIER COULDN'T FACE another funeral for yet another friend. Truth be told, he didn't care if he ever set foot in that church again, but he had to pay his respects to Memo's family, so he put on his jacket and tie and made his way to Amapola for a gathering at their home. He liked going to Memo's gated community in Amapola. It was as if the darkness of the island's financial ruin couldn't reach over the high-security fences, get past the guards at the entrance gates. The houses were freshly painted and surrounded by beautifully landscaped lawns. Children played in the street and waved as he went by. When he was little, his own block wasn't all that different. Not as fancy, but it looked like it was loved and cared for.

There were cars parked up and down Memo's street, well-dressed mourners walking in and out. He really wasn't up for this, but he figured twenty minutes, tops. He'd pay his respects, say a few hellos, then book. He got out of his car, adjusted his tie, and froze.

Something had brushed the back of his neck.

He whipped around. Nothing was behind him. The sun retreated and he stood in shadow, spinning like a top. Nothing.

"You're losing it, Utierre," he mumbled.

He shook himself a bit, closed the car door, and started walking across the street. He looked up and noticed there wasn't a cloud in the sky. Javier shuddered and ran his hand through his hair.

He made his way into the house, nodding at people as they passed. The house was packed: a sea of black clothing, the smell of a dozen proffered food platters heavy in the air. Javier had seen classic American wakes in movies and on television. The attendees spoke in hushed tones, their faces serious and sad, eating small, pale sandwiches with no crust. In other words, pretty much the opposite of a Puerto Rican wake. Loud voices, heavy food, laughing, crying, singing. Whatever you were feeling you expressed it. If he had to go to a wake, Javier preferred the Puerto Rican version. It was just more honest.

He spotted Memo's mother near the kitchen. She was surrounded by a group of older women, clucking and fussing over her like hens. There was no way he was throwing himself in the center of *that*. He'd wait until the group moved on, say a few words to Memo's mom, then sneak out. He noticed Padre Sebastian at the buffet and was about to make his way over when Memo's mother, Señora Lopez, looked up and caught his eye. Her lip quivered and she parted the group of ladies to meet Javier in the middle of the room.

"Oh Javier, I'm so glad to see you!" She grabbed him in that crushing hug only Puerto Rican mothers can give. He held on tight as her thin body shook. He wished he could tell her that he'd tried with Memo, tried to get him to clean up. But she didn't want to hear that now.

She pulled back and put her hand on his face, the other over her heart. "You were always such a good friend to Guillermo. He was such a sensitive boy, you know."

Javier forced some words through his tightening throat.

"Señora Lopez, I'm so sorry about Memo. He was a good friend."

She nodded and closed her eyes for a second.

There was a commotion by the entrance. Voices raised, a crowd gathering. A small group of people made their way in, the mourners parting to allow passage. Javier saw Señora Lopez's eyes go wide as she saw who was in front: Keno.

She pulled herself up and pointed.

"You have some nerve coming to my house! Dirtying my son's wake with your filthy presence!"

Keno stopped short and just looked at her for a moment, then he bowed at the waist. "Memo was my friend and I just wanted to pay my respects, Señora—"

"Respects? Respects? What do you know about respect? You're the reason my sweet Guillermo is dead! You and your sinvergüenza friends!"

Javier noticed a girl pushing her way from behind Keno. Marisol. Lord, did that loca stalk funerals or something?

"Don't yell at him! It's not his fault! It's him"—she pointed at Javier—"and those damn cangrejos!" She spit the last word at Javier's feet, and anger flamed behind his face. She was crazy as a bedbug, and she was pointing fingers at him? He was the one who'd gotten clean, who'd pulled himself out of that vortex. But the priority now was protecting Señora Lopez. He owed Memo that much. He put his arm around her thin shoulders.

"Don't listen to them, Señora. Why don't you sit down over—"

"Oh right, Javier the good boy, Javier the angel." Keno took on the same tone as Marisol. "Well I remember when you weren't so good, pendejo!"

Javier pushed Señora Lopez behind him and faced Keno for the second time that week. "Watch your—"

He didn't get another word out before Padre Sebastian

pushed his way into the center and put a palm in the center of Keno's chest.

"That's enough." His voice was calm, low, but commanding. "Don't you think Señora Lopez has been through enough losing her son? Starting a fight in the middle of this poor woman's living room is no way to pay respects on any planet." To his credit, Keno looked at the floor, appearing appropriately ashamed. "Now, I think it's best that you and your friends pay your respects and leave."

Keno looked at the priest, and Javier could see him weighing his next response. But besides being a man of the cloth, the Padre had enough of a rep for not taking shit that it was clear to everyone present that it would not end well. Finally the gang leader nodded, turned to Señora Lopez, bowed his head, and said, "Lo siento, Señora. I only wished to offer my condolences. Memo was a like a brother to me."

Señora Lopez clearly didn't buy it. "Ha!"

Javier had to admit, Keno did look regretful. "We'll leave now."

But Marisol wasn't going to let him off that easy. "No, Keno! We're not talking about who is behind all this! It's the rich gringos moving into the neighborhood, driving up the prices, pushing out the people who have a right to be here! Pushing Puerto Rico's men like you and Memo toward drugs! Pushing us out of our island, like Vico and me! And him!" She pointed at Javier. "He's teaming up with that gringa and her uncle!"

Javier stared at her. "What?" It was like she was a politician at a podium.

Keno turned to her and scowled. "Shut up, Mari! What the hell are you even talking about?" He turned and stalked his way out the door with Marisol following behind like a small, barking dog. The last of the group made their way out, and the people in the house let go of a collective breath and conversation started up again.

Javier pushed a breath out and felt the adrenaline seep out from his pores. The gaggle of women pulled a shaking Señora Lopez into their midst, and moved her toward the living room and a comfortable chair.

Javier watched out the window as the group dispersed to their cars. His heart stilled when he saw Keno shove Marisol into a blue, beat-up hatchback.

Old San Juan. Could that be the same car?

Sebastian put his arm around Javier's shoulder and led him to the food table. "Why don't we get something to eat, huh, Javi?" For a lean man, the padre was always focused on food. Eating was the last thing on Javier's mind. Lupe had mentioned something about Marisol being involved. . . .

Javier was distracted as the priest dished out food on a paper plate for him. He picked at some roasted pork and sweet plantain as Sebastian chatted, but he couldn't summon an appetite. Sebastian was watching him out of the corner of his eye.

"In Jamaica a fight during Nine-Night is a dangerous thing."

"What's Nine-Night?"

"It comes from African tradition; the belief is that the deceased's duppy—"

Javier nodded. "Their spirit."

"Exactly, the duppy takes nine days to return to Africa. So family and friends gather for nine nights. You're supposed to give the deceased a good send-off to the next world or the spirit stays around and bothers the living, so fighting is a big no-no."

"Did you ever see a fight at one anyway?"

Sebastian chuckled. "Oh yes. The tradition also includes hundred-proof rum so, as you can imagine, that isn't very conducive to quiet reflection."

Javier chuckled. Sebastian was smiling, but staring at him.

Staring at him in that man-of-God-sees-all type way. "¿Qué, Padre?"

"Just wondering how you're dealing with all this. First Vico, now Memo."

Hearing the names brought back the feeling of being in a shadow, the memory of fingers across his neck. He shoved a piece of plantain into his mouth and choked it down to buy a moment. He swallowed and felt it trudge its way down every centimeter of his gullet. "I'm fine, Padre." Lying to a priest now, ay Javi? Add that to his long list of transgressions.

The priest looked at him again. Nothing got past the man. Javier didn't know why he even bothered. But Sebastian's voice was soft. "Why don't you go up to the retreat for a few days, son? I think getting out of town might be a good idea."

Just the thought of the parish's retreat center in the mountains brought a smile to Javier's face. High in the mountains where it was always cool, waterfall-fed pools in the backyard, eating fruit fresh from the trees that hung over the patio, the song of thousands of coquís singing you to sleep at night. It was the closest to heaven Javier had ever experienced. It was tempting, but he had work to do. He had to talk to Lupe and soon.

"Thanks, but I can't."

"Sure you can, I gave you the week off, remember?"

"No, I mean I have *other* work to do."

Sebastian was giving him that look again.

Javier had to admire the man's tenacity. "Look, Padre, it's nothing terrible, I promise. I just . . . I need to find Izzy, before . . . well, just before."

"Gracias a Dios. You had me worried! Yes, I think finding Izzy is a good idea."

"You do?" Did the priest have some idea what was going on?

"Yes, you can help each other through this difficult time. Maybe once you find him you could both go to the mountains."

"Oh. Right." Javier was kind of relieved when an older woman pulled Sebastian away to introduce him to her husband. For a moment he'd thought that Sebastian was going to help him understand what was going on. It was too much to hope that someone would just hand him the answers. When Javier was little he worshipped his father, thought that he was impossibly strong and smart, that he knew the right thing to do at all times, knew all the answers.

But then again, he'd also believed in the Easter Bunny.

Lupe

AFTER GETTING JAVIER's text, Lupe managed to talk her uncle into giving her a lift to Old San Juan again when he came home for lunch. She worried he might be suspicious, but counted on the fact that he would be glad she was not asking about Izzy or the case and instead wanted to do something "normal." Whatever that was.

"More shopping, sobrina?"

"Yes, I saw a cute sundress that I want to try on." She said it with a highish bouncy voice that might have lowered her IQ several points.

Ten minutes and one iced latte later, Javier's car pulled up to the small park in front of Starbucks and Lupe felt her pulse go from zero to sixty. Because of the two shots of espresso, not the boy, she convinced herself. She knew this whole fiasco was totally crazy, even for her. He hadn't seen her yet. She could still turn around and walk away. Run, even. That would be the sensible thing to do. Yeah, no. She was no coward and something bad was coming, she felt it in her bones.

Lupe stood up straight and as tall as she could get at 5'1", and strode toward the car. She tried not to look at Javier as she opened the door and dropped into the passenger seat. So much for not taking rides from strange guys. That rule lasted, what, twenty-four hours? She looked over to see Javier's whole body turned toward her and he was smiling big.

Getting into a car with a demigod, however, was the thing of bucket lists.

She tried to smile back, but it felt more like a grimace. "Where are we heading first?"

"Miss Lupe gets right down to business. I like that." The two-hundred-watt smile lit up the car again and Lupe felt the whole block spin. She put her hand on the passenger door, trying to steady herself. Addict, remember? She already had one of those in her life and that was enough.

"Izzy isn't going to be easy to find. He's kind of a vagabundo." He pulled the car around a sharp turn near the parking garage and they began to make their way out of the city.

"Vagabond? Like, homeless? Izzy?" She pictured his mother's comfortable home. It had a pool in the backyard, for God's sake.

"Yes. I mean, he lives with his mother, but over the last few years he stayed wherever he does his drogas. I hear that he's been trying to get clean, which makes it even more difficult to guess where he'll be. But we can start with her."

"No!" It was so loud even Lupe jumped at the sound of her own voice. "I can't. Izzy's mother is my uncle's sister-in-law, and she would tell her sister. . . ." Her voice trailed off.

Javier looked over at her until the traffic started moving again. "So your uncle doesn't know you're here? That you're with me?"

Lupe didn't want him to think she was ashamed of being with him. She had *so* much more to be ashamed of. "No. He wouldn't understand."

His jaw was twitching. "Because of my past?"

"No! Well, yes. But mainly he can't know I'm looking for Izzy, or the murderer. Especially the murderer. And it's not just you, he wouldn't approve of me riding alone with anyone of the male species other than him."

The corner of his mouth twitched. "Species? Is that what you consider me?"

"Well, yes. You can't help it if you're a member of the inferior gender."

He chuckled at that. The sound was warm and clear, like water tumbling over rocks.

She smiled back. "Besides, if we're going to hang together, you should know that I'm good at ignoring authority. Even if he's the chief of police *and* family."

"Well, that we have in common." He took an exit off the highway. "There are a few areas we can check, places Izzy liked to go."

"Okay, so I thought we could talk strategy."

He smiled as he drove. "Strategy, huh?"

"Uh, yeah. Like, who might want your friends dead."

Javier's jaw tightened.

Lupe's hands flew to her mouth. "I'm sorry, I'm so sorry. My father says my mouth goes faster than my brain. What I meant to ask is . . . is there anyone who might have a grudge against Vico and Memo?"

Javier sighed. "I don't know. Like I told your uncle, addicts travel in dark circles."

"Yes, but what connects them? Being cangrejos?"

"But that would mean . . . me, Izzy, and Carlos would be at risk."

She sat quietly, wishing she could press Undo. But it was the truth: it could mean that. "Well, hopefully we can find Izzy and put together this puzzle."

"I hope so."

They proceeded on a tour of the sketchier parts of the

island. To Lupe, the streets looked sucked dry, like a snow cone that you'd drained all the syrup from and all that remained was pale, sad shards of ice.

"Bet these places aren't in the tourists' guides."

"We don't have the resources that you take for granted on the mainland."

"I can't speak for my *entire* country, but *I* don't take anything for granted." She slumped down in a sulky slab against the car door. But she did take it for granted, didn't she? There were always dinners out in Stowe, good clothes, a nice house and truck. It made her even more angry that he was right.

The lunchtime traffic crawled to a stop on a block where it seemed all the store windows were crisscrossed with graffiti-decorated wooden boards. The signs above the windows were reminiscent of a better time: BORICUA GROCERY, TROPICAL NAILS, and CARMEN'S FASHION. Lupe wondered where Carmen was now. "Wow, the recession has really hit hard here."

"We're in a depression here, not a recession. We have a saying in Puerto Rico: 'Cuando Los Estados Unidos tiene catarro, Puerto Rico tiene pulmonia.'"

Lupe just nodded. She understood most of it, but was damned if she was going to admit there were words she didn't know. She always failed that *How Puerto Rican are you?* test.

"That means, 'When the U.S. gets a cold, Puerto Rico gets pneumonia.'" He looked around, his gaze resting on a trash-strewn lot out Lupe's window. "Whenever you think it's bad on the mainland, you can guarantee that it's worse here."

She was furious she didn't know this. "Why doesn't my father talk about these things? Doesn't he think that what goes on down here is important to me? It's half of my blood!"

They drove in silence while Lupe fumed. As she looked out the window, the scenery changed, the scent of salt in the air got stronger, and she felt her anger begin to dissipate. She sat up higher as a bright turquoise bled into the horizon.

"The ocean!" The minute the words left her mouth she was embarrassed. Of course it was the ocean: it's an *island,* after all. But she couldn't contain her glee as cinnamon-sugar beaches came into view.

Javier turned left onto a street that ran parallel to the beach, small wooden shacks appearing on either side of the road, the smell of fried foods reaching for her through the open windows.

"This is Piñones. Izzy sometimes comes here to hang at the kioskos." Javier was ducking his head to look out the windows, the traffic weaving slowly through the strip of rustic restaurant and bar kiosks.

Lupe noticed a souvenir stand with brightly colored swim rings hanging from a rope like party garlands, rows of rope hammocks with the Puerto Rican flag printed on them leading to the entrance. A memory of going into a similar place with her parents—her mother was still around in those days—flitted just out of reach, an image of a Spanish doll with a red flouncy skirt and tiny castanets glued to her hands. She remembered wanting it so badly. Was a descendent of that Spanish dancer still there, looking down from the sand-dusted shelf at another sun-burned little girl? Lupe was comforted by how little things changed here, how something from her childhood could look exactly the same.

Javier pulled the car over to a seedy open-air bar and turned to face Lupe. "I'll be right back."

"I'm going in with you." Lupe grabbed the door handle just as Javier clicked the locks. She shot him a look that would melt stone. "I know you didn't just lock me in this car."

"Lupe, it's better if I go in alone."

"Why? Your girlfriend work there or something?"

"No, but they're much more likely to talk to me alone."

She glared at him. "Why?"

"I speak Spanish—"

"I can manage! Sort of."

"I'm *from here*."

She couldn't argue with that. She let go of the handle and crossed her arms over her chest like a petulant child. "Fine."

He had the nerve to smile that smile at her. "I'll be right back."

"Okay, *Dad*." She hated the way her voice sounded, but she hated the feeling of not belonging more. She was half Puerto Rican! Half! If only she actually looked it. When she was little she used to rub her hands over her freckle-covered, pale arms as if that would spread the freckles around and give her skin the same warm color as her father's.

As she watched Javier walk away, it was hard to stay angry at him when she was fascinated by how his jeans fit his body perfectly without being too tight or fussy, by how his curls tumbled in the ocean breeze. The midday light was weird, though. His shadow was a bizarre shape, stretching and pulling like it belonged to someone else, like his shadow was stalking him instead of following. A horn honked nearby and Lupe jumped, glaring at the impatient businessman who shook his fist at another car, and when she looked back, Javier's shadow was normal.

A trick of the light.

Had to have been.

After she lost sight of Javier, she stared out the window at the scrawny men leaning on the wooden bar rail like sad, scruffy lions in the midday heat, slowly lifting brown beer bottles to their lips, Bacardí and Medalla banners stretched below them like safety nets. She imagined that once they had been bold lions, full-maned and strong.

She thought of her father sitting in the dark interior of the Vermont version of these bars, his brown skin standing out among the pale New Englanders around him. It was like he was feeling the hopelessness of the island despite his lake house, shiny new truck, and full-time job, like an amputee still feels ghost pain from a long-missing limb.

Lupe was lost in thoughts of her father when the *click* of the locks and the sudden opening of the driver's side door made her jump. She yelled, loudly, before she saw Javier slide behind the steering wheel, balancing packets of tin foil in one hand.

He stopped and smiled at her. "It's just me."

She narrowed her eyes at him, embarrassed, when the smell reached her, the oil-soaked heavy scent of deep-fried Puerto Rican goodness.

"No one has seen Isadore, but I thought you might be hungry." He opened the shiny silver envelopes exposing the golden banana shape of her favorite island food.

"Alcapurrias!" Lupe said, the *r*'s rolling off her tongue as her father had taught her. She gleefully took one of the packets from Javier's hand and realized he was staring at her.

"What?"

"The way you said that—"

"What?" Why were people always surprised when she spoke Spanish without an accent? She didn't feel confident enough to speak it often, but she had heard it spoken her entire life, so of course she had picked up the Puerto Rican pronunciation.

He shook his head and smiled. "Nothing."

The smell of the food was smoothing out her annoyance. Who could stay irritated with someone who brought you food like this? She took a bite, reveling in the deep-fried goodness of the plantain exterior, the savory picadillo beef spilling on her tongue. She was pretty sure she scalded her mouth but didn't care. It was worth it.

Javier took a bite of an alcapurria as he threw the car into drive.

Back to the business of finding Izzy.

Javier

💀

JAVIER WAS TRYING to put himself in Izzy's place. Lord knew he had spent enough time thinking like Izzy, but luckily he'd met Padre Sebastian and things had changed. Now he worked hard to *not* think like that again. It made him feel raw, like ripping a bandage off a not-yet-healed wound. But he had to find him. Together the three of them would figure out what the hell was going on.

They had looked in every spot Javier could think of: parks, bars, flophouses. Javier had to admit, there was a part of not finding Izzy he liked, spending more time with Lupe.

Focus on Izzy, idiota! The last resort would be Omar, the dealer he and Izzy went to in El Norte, but Javier was hoping to avoid that. There was no way he was bringing Lupe to that snake pit no matter how much she would insist she could handle it. And he hadn't known her long, but he knew that she would. Besides, going to one's dealer two years after getting clean was not a good idea. He'd been so relieved when word reached him that Izzy had started recovery. El Norte was the last place—

Wait, El Norte.

"I know where he is!"

"Great! Where?"

"He probably heard about Memo and went to where he feels safest. I don't know why I didn't think of it earlier." Javier had to consciously keep himself from pushing the car's accelerator all the way to the floor.

The heavy afternoon air dragged through the windows as they weaved in and out of afternoon traffic along Expreso Baldorioty toward Amapola's north side. He leaned forward in his seat as the white columns of the Museo del Arte came into view on their left and squealed the tires in his rush to get to the parking garage. As they pushed through the glass doors to the museum, Lupe stopped to read the sign.

"An art museum? This is where you think Izzy is?"

Javier was already wound pretty tight, but this made his blood pressure rise even higher. "What, just cause someone does drugs they can't appreciate art or culture?"

"Excuse me?" She stopped short and her hands were on her hips. "Whose cousin is Izzy, hmm? I think I know my family."

"Izzy is the closest thing to family I had growing up. Day in and day out."

"And I'm glad you had each other, but don't assume I don't understand my cousin just because I didn't grow up here."

Something about her tone felt like he was being lectured at. Javier hated being lectured at, that's why he wasn't applying to colleges. He felt the heat in his head rise. "How can you say you understand? You come down here once a year and think you understand us?"

"'Us' again? Who the hell is 'us'? I've known Izzy my entire life. When we were kids we were—"

"Right, when you were kids. You have no idea who he is now."

"Look, Izzy has always been wild—"

Javier pointed at her. "See? Right there. That shows you don't really know him. Izzy might be a total smart-ass, but among los cangrejos he was the diplomat, the one who was always diffusing conflicts, knowing the right thing to do. Trust me, you don't know Izzy like I do."

"Oh what, since I don't shoot up with him I can't know him?"

Javier felt a boiling feeling in his chest. He made his voice slow and measured as if he were talking to a five-year-old. "All five of los cangrejos, we went to good private schools, our parents took us to art shows and symphonies. My dad is a goddamn lawyer. Smart middle-class kids never go off the rails in your perfect world?"

Lupe crossed her arms. Javier wouldn't have been surprised if flames started shooting from her eyes from the look she was giving him.

"Don't you go putting words in my mouth, Javier Utierre. Just because I didn't expect it doesn't mean I'm passing any kind of judgment." She took one hand off her hip and pointed at him in a very pissed-off-Latin-girl kind of style. "And by the way? My world is about as far from perfect as you can get, so clearly, *you've* passed some kind of judgment about *me* and I don't appreciate it."

The boiling was starting to reach his eyes. He was afraid he was going to say something he would really regret. "This was a bad idea. Why don't you go back to your safe little town in Maine—"

"Vermont!"

"Whatever!"

Their last words were followed by squeaking shoes on marble floors.

"Excuse me, jóvenes, you have to keep it down if you're going to stay here. This isn't a sporting arena!" the old lady said through pinched lips, her judgment peeking its way through the small lenses of her eyeglasses.

The two of them were blinking and looking around at the museum hallway as the woman squeaked her way back to her desk, and it was as if they both just realized where they were, in the lobby of the museum. They looked at each other and burst out laughing, quickly trying to stifle it as the lady glanced back over her shoulder. This only made it worse, to the point that they were holding on to each other, tears running down their cheeks. Just when they caught their breath, Lupe whispered, "This isn't a sporting arena!" and they both dissolved again.

They pulled it together as Javier paid admission for them both and the mood turned solemn as Javier led Lupe to the wing that held Izzy's favorite exhibit. He started filling in the blanks as they walked. "Izzy likes to paint, always has. He's been coming here since it opened when we were, like, four. His father used to take him here, que descanse en paz"—he quickly translated the phrase for Lupe—"may he rest in peace."

"Oh." Lupe just nodded and for a moment the only sound was the occasional squeak of other people's shoes on the white marble floors. She glanced at one of the signs near the permanent collection. "José Campeche. Who was he?"

"He was a Puerto Rican artist. Son of a slave. Never left the island, but was known worldwide. I think that's why Izzy likes him so much. Even after his father died and Izzy's dreams of traveling and painting fell apart, hermano still has hopes of being a real artist one day." As Javier talked about Izzy it weighed him down like he had a cinder block on each shoulder.

Lupe seemed to think about that, then said, "I remember Izzy painting when we were younger. I didn't know it meant that much to him. I thought it was just something he did for fun. I guess I don't really know him like I should. Like I'd like to."

They turned the corner into the main exhibition room and

saw the back of a lone figure sitting on a bench near the far wall. Javier let out a big breath. Izzy was parked in front of one of Campeche's most well-known paintings: a man being rescued at sea, the water churning and wild while two men reach into the waves trying to save him. Izzy sat with his body bent, elbows leaning on his knees, eyes glued to the image of the flailing man. Javier stopped, not wanting to disturb his friend. He could see Lupe pause next to him. He looked over with a smile that seemed more of a nervous tic, and she nodded at him. They started to walk again, their steps silent on the shining floor.

"Izzy?" Javier's whisper sounded amplified in the silent room. He thought Izzy would start at the sound, or at least turn, but he simply smiled without taking his eyes from the painting. He didn't seem surprised at all.

"What up, Javi?"

Javier sat down next to Izzy on the upholstered black leather bench, Lupe next to him, perched on the edge of the seat. "Your mom is worried about you, hermano."

Izzy chuckled. "Mom's always worried, bro. She thinks that's her job. I can't believe she didn't give up on me years ago." He turned then and Javier looked deep into his friend's eyes, searching for telltale signs of junk, but Izzy's golden brown eyes were clear. Tired, but not stoned. At least Izzy wasn't using. That was something. Then Izzy noticed Lupe and his grin widened.

"Holy shit. Is that you, prima?"

Lupe smiled back at him. "Yeah, cuz. Long time no see."

Izzy looked back and forth from Javier to Lupe and back again, his smile widening. "Girl, does your tío know you hanging out with this loser?" He jerked a thumb in Javier's direction.

Lupe's face grew red and she looked at the ground. She might be strong, but she couldn't hide her feelings for shit.

"I'd say that's a big-ass no. Man, Esteban's going to lose it when he finds out his precious lily-white niece is spending time with the likes of us."

Lupe's face was still red, her eyes filled with flame. "Lily. White? What the hell, Izzy? You've always worked real hard to make me feel different—"

"*Feel* different? Newsflash, prima. Down here you *are* different."

"Well, maybe if everyone would spend less time telling me I don't understand and help me *to* understand, I would."

Javier looked from one to the other. He was going to have to switch roles with Izzy and play the diplomat or they were going to get thrown out. "Tranquilo, Izzy. Lupe is here because she's worried about you. So am I."

That laugh again, that sounded like it was on the edge of being a groan. "Why you worried about me? Did Padre Sebastian send you? Man, I been clean and sober for three months now." Izzy waved his hand in a way he always did when he was getting pissed. He'd been doing it since they were kids.

"Yeah, but remember who you're talking to. I know you only come here when you're in a bad place, man."

Izzy stood up abruptly, his arms flying from his sides as if he were plunging off a cliff. "Why the hell shouldn't I be in a bad place? I mean, shit. Vico and Memo dying like that, one after the other. It's a nightmare, man."

"I know, pana, I know. But that's what we're here to talk to you about—"

"But nothing. This shit is messed up." He paced back and forth in front of the painting, his sneakers squeaking with each pivot. "I've spent days going over and over the last few months in my mind, the last few years, trying to figure out when the darkness that's following los cangrejos came. Sometimes, when I think about what's going on, it feels like my lungs are being squeezed, like I can't breathe." He put his face right into Javier's, his eyes pleading for answers, for release. "Javi, with all our friends dying, why not use? Horrible things still happen, how do we stay straight? *Why* should we stay straight? The pain would stop, at least for a while."

Javier froze. He wanted to give the right answer, but what *was* the right answer? He hated to admit that Izzy had a point. What would Padre Sebastian say? As he stared back into the swirling brown of Izzy's eyes, he wondered if they were both fighting a losing battle. Like the guy in the painting, gasping for breath, barely keeping his head above the waves, the depths calling for him.

"Izzy, we think there are patterns in the killings. . . ."

Lupe nodded. "And we're going to figure it out."

At that Izzy snorted and looked his cousin in the face as if he were a pit bull deciding whether to bite. "Well, óyeme, 'cousin Lupe,' I think you'd best get your ass back on a plane."

"Oh, you think so, 'cousin Izzy'? Maybe I should do that and leave you to get gutted by some psycho."

"Psycho? You've never seen a real psycho. If you'd like to keep it that way you'd best stay the hell away from this guy"— he jabbed his thumb at Javier—"or any of us, for that matter." He started to pace again, his attention moving away from Lupe. Izzy stopped, looked at Javier with sad, old eyes. "Believe it or not"—his gaze still on Javier but also looking down into him— "we're cursed."

Izzy stared at Javier for a few more seconds and then he was up and walking, strolling across the museum floors with his hands in his pockets, his last words hanging in the air like a coming storm.

Javier sat for a moment, examining the painting in front of him. He wasn't sure if he related more to the man about to drown in the water or the sailors on the boat reaching in vain for their comrade.

He stood, offered Lupe his hand. To his surprise, she took it, and the two of them followed Izzy out.

Lupe

💀

WHEN THEY WALKED out of the museum, Lupe spotted Izzy sitting in the middle of a bench out front.

She walked to the bench, stopped, and stood staring down at Izzy, her hands on her hips.

Without looking up, Izzy chuckled. "You always stand that way when you're pissed. Even when we were niños."

"Yeah, well, you're acting like a niño, taking off like that without a word."

Izzy sighed. "Lately the air gets hard to breathe when I'm inside."

"Yeah, I get that." Lupe sat down next to her cousin, her anger dissipating. He seemed so defeated, which only worried her more. She may not know him like she thought she did, but she knew Izzy was not a quitter.

Javier joined them on the bench, sitting on the other side of his friend.

Izzy shifted over until his shoulder bumped hers. "Do you remember the last time me and my dad came up to Stowe to ski?"

The image of her dad loading suitcases in the back of his truck outside the Burlington airport brought along the memory of a blast of icy, late-night air. She involuntarily shivered. "Yeah, I thought you were crazy. It was, like, ten below zero."

Izzy chuckled. "Yeah, it was effing frio, but I remember that day like it was yesterday; his yellow ski jacket, the smell of the pine trees." He smiled more to himself than anything. "I think that was the last time I was *really* happy."

Lupe's throat caught. She felt bad for thinking her life sucked. Her dad was a drunk but at least she still had him.

Javier coughed. "Hermano, why you want to sit around and wait for shit to happen? That's not you, man."

Lupe noticed Javier spoke differently around Izzy.

Izzy looked up at Javier, his eyes red and old-man tired. "What's the point?"

"The point is, you might be in danger. Let's figure out what's going on and stop it. We need The Diplomat in on this one. Lupe and I have . . . shorter tempers than you do."

Lupe snorted, smiling. "Ya think? And I'm going to help, too."

"Oh, I'm sure tío will love that."

"He won't know. I'm going to show you there's no such thing as being cursed. Besides, remember who it was that saved you from the fire ants that time?"

Izzy laughed. "Yeah, by blasting me with cold water from the garden hose!"

"Cold? That was not cold. Now *Vermont* hoses are cold. Besides, it did the trick, didn't it?"

Her cousin finally looked at her, and gave her that lopsided smile like he had since they were little. Esteban called it Izzy's shit-eating grin.

Javier put his hand on Izzy's shoulder. "So what's the verdict, hermano? You joining us?"

Izzy nodded his head, still smiling. "Yeah, man. What a trio of losers. A pair of Boricua addicts and the Gringa-Rican from Vermont."

Lupe smiled back at him. "That's the first time you called me Puerto Rican. Even if you started with Gringa."

The three of them drove around for an hour while they talked about the little they knew. They discussed the possibility of revenge, rival dealers, and enemies. Nothing seemed to fit. After they exhausted their ideas, they sat in a moment of frustrating silence as they cruised down the highway. That's when Lupe saw the Papi Gringo billboard.

"El Cuco!"

Both boys looked at her. "What?"

Lupe was talking fast, but she couldn't help it. "Just hear me out. Vico's grandmother talked about retribution when I saw her in El Rubí—"

Izzy scoffed. "Vico's abuela? She must be 106. And what the hell were you doing in El Rubí?"

"She seemed pretty sharp to me. Plus, there's the words to that Papi Gringo song. . . ." They stared back at her.

"Oh, do *not* tell me you haven't listened to the lyrics?"

Javier shrugged.

Izzy said, "Hey, I been busy."

"Wait, there's a photo of you with Papi Gringo online! I saw it! At one of his concerts!"

"I didn't stay for the actual concert."

Lupe sighed. "Some friends you guys are. The song is all about retribution. . . ." She loved knowing more about something Puerto Rican than they did. They didn't have to know she'd only learned about it yesterday from Tere. She pulled out her phone and pulled up Spotify. "Let's just play it. Does this car have Bluetooth?"

Izzy and Javier looked at each other for a second, then burst out laughing. When they could finally breathe again, Izzy said, "Girl, this car don't have a single tooth!"

Javier added, "It's toothless!" They started laughing all over again until tears were running down their cheeks.

"Oh, for God's sake." Lupe reached for the radio dial, and searched through the stations as the guys did the high-five 'good-one-bro' thing over her head. They were lucky she didn't punch them both toothless. It only took a few minutes until a station was playing Carlos's hit. Lupe waited as the boys listened to the lyrics. She had to bite her tongue after the closing notes. Did they hear the connections she heard?

Javier clicked the radio off.

Izzy took a deep intake of breath. "Damn."

Lupe smiled wide. "Right?"

"Carlos doesn't suck."

Javier responded. "Yeah, homeboy's got some talent."

Lupe was dumbfounded. "What? That's all you got from that?"

Javier shrugged. "It's just a song."

"Wait, hold up. Lupe 'the sensible' isn't suggesting that El Cuco is after us? Are you?" The smile threatened to split her cousin's face.

"No! What about all that talk of retribution? Of life 'pumping through a needle' and 'El Cuco's cure will conjure that'? What if someone is trying to reproduce the myth of El Cuco?"

"It's just Carlos, writing about how we grew up."

Lupe slumped down in the seat.

"I'm sorry. I just don't think it has anything to do with what's going on."

"Yeah, cuz. You been watching too many movies. Things just aren't that interesting in real life."

As she sulked in silence, part of Lupe agreed with them that it was crazy to believe there were clues in a song. But another part, a deeper, older part, knew that unconsciously or not, Carlos had hit on something in his song.

Something bad.

"Grrr!" Lupe growled at her phone as Javier inched them through traffic.

"What're you growling about, Lupe?" Javier asked, the only one who wasn't completely absorbed in a phone.

"There's, like, next to nothing about El Cuco on the internet! I mean, chupacabras are everywhere! Why not this legend? Dark bullshit like that sells."

"There isn't a lot about the island on the internet. When I did a paper on the Taínos I had to go and talk to people, visit historical sites. There was some information, a few books, but more often than not I got much more information talking to people."

"Speaking of which . . ." Izzy handed Lupe his phone. She read the text as the car inched through traffic. It had to be from an adult, it was in complete sentences:

> Isadore, I got your message about the legend of El Cuco. It might help if you talk to a gentleman who is an expert on the subject. Ernesto Quiñonez is a professor of anthropology at the University of Puerto Rico, semi-retired as he's very elderly. His specialty is island mythology and he wrote many of the articles you accessed through the library. Perhaps it would help to go straight to the source? I have pasted his contact information below. I hope this is helpful.

She smacked her cousin on the shoulder. "You were researching El Cuco? After laughing at me when I brought up Carlos's song?"

Izzy shrugged. "I got a librarian friend."

Javier smiled. "'Friend'?"

Izzy sneered. "Not like that! She's like, fifty. She just likes me. I read a lot."

Javier looked over at him. "What did your *friend* say?"

Lupe read him the text. Javier took the next exit to head in the other direction. "Let's go talk to this professor."

The campus was a half hour away in Río Piedras and, luckily, traffic was light. They parked and made their way across the campus to the main building. It felt like any college campus she'd seen in the past; the daily life of the university buzzed around them, but she was surprised by the cracks in the sidewalk where tree roots pushed through, the minimal landscaping, bald patches in the grass. When they arrived at the main building, the ornate painted carvings on the columns caught her attention. It was like a scruffy peacock, rough around the edges, but still parading around with its colorful tail high. The guard pointed to some stairs that led to the professor's office. The three of them made their way up an ornate staircase, surrounded by rich murals featuring images of the arts, science, and culture. Lupe was mesmerized. The hallway to the office opened on one side to the courtyard, sunshine, impossibly blue skies, and palm fronds blowing in the breeze. The side of the building with the offices was stone, dark, and somewhat forbidding.

They found the large green wooden door, framed on either side by slatted windows, the shutters closed tight. As Javier knocked, Lupe whispered, "I hope to God there's air-conditioning in there."

After a minute or two of silence, a very handsome young man with dimples opened the door.

"Can I help you?"

"We're here to see Professor Quiñones. We have an appointment."

A crackly voice yelled from farther inside, "Let them in, Armand! Let's get this over with!"

Izzy snorted. "Oh I have such a warm and fuzzy feeling about this."

When they stepped inside, it was like entering a different world. No air-conditioning, the room was like a sauna, and lit only by ornate lamps positioned haphazardly around the room. If there were any windows they were shuttered like the ones in front. The office appeared to be two rooms; the first, the one they were in, had a worn wooden desk, behind which Armand looked bored, but what was most striking was that almost all the surfaces of the room, including the floor, were covered with saint statues of varying heights. From six inches to six feet, there were hundreds of them, rustic wood, ornately painted ceramic, pockmarked gray stone. Every one was different, but one thing they all had in common: their eyes were looking at them. Their rapturous gazes followed them around the room, until Lupe thought she might crawl out of her skin. El Cuco himself could be hiding among them and she'd never know. She noticed rows of darkened fluorescent lights above and for a moment considered finding the switch and flipping them on, just to shine some light on the creepy scene.

An impatient voice barked at them in Spanish from the interior room.

Lupe couldn't wait to see what was in there.

She let Izzy and Javier go first, following quietly behind, taking everything in. The light in this room was limited to small spotlights shining on the walls, showcasing the incredible art from floor to ceiling. Oil paintings of blazing orange flamboyán trees, spiky vejigante festival masks in bright colors, pencil drawings of men working the sugar cane fields. Every piece tied to the culture of the island. The room was dominated by a huge, ornately carved, dark wooden desk at its center, its top obscured by piles of books, papers, and an ancient typewriter. The room smelled like old newspapers, leather, and menthol. If you bottled it you could call it "Eau de Old Academic." She almost giggled at the thought.

Lupe realized everyone had gone silent, and looked over to find Javier, Izzy, and a tiny man with a full head of wild white hair behind the desk staring at her.

"Sorry. I was distracted by the incredible—"

The old man waved at her impatiently, and asked in slow, precisely enunciated Spanish, "I was asking who you were, dear."

"Lo siento. Yo soy Lupe—"

He cut her off in clipped British-tinged English. "Why don't we stick to English for her sake, hmm? I have no desire to listen to yet another gringa massacre our beautiful language."

Lupe narrowed her eyes at the old man.

Izzy snorted and Javier's eyes darted to her. "Profesor, Lupe's father is from—"

"It doesn't matter, she's still a gringa. Pity so many islanders with good Spanish blood had to muddy the waters by intermarrying and . . . breeding."

He pronounced the last word as if just saying it repulsed him. Lupe had had enough. "Look, I don't need—"

"Yes, yes, I know you North Americans offend easily, so let's just get this over with before your little blond friend winds up and hits me, yes? What is it you young people want from an old man?"

For a beat they all just stared at him, mouths open. To say that Professor Quiñones was not what they expected would be the understatement of the year.

Javier coughed. "Yes, Señor, we—"

"Uh-uh. Doctor, please. I didn't spend all those years in graduate school at Oxford to be addressed without the proper respect."

Lupe could see Javier's jaw tighten. At least the old man was getting on *all* their nerves. Well, maybe not on Izzy's. He seemed to be enjoying himself. He noticed Lupe looking at him, coughed and wiped the smile off of his face, then pulled out The Diplomat side that Javier was always talking about.

"*Doctor* Quiñones. Por favor, we're trying to learn more about the myth of El Cuco."

The professor held up his index finger as if lecturing to a room of students. "Myth? Men have always relegated whatever they don't understand to myth. I would wait until you learn more before you call it a myth."

Lupe scoffed. "You're not saying that you believe in monsters? You, a fancy college professor with all those letters after his name?"

The professor tented his fingers below his chin and stared at Lupe, looking into her eyes until she started to squirm. "Not only is that what I'm saying, but if I were a betting man I would wager my rather meager retirement savings that your two handsome friends here have actually seen monsters, in the flesh, as it were."

Lupe looked from Javier to Izzy, the old man's words sitting on the desk like paperweights. "Well, sure, metaphorical monsters—"

The professor cut her off. "Right, I thought so." He went back to addressing Izzy. "So you seem like a reasonably intelligent young man—"

Lupe snorted.

Izzy leaned over and whispered, "You're not helping."

The professor continued, but she could tell he was getting truly aggravated. "What is it you want to know about El Cuco that she hasn't already found on the internet and dismissed as Hispanic superstition?" He gestured in Lupe's direction. Lupe could feel her face redden. It only made her angrier that he seemed to know so much about them.

He didn't seem to expect an answer, though, because before Izzy could say a word he continued in full lecture mode. "I assume you know his origins? That the legend appears in almost every Hispanic culture, though his name varies? He's called El Cucuy in Mexico, for instance. The legend was first encountered in Portugal with the 'Coco,' referring to the slang word for head or skull. Parents in Hispanic cultures threatened children with some version of the same monster. They'd tell their offspring that the monster was lurking on the roof watching to see if they misbehaved."

"Talk about giving kids something to bring up in therapy."

"Young lady, there are thousands of scary tales used to frighten small children. 'Hansel and Gretel,' 'Little Red Riding Hood,' why, Jamaica's duppy—"

"Yeah, I got it."

He sneered at her. "You Norteamericanos are raised to be *so* polite."

Lupe grinned. "About as polite as college professors, it seems."

Izzy stepped forward. "Okay, children, let's calm down."

Quiñones ignored that comment and turned to Izzy. "It seems you know everything. So? What more can I tell you?"

Izzy spoke, serious now. "Why does he come? El Cuco, I mean."

The professor stood and Lupe was surprised at how tall he was. His long, lean frame had been so folded in the overstuffed leather chair she'd thought him tiny. He was thin and impeccably dressed in a white suit with a black tie. He straightened up with some effort, then began to pace along the far wall, one hand in the pocket of his suit vest, the other occasionally brushing his neatly trimmed white beard.

"There are theories among cultural anthropologists and psychologists that he represents a supernatural manifestation of childhood fears and that 'sightings' of him increase with the unrest of the culture, much like the zombies and vampires that have had their own renaissance of late. And can you think of a time in which our poor island has been in a higher state of unrest? In the late—"

It was Javier's turn to cut *him* off. "But *why* do you think he comes?"

Quiñones stopped pacing. After a moment, his face rearranged itself into a smile. "I think it's very simple, my boy. He comes because he's called."

Izzy stepped forward. "But by who?"

"Whom, by whom. I insist on proper grammar in my office." Izzy gave Lupe a look as if she should be enjoying this. The professor continued. "El Cuco has always been what parents threaten their children with, in order to get them to behave. My theory is that he's a physical manifestation of the very limits of a parent's control over their children. It is he they turn to when they no longer have any influence. And in calling him, they hand the power over to him."

Lupe saw Javier and Izzy share a look. Something struck a chord with them and she was going to find out what it was the minute they left the old kook's office. Which she wanted to do sooner rather than later, so she put her hands on her hips and stood in the way of the professor's pacing. In the interest of getting the hell out of there, she decided to just play along. "Okay, so *hypothetically*, how does one destroy El Cuco in these legends?"

Quiñones put his hand on her shoulder and laughed. Loud. And long. The three of them just looked at one another as tears ran from the man's wrinkled eyes. Oh, this was getting old fast. She was about to take his hand and judo-throw the geezer onto the hard floor.

Finally he caught his breath, took a bright white handkerchief from his jacket pocket, and wiped his eyes. "I'm so sorry, dear. But it's so amusing how you North Americans are so anxious to destroy everything that gets in your way. It's so very . . . John Wayne of you." He then began to clean his glasses with the handkerchief. "Most cultures live quite contently with their monsters. Except yours, of course." He put his glasses back on and regarded Lupe. "You can't destroy El Cuco. He's woven into the very fabric of the island's culture."

Izzy's hands clenched into fists. "Then how do we call him off?"

Lupe put her hand up. "Now wait a minute, you don't really believe that a monster is—"

The professor ignored her once again. "You can't. You have to give him what he wants."

Javier's turn. "What does he want?"

"Retribution."

They all looked at one another. "Retribución" from Carlos's song ran through Lupe's head, as she was sure it did in both of theirs. What did it mean, though? She had to ask. "Retribution for what?"

"Ah, that's the question, isn't it? When you think about it, the cuco is rather gorgeous in his simplicity. He manifests for one purpose and one purpose only. As for your query, retribution for some transgression, whatever a parent might consider 'bad' behavior, I imagine."

"Bad? But that's way too subjective and vague a descriptor on which to base supernatural vengeance!"

The professor clapped his hands. "How delightful! The gringa is intelligent! My dear, you must be like a unicorn in your hometown. I'm guessing somewhere in northern New England?"

Lupe had had it with the old man's crystal ball reading. "Look, Professor Ass Hat, my friends, my family"—she gestured toward Izzy—"are in danger. There's somebody masquerading as El Cuco, and we just want to know how to stop him."

"Now see here, young lady!" There was fire behind the man's eyes, his pale face reddening as he yelled. "You can't come into an old man's office, insult him, and demand information! So typical of Norteamericanos, so self-righteous! If I had my way—" He stopped and staggered a bit, and Javier reached out to take his elbow but the professor ripped his arm back, losing his balance again.

The assistant appeared in the doorway and rushed to the professor as Quiñones whined, "Armand! Armand! Get these ingrates out of my office!" Armand talked softly and coaxed the professor back to his chair.

Armand turned toward them, but they were already ducking for the door, happy to be leaving Professor Quiñones's depressing cave. Armand followed and pushed them out the door, and they heard the lock *click* after them. All three stood in the hallway, stunned, mouths hanging open again.

"Well, that was helpful." Izzy's voice was flat.

July 8, 4:31 P.M.

Lupe

💀

JAVIER DIDN'T SEEM to be paying attention. Lupe watched him step away from the academic's chaotic office, lean on the waist-high wall, and stare through the arch-shaped opening toward the courtyard.

"You okay, Javier?" Lupe touched his arm and the contact made him jump.

"Yeah. It's just . . . I keep thinking about what the professor said about parents and kids being bad." He turned to Izzy. "Do you remember anything about our last birthday party?"

Izzy was staring out, too. "Yeah. The last cangrejo birthday."

"Right. Remember my mother found us in the backyard?"

"Under the flamboyán tree."

Lupe watched them go back and forth, their eyes faraway, traveling back five years.

"And we got a lecture from our mothers. What did they say to us that night?"

Izzy's voice grew edgy with impatience. "Man, I don't know. In those days our parents might as well have been speaking Chinese for all I understood them. I wasn't listening."

As Lupe watched Izzy stare blankly, she knew that he wasn't telling the truth.

Javier touched Izzy's shoulder. "Maybe we should talk to our mothers. See if we can't get to the bottom of this."

Izzy's voice was quiet, like he was talking to the courtyard, not to them. "They can't help. No one can."

As they headed back to San Juan the sun was starting to make its descent and it wouldn't be long before her uncle would start to suspect something.

A text came in on Javier's phone. He glanced at it as they sat at a light. "Ángel is out of the hospital and home."

Izzy sat up straight. "Finally we catch a break."

Javier started shaking his head. "No. No way. I know what you're thinking and we're not going there."

"What? Why not? Man, he was there when Memo died! He's our only lead."

"Rumor has it his mind is gone. He repeats stuff over and over. It would be a waste of our time." Javier's patience seemed to be wearing thin.

"Let's see for ourselves! You know half the shit that gets talked around is fiction."

"Who's Ángel?" Lupe felt like she was five and trying to get her parents' attention. They were talking over her. She hated that.

Javier was still shaking his head. "No way I'm taking Lupe to El Norte."

"Um, excuse me? I'm sitting right here—"

"Yeah, man. I think she can make her own decisions."

"We can go talk to him after I take Lupe home."

She couldn't believe it. "Spare me your sexist bullshit. There's no way you're doing anything without me."

"You don't know what El Norte is like. It's a side of Puerto Rico you've never seen."

"Oh what, are there drugs there?" She pretended to bite her nails. "You do understand that Vermont is the heroin capital of the U.S., right?"

Izzy snorted. "Maybe they should put that on the tourist brochures."

Lupe shot him a look. "You think Puerto Rico is special because of its drug problems? I can buy methamphetamine a block from my house."

"And maple syrup. You could buy that, too."

Lupe growled at her cousin.

Izzy grinned. "I mean, if you wanted to save yourself a trip."

Lupe felt her jaw tighten, her teeth grinding against one another like a boat scraping along a dock. She pointed at Javier. "Drive." Her voice was calm, scary calm, but forceful.

Javier's hands twisted around the steering wheel.

"You heard the woman!" Izzy put his feet on the dashboard and crossed them at the ankles, clearly entertained by the tension in the car.

Javier appeared to reach a decision, and squealed the car toward the exit they were just passing, other cars laying on their horns as he veered across the other lanes.

As he steered the car back onto the highway in the other direction, Lupe chewed her lip and hoped her mouth hadn't gotten her into something she'd regret.

July 8, 4:48 P.M.

Javier

☠

JAVIER TRIED TO slow his breathing as the scenery began to change. The music got louder as they inched toward town, the colors more intense, the smells stronger. There was always something about El Norte that seemed, just, *more*. More everything. Except safe. The undercurrent was one of being on the edge, the precipice, of something happening, something about to be out of control, something dangerous. When he was using, Javier had welcomed that feeling. It was like riding a bike down a hill and letting go of the handles. Freedom, that's what it felt like. Now he knew that it was pretty much the opposite, but it was still damn exciting.

God grant me the serenity to accept the things I cannot change. Javier started repeating the Serenity Prayer from Narcotics Anonymous over and over in his head like an incantation. It was something he used to bring himself back, away from the edge. He waited for his breath to even out, his heart to slow its rhumba beat.

It wasn't working.

Lupe was quiet, looking out the windows with big eyes. For

all her tough talk, he bet her family never took her to El Norte on her summer vacation. He chuckled to himself. He liked this girl, a lot, but he felt superior in his Puerto Ricanness compared to her. His roots dug deep in the magical Caribbean soil.

God you're an asshole. Javier was often grateful no one could read his thoughts. This was why he preferred doing things solo. He just wanted to get this over with. The sun was sinking and in El Norte the bad things slithered out at night under cover of darkness. "Where does Ángel live?"

"In The Factory. Take the next right, and a left on Calle Alameda." Izzy was shifting farther forward on his seat, like the junk was pulling at him from the street corners.

The Factory. Lord. An infamous drug den and home of the Calaveras. It was worse than he thought. Beads of sweat formed on Javier's forehead. It was as if he were going backward with every block, deeper and deeper into his past.

As he slowed down at a traffic light, he was distracted by something moving on his left. He swung his head around, swerving the car a bit with the movement, his heart racing.

There was nothing there.

As they sat there waiting for the light to change, he could see the movement out of the corner of his eye again, whipped his head around. This time he could see part of a black shape, just at the edge of his vision. The darkness was spreading. It was on the right side, too! The breath was squeezing from his body and he was shaking his head left and right, but the darkness only moved with him.

Lupe's voice broke through his panic. "What is wrong with you guys?"

Guys? Plural?

Javier looked past Lupe and saw Izzy looking left and right, his eyes wide and filled with terror. They caught each other's eyes, and Javier could feel the fear arc between them.

Lupe peered at one, then the other. "Am I missing something?"

The darkness slowly receded, but still remained, just beyond his vision. He could feel it lurking.

Izzy looked around as if waking up and pointed to a pockmarked, three-story industrial building covered with layer upon layer of graffiti and torn political posters. "Here."

Javier recognized the trio of junkies from the neighborhood who called themselves "the three kings" draped across the steps to the front door with missing glass panes. They spotted Izzy getting out of the car and greeted him with exaggerated movements like they were all underwater. Izzy looked a bit too comfortable.

Javier rushed to catch up with Lupe as she got out of the car. He realized she was watching him as they started to walk. "What?"

"Why didn't you argue with me about going in?"

Javier shrugged. "Because it would be much more dangerous for you to wait in the car, looking like you do."

She stopped walking. "What? What the hell does that mean?"

He smiled. "You know, white. Blond. A gringa."

She gave him a look that could wither flowers. "Why do you do that?"

"What? What'd I do?"

She gritted her teeth and put her hands on her hips. "Make sure you make me feel different, an outsider, over and over."

"I— But you are." He was baffled. She knew she wasn't from here, right?

She raised her voice and even the three kings were looking now. So much for not calling attention to her. "You think I don't know that? You think I'm happy about having the skin color of my mother who took off? It's the only damn thing she left me and all it does is make me feel like I'm not part of the only family I have!"

Her eyes were getting glassy and Javier's throat tightened. He wasn't trying to hurt her. "Look, Lupe, I—"

But then she was moving. "Forget it."

When they got to the building staircase, the three sleazes leered at Lupe like she was a plate of tres leches cake. But they had no idea who they were dealing with. She stopped for a split second, turned her withering glare on them, and without a word from her they went silent.

Javier smiled to himself. He guessed she *was* a Puerto Rican woman.

Izzy was still jawing with the three kings, so Javier grabbed his arm and peeled his friend from them like a Band-Aid. "C'mon man, let's get this over with."

"Catch you later, panas!" Izzy called back as he walked through the doorway.

Lupe was staring at her cousin. "Friends of yours?"

Izzy shrugged. "The Diplomat gets along with everyone, cuz."

"Yeah, well, I think you should be more discerning in your friendships, cuz."

They stopped at the bottom of the steep, wide staircase. It was dark, spray-painted, and smelled vaguely of vomit.

Javier pronounced, "I would just like to say again that I think this is a bad idea."

And with that, Lupe stormed up the stairs with Izzy following behind.

The ceilings were very high, the walls concrete and crumbling. "What was this building?" she asked.

"It was a factory back in the day. Closed and moved to Mexico when NAFTA was signed." Izzy's voice echoed.

They arrived at a massive sliding metal door, sounds of music, voices, and crying coming from inside. Lupe looked even paler than usual. "What kind of factory?"

Izzy smirked. "Pharmaceuticals. Now that's what you call

'ironic,'" he added in his best pirate accent. Then he pulled open the sliding door, revealing a large room filled with random scavenged furniture, people draped all over them like lizards in the sun. There was a reggaeton heartbeat thrumming in the floor, the walls; those who were standing seemed to move with it.

Javier froze. He sniffed and under the scent of cigarettes, sweat, and decay, he detected the unmistakable vinegary essence of black-tar heroin.

He could feel his heartbeat behind his face, his arms going numb. As he looked around, he noticed that the blackness was leaking into his vision again, farther this time.

He jumped when Lupe grabbed his arm. She pointed toward Izzy who had stopped walking also. Javier glanced over to see what his friend was looking at and saw a skinny guy with a rubber hose tightened around his bicep, a needle hanging from the crook of his arm, a look of total vacancy spreading in his eyes. Lupe was watching with a fascinated horror while the look in Izzy's eyes was that of a starving man watching a suckling pig on a spit. Javier would be willing to bet the shadow was spreading even farther in his fellow cangrejo's head. He herded them both along toward the back, wondering if even worse sights awaited them there.

Izzy seemed to wake, and pushed in front of them, knocking on a scratched gray metal door in a hallway lit by a bare blue bulb, the colored light giving their skin a drowning hue.

"¿Quién es?" a gravelly voice called from within.

"Izzy. Open up."

The door opened slowly, and the three of them entered a surprisingly bright room, rows of fluorescent lights beaming from among the maze of pipes that covered the ceiling. The room was filled with people who were all circled around a guy lying on a bare mattress that topped a stack of wooden pallets. There was nothing in the room other than the makeshift bed and a paint-splattered ladder against one wall.

A girl who held the boy's hand gestured to Javier and Lupe. "Who the hell are they?"

Izzy answered, "They're cool. We're here to talk to Ángel."

She looked back into the guy's blank face. "Good luck. My brother's not himself."

Izzy pushed through the people, leaned over, and looked into Ángel's face. "Ángel, man, it's me. Izzy."

Nothing, no reaction.

Izzy looked back at Javier and shrugged. He tried again. "We want to talk to you about Memo."

Ángel's eyes shifted and caught Izzy's gaze.

Izzy nodded. "That's right, you remember Memo."

It was as if Ángel had been plugged in; he started to shake.

His sister stepped back. "What did you do to him? You're wasting your time. The cops tried to get him to talk, but—"

She stopped and they all stared as Ángel grabbed Izzy's shirt, pulling him right up to his face, eyes shifting wildly, pupils huge. "Memo . . ."

Izzy put his hand on Ángel's shoulder. "Yes, what about Memo?"

His voice was uneven, like it was being dragged over gravel. "*He* took him."

Javier stepped forward. "Who took him?"

Ángel's eyes were darting, like he was seeing it all play out again. "We'd just done a job. Memo stepped up. Saved my life, even. But then . . . man, we were just drinking a cerveza . . . I started to get this feeling . . ."

"What kind of feeling?" Javier could tell from Izzy's voice that he was trying to be patient, but it was getting harder and harder.

Ángel pulled Izzy close again. "It was like a black hole, you know? I could feel it pulling, pulling in toward its nothingness, its darkness."

Izzy looked back at Javier and they shared an uneasy look. Izzy asked, "It was pulling at you?"

Ángel shook his head hard. "Not me. It didn't want me." He looked back into Izzy's eyes. "It wanted Memo. It wrapped its thin, black shadow tendrils around him, and . . . and . . ." His face collapsed and he started to sob, his sister pulling him into a hug, whispering comforting words.

She gestured toward Izzy and Javier. "Get out of here! You're upsetting him all over again!"

But over his sister's shoulder, Ángel seemed to notice Javier for the first time. He pointed back and forth between Izzy and Javier. "You two, do you see the shadows behind you?"

Javier spun around like there was a spider on his back, and he saw Izzy do the same. How could Ángel know? The shadow, the darkness . . . they weren't real.

"What're you talking about, Ángel?" Javier didn't bother to hide the irritation in his voice.

"It's the same shadow *he* had. Right before . . . before . . ." Ángel whispered.

Izzy's voice tightened. "*Who* had? Before what?" This time he was grabbing Ángel's shirt.

"Memo." After that one word the room went silent, the only sound a speaker in the next room blasting, of all songs, Carlos's hit "El Cuco."

Everyone jumped as Ángel screamed. "El Cuco! He's coming!" His wild eyes focused just over Izzy's shoulder toward the corner of the room. They all followed his gaze, but there was nothing there but stained ceiling tiles. Then he just pulled back into himself, returning to the same position where he had been when they came in, like a toy soldier winding down.

He was just repeating the words to the song . . . right?

There was a beat of stunned silence, then Ángel's sister began to shout.

"Why the hell did you come here, Izzy? Your idiota friend Memo almost got him killed!"

Javier stammered. "Memo almost got *him* killed? Mira, it's his so-called gang that got *Memo* killed! He was a good kid until he got hooked up with them!"

"Forget it, pendejo! You and your 'cangrejo' friends got him into drugs way before he joined the Calaveras."

Javier pushed closer but he could feel Lupe tugging on his arm. He yanked it back. He and Ángel's sister were face-to-face when a group of people streamed into the small room led by Keno, his "soldiers" lined up behind him like pool balls.

"Izzy, what you bringing this trash around for?" He pointed to Javier. "I thought you were too good for this neighborhood, Javi?" Then he noticed Lupe standing behind Javier. "And you bring Dávila's niece here, too? Are you crazy?"

The sister yelled, "She's cop family?"

People in the crowd started pointing to Lupe and whispering. Great. Now they all knew she was related to the chief. They might not live to be killed by whatever the hell was stalking them.

Javier noticed the people coagulated in the hallway outside the door and confirmed that they'd voluntarily walked into the lions' den. Keno's eyes were still on Lupe, and though she was standing strong, chin held high, Javier could feel the tight grip of her fingers around his arm. She was brave, not stupid.

"Well, Lupe Dávila. Marisol's been looking for you."

"Yeah? She must not be looking hard, I'm right here."

Wait, maybe she was stupid, too. Girl didn't know when to keep her mouth shut. No shake to that voice, though. It was like she was at her most comfortable talking smack.

"Not for long, gringa!"

Keno stepped closer to her and Javier noticed he was pulling a revolver from under his arm. Javier moved to intercept Keno when all hell broke loose.

Keno's men pressed in behind Javier, shouting threats; the people from the hall poured in hoping for a show, blocking the only exit. Javier was trying to figure a way for them to get out. The window? No, there were three guys between them and the window and they were on the second floor. No way could he fight his way out, not with these numbers—

An ear-splitting siren blared from above and everyone slammed their hands over their ears.

Then it was raining.

Water came down from everywhere, pouring onto their heads, the siren continuing above, pieces of plaster falling with the water like wet snow.

It was then Javier noticed Izzy perched on the top rung of the rickety ladder against the wall, a lighter held high over his head, flicking the fire detector above. He looked at Javier and mouthed *Go*.

Javier grabbed Lupe's hand as the room came to life once again, people running to and fro as if the water were acid, confused yelling.

They ducked their heads and joined the crowd straining to get out of the room. Then their wet feet were pounding down the stairs, finally breaking out onto the sidewalk.

Lupe was breathless, but still moving toward the car. "What about Izzy?"

Javier was turning the key in the ignition before the doors were even closed, peeling out of the parking space and onto the empty street. He remembered the hunger with which Izzy watched the guy shooting up, and felt an emptiness in the pit of his stomach.

"Izzy can handle himself."

But he wasn't at all sure he could.

Lupe

💀

LUPE PICKED AT her codfish as if dissecting it. Normally she loved her aunt's bacalao, but that night she was having trouble eating. She was ignoring a text from her father, and he never texted. His fingers were too big for his flip phone. And, well, it was a flip phone.

> Our neighbor Linda told me she saw online that you were hanging out with music stars down there! I take it you're having fun?

She imagined her response.

> Yep! And tonight I visited The Factory, a major drug den in El Norte! A gang leader pulled a gun on me and I saw someone shooting up!

Yeah, no.

Best ignore his message altogether.

She almost told her aunt about leaving Izzy at the drug den several times, but the woman was already pissed she'd been so late for dinner and anxious about her husband without knowing that her nephew might be in danger. Oh, and then there was the issue of Lupe being right in the middle of it all. Yeah, her tía was a handwringer at the best of times; this news might send her off the edge. No, she'd wait until her uncle got home and talk to him.

They cleaned up in silence, wrapping up a plate for Esteban to heat when he eventually got home. When the kitchen was back to its normal immaculate state (Lupe had determined years ago that cleaning was an Olympic sport in Puerto Rico), her aunt made her way to the stairs.

"I'm going to go to bed and read. Buenas noches, Lupe." Her eyes were so sad, so powerless. How did she live like this all the time? Maria and her uncle had been high school sweethearts, the great loves of each other's lives. How did she handle him being in danger every damned day? It must feel like living with your heart in a vice, tightening and releasing, then tightening again.

"It will be okay, tía. I promise," Lupe called lamely, though she didn't believe it herself.

"Querida Lupe, don't make promises you can't keep. Though I pray to Díos you're right." She smiled that sad smile, and started to take a step.

Lupe lurched forward on impulse. "Tía!"

Maria turned with her hand on the railing. "¿Sí?"

For one second she thought of saying "nothing," but instead she said, "Thank you."

Her aunt tilted her head. "For what?"

"For caring that I was late for dinner. For worrying about me. About everyone." Her voice caught. "For being like a mom."

Maria's face melted and she turned and pulled Lupe into a hug, her tears wetting them both. Then Lupe did something totally uncharacteristic for her.

She hugged her aunt back. A big, bear-like, tío-type hug.

When Maria spoke, her soft voice vibrated at the top of

Lupe's head like a hymn. "I wish I were your mamá. I would never let you go."

Lupe whispered into her aunt's clean-smelling blouse. "I wish you were, too."

Maria kissed her on the forehead, held her at arm's length, then let go. Lupe watched her walk up the stairs, the framed photographs of her wedding, of Esteban and Lupe's father, of her and Izzy as children, disappearing behind her and reappearing as she passed.

Lupe stood there at the base of the stairs for some time, then she texted Izzy again.

And again.

Look out the front window.

It was a text from Javier that woke her up.

Huh? She sat up. She was on the couch, a 1950s horror movie flickering from the television in black and white.

I'm here.

Lupe looked at the time on her phone. 10:18 P.M. Huh? She moved the front window curtain aside and saw the shadowed figure on the sidewalk in front, the glow of a cell phone gently lighting up his face. Her heart started beating faster.

Her aunt had to be asleep by now. But waking up and finding a boy—particularly *that* boy—in her house would not be a good thing. She responded.

Backyard.

She pulled open the sliding glass doors with a *whoosh* and stepped out onto the stone patio. The moon was not quite over the trees yet, but its glow lit the palm fronds from behind. She heard the metal gate squeal like it was in pain and Javier turned the corner of the house, hands in his jean pockets, hair all tousled from the wind.

"What are you doing here?" she whispered. "Is something wrong? Have you heard from Izzy yet?"

Javier shook his head. "Izzy isn't answering his phone."

Lupe pictured him on that ladder, the gang members moving in like lions feeding on a carcass. She looked back at the darkened house, afraid her aunt could even hear Lupe's thoughts.

"I've been driving around looking for him. I don't know where else to look. And this whole thing . . . it gives me such a bad feeling."

"Of course you have a bad feeling. Two of your friends were murdered."

"No, you don't understand. It was what Ángel said. What if it really is El Cuco? What if he really is coming for us? Izzy and me?"

"But you both cleaned up! I mean, if it's about bad behavior, doesn't that count?"

Javier shook his head. "I don't know."

It was Lupe's turn to shake her head. "No, I refuse to give up. There has to be something we can do."

Javier was staring at the ground, kicking at the stones in the path with the toe of his shoe. "Look, I appreciate all you've done—"

"I've done nothing yet!"

He looked up at her and did that sad smile thing. Too many people were giving her that kind of smile lately. "You tried to help, you care, that matters." His eyes darted down to her lips.

Just that small shift of his eyes brought a warm hum to her

chest. She was suddenly aware of how close his body was to hers, that she could feel the heat coming off of him, smell the light spice of his cologne.

Then he stepped away and she almost stumbled. He moved over and sat down on the patio bench with a sigh. "Lupe, I know if I asked you to step back and let Izzy and me worry about this situation you'd probably punch me."

"Most likely."

"It's just, it's getting harder. The more I care about you."

She gaped at him. No boy had ever spoken to her like this, about feelings. Feelings for her.

"What if something happened to you? I mean, whatever this is, los cangrejos brought it on ourselves."

She tried to stay on task. "I don't know about that. So we have to worry about Carlos on Saturday, too, right? I mean, if this is about the birthdays."

Javier looked up at her. "Oh shit."

She nodded solemnly. "Yeah, his birthday is the same day as yours, right? The street party?"

Javier's eyes lit up as he shook his head. "No, they're just having the party on Saturday because it's sure to get more attendance on the weekend."

"What does that mean? When is his actual birthday?"

"Lupe, his birthday was the first."

"Wait, it passed already?"

Javier nodded.

"Does that mean the dates are just a coincidence? That you and Izzy aren't in danger?"

Javier shrugged, but she could tell from the look on his face that he didn't think so.

"So why did nothing happen to Carlos?"

"I don't know. I mean, he left Amapola right after that last birthday party. Maybe because he got out?"

"Or because he didn't do drugs. Wasn't addicted." Lupe folded her arms, thinking. "But again, you and Izzy straightened up. You should both be safe from whoever is doing this. Right?" Her mind buzzing, she sat down next to Javier, not realizing how close they were until she felt her arm brush his. Suddenly feeling awkward, she pointed up to the huge white moon, its double rippling in the dark water of the pool. "The moon is nice tonight."

He didn't answer. She could feel his eyes on her like a touch. A tingling spread over her arms, her legs. Suddenly she could hear the music of the coquís, smell the night-blooming jasmine that ran along the fence. When she finally got the nerve to look over at him, he was standing up.

"I—I should go, I'm going to keep trying to find Izzy. Just in case."

"Right. Of course. Just in case." She felt like a total idiot. Here she was, melting when this boy just looked at her while her cousin might be in danger. She walked next to him as he headed toward the gate. "I've decided I'm going to talk to my uncle when he gets home tonight, tell him everything."

"You're sure? He'll probably think you've come all the way to la isla just to lose your mind." He was quiet for a minute. "Does that mean you're going to tell him about us?" He gestured between them with his index finger.

"Of course! I mean . . ." Wait, what did he mean by "us"? She stammered as he smiled at her. What was he smiling about? She felt the heat rise behind her face. Thank God for the darkness.

A car door slammed out front. They froze. Her uncle couldn't find them together, alone, in the backyard. They tiptoed to the fence, Javier slipped open the latch silently, and they made their way on exaggerated cat feet around the house. The light on the porch of the neighbors' house across the street went on, the front door opened and closed, the light went off.

They sighed a simultaneous breath of relief. Then started laughing, covering their mouths so her aunt wouldn't hear them. Javier waved and went toward his car, lifting his legs up ridiculously high in a dramatic tiptoe.

She smiled as she started toward the backyard. For a minute she almost forgot about the ticking clock.

Almost.

Her phone buzzed in her back pocket. Izzy! She pulled it out and glanced at the screen.

I'm coming for you next bitch

She stopped.

Looked at the screen again.

It was from a Puerto Rico area code, not a number she recognized. She was pretty sure El Cuco wasn't texting her, so who was this? Lupe's muscles tightened as if ready to run. But she might not be sure how she fit in down here, but there was one thing she was damn sure of: she was not a runner.

Not now, not ever.

She typed two words in response.

Bring it.

July 8, 10:54 P.M.

Marisol

☠

MARISOL GLANCED AT Keno in the passenger seat. At least he'd finally dried off. When she picked him up at The Factory he was soaked to the bone and she was surprised the water wasn't steaming off him he was so angry. But after he told her what had happened, she joined him in his anger. She had spent the evening at a rally for Puerto Rican independence and she was already worked up, but hearing about the visit from los cangrejos and that gringa tipped her into fury.

She'd tolerated enough of Keno's brooding for the evening. It was time to take action. "So what's the plan?"

His head whipped in her direction. "Plan? I don't need a plan." He padded the bulge of the revolver under his arm. "I'm going to plug that pendejo, Javier. Simple. Probably Izzy, too, for bringing him there." He smiled for the first time that night.

"But what about the gringa?"

Keno grinned at her. "You want a part of this? I'll leave her just for you, baby." He reached for her hair, rubbing the long black strands between his fingers. Just the thought of violence seemed to turn him on. She shoved his hand away. Generally she tolerated the physical part of their relationship, but now was not the time.

"Guns aren't my thing, you know that."

Keno threw up his hands angrily. "I forgot, you think you're too good for my 'thing,' huh? Particularly after you go to one of your 'political' meetings."

He stared at her in that way that both excited and frightened her, like he was on the edge of something . . . dark. It was like the thumping in her head, they shared that feeling of teetering on the edge of a free fall into the soft, dark abyss. He "got" her in a way no other boy had. And though most of Las Calaveras were morons, Keno and the gang accepted her, didn't treat her just like Vico's little sister. Like los cangrejos had. When your family is dropping like flies, that counts for a lot.

He straightened his jacket and lifted his chin. "Forget politics, Marisol. Sometimes the only solution is a piece of lead between the eyes."

She drummed her fingers on the steering wheel. He was *so* one-note at times. "So Ángel's talking again?"

"Nah, man. Just when Izzy asked him about Memo. He woke up just long enough to talk some wild shit about Memo getting 'taken.' Ángel's a few cans short of a six-pack."

"Taken?"

"Yeah, and he actually screamed 'El Cuco!'" He snorted.

Marisol sat up straight, pulling the car to a stop. "El Cuco?"

"Yeah, loco."

Marisol's mind swam with memories, like she was inching through a thick fog, trying to find her way. She could see a cake, one of the cangrejo parties. The mothers were angry at the boys for something. . . .

"So, you pull over so we could make out, or what?"

Marisol jolted out of her memory as Keno pawed her from

the passenger seat. "No!" She shoved him off and pulled back into traffic, horns sounding all around them.

"Fine. I don't give a shit." But she could tell by his defensive tone that she'd hurt his fragile male ego. Sigh.

"Look, I'm thinking."

He looked into the visor's mirror and primped his now-dry hair. "Yeah, well I think you do a bit too much of that, if you ask me."

Nobody asked you, Keno. But she didn't say it aloud. Instead she said, "Well, I have a plan that will take care of all of them."

He snapped up the visor and smiled over at her. "Now you're talking."

As she drove she realized that the darkness was starting to edge into her vision again, the thumping like the footfalls of a beast pounding inside her head.

July 8, 11:54 P.M.

Izzy

💀

IZZY FELT AS if he were walking underwater, like he was in Campeche's painting. In fact, he'd have sworn he was if it weren't for the hardness of the sidewalk beneath him and the storefronts passing by on his left. He looked down and could see his body moving, but he didn't feel it, as if the water was really cold and numbing. But the heroin in his veins carried him on its own wave.

Damn, he'd forgotten how good it felt to be high, the pain receding into the background while the glowing took over, that feeling like everything was going to be okay. Heroin was your mother, your father, your girlfriend, food, water, oxygen. Why had he stopped? It was as if this were the way he was supposed to be, not slithering through his life on his belly, just trying to get through each day.

There was no one else on the street, but then there usually wasn't in that part of Amapola after sundown. On the other side from El Norte in more ways than one, downtown is a business area, bustling during the weekdays, dead at night. Not that he had any idea what day it was. That had ceased to matter since he'd grabbed that kit from Ángel's apartment a few hours . . . or was it days . . . before. For a few hours he'd tried to figure it out with Lupe and Javier, tried to fight it, but when he was in The Factory, well, it had felt like home. Besides, he got Lupe out. That was the most important thing. Probably the only reason he made it out at all was because he didn't care if he didn't.

It was so easy, shooting up was as normal to him as breathing. He'd tried to stop, had promised his mother he would, but Vico . . . then Memo. . . . well, let's just say he preferred his life and his mind buffered, wrapped in a blanket. After the first few weeks of being clean, the darkness seeped in like an oil spill, coating him, pulling at him, bleeding into his mouth and nose until he could no longer breathe. He hadn't expected that he, Javier, and Lupe would find anything, but unfortunately in just a few short hours a strand of hope had wrapped its way around his heart. The same strand that was now pulling tight, the pumping blood slowing under the pressure.

He wasn't walking, really. More like falling forward. *But that's okay, at least you're moving,* he thought. Izzy was weaving back and forth across the squares of concrete, like when his father took him skiing before he died. He remembered side-winding down that mountain, the cold New England snow almost like the sand on Vieques island, the skis an extension of his feet, the fronts pointed inward in a V in front of him. His father complained about the cold, but Izzy kind of liked it. He watched the back of his father's yellow ski jacket, following it as it snaked down the trail in front of him, and thought his father was like the sun. In fact, that was the last day Izzy could remember feeling truly warm.

Izzy lifted his head up and looked around. He was surprised to see the darkened street and not the brilliant white blaze of snow. As the drugs made their way through his body it was getting harder and harder to tell memories or dreams from reality. In fact, he often wondered whether they were the same thing anyway. He stopped with a profound thought—he seemed to be having a lot them that evening—what *was* real, anyway?

He looked down to the sidewalk and noticed an uncrushed cigarette butt with at least an inch of smokable tobacco. Tsk, tsk. People were so wasteful these days, but hey, more for him. It took a few tries, but he picked it up between his fingers and stumbled back to his feet. As he was struggling to get the hand with the lighter to meet the cigarette butt, he heard footfalls behind him. He wheeled around and saw a figure a block away, moving from a pool of streetlight to darkness to streetlight. A man in a dark suit like the ones his father used to wear to work.

Izzy sniffed and wondered if he was dreaming of roasting meat. He looked down and saw that the lighter was under the wrist holding the cigarette and his dark brown skin was beginning to crackle and shrivel, turning black. He lifted his finger from the lighter switch, the flame sucking back into the clear red plastic base. "Ouch! Motherf—" he yelled, though he wasn't sure if he really felt the pain, or if he just felt he *should* feel it. *Damn, that's deep.* He stared at his arm for a while, only breaking away at the continued sound of footsteps, louder now.

The suited man was coming closer, his shoes making a clean, clipped sound as they hit the pavement. Izzy was just about to look back at his now truly hurting arm when he saw that the man's shadows were in front of him, though the light was above. And they were odd, moving differently from their maker, stretching and reaching with thin fingers. Just then the man lifted his head before stepping out of the circle of light from the last streetlamp. He had glowing yellow snake eyes.

Izzy took a huge gulp of air and felt his chest tighten. He lurched forward again, trying to make his legs run. As he went, he saw movement on either side. He swiped left, then right, his body weaving across the pavement. But the darkness was creeping from the corners of his eyes like shadows reaching for him from within his own skull. His lighter clattered to the sidewalk and he willed his body to move faster, his feet dragging behind him. He could feel his heart beating a fast rhythm in his chest and terror gripped the sides of his head as if to crush it. He could only see a slice of the street ahead, his vision swallowed by the blackness. Izzy wished the sidewalk that was moving beneath his feet would go faster; he had to get away. He stumbled off the curb, catching himself just before he tipped over, and hurled himself across the street. Up ahead, through the small hole he had left of sight, he could see rows and rows of buildings, the fire escapes zigzagging down the stone facades like the Erector set he'd had when he was a kid.

He stopped in front of a building, and he could see a pinpoint of the streetlight's bulb dully flickering in its halogen death throes above him, the bodies of trapped insects pooled in the bottom of the frosted glass globe. He leaned out from the building's shadow to see where the man had gone, whether he was following. He used what vision he had to scan the blocks behind him but no one was there, the yellow pools of light were empty, the only sound an occasional car that swept by, billowing up garbage and newspapers in their wake. The fire escape above him made crisscrossed patterns on the sidewalk in the flickering light that reminded Izzy of the bars of a cage.

Then the darkness filled out the last of his eyes.

He was blind.

Izzy dragged in ragged breaths, his lungs reluctantly filling.

Izzy opened his mouth to scream, but his throat was so tight with terror all he could do was gasp.

He wished he hadn't shot up, that his mind was clear.

Izzy knew he should keep running, but all he could do was shuffle along with his back against the building, his fingers running across the brick, desperately feeling his way.

Silent sobs wracked his body as he imagined the man's shadows growing, stretching, as high as the building behind him, reaching for him.

Izzy moved his eyes back and forth in his head. He could feel them moving, but all they could see was an inky blackness. He could hear the sounds, feel the breeze of an occasional car zip by. There were no footsteps that he could hear. Should he run forward to the street the next time he heard a car? Try to get help? But how would he stop when he got to the street and not get run over? Would someone even be able to save him?

Was he worth saving?

He heard the groan of shifting metal from the fire escape overhead. He whipped his head up and was surprised he could see movement above him in the dark. He dug his fingers between the bricks as if he could ooze his body through them and away molecule by molecule.

Then the hissing sound reached him.

His lower body was itching to move once again, his feet shifting back and forth, but he couldn't look away from the slithering shadow above. It was like a shadow within a shadow. Like the iron bars themselves were moving, pooling together in a melted mass of darkness and reaching for him. His blood pulsed in his veins like waves pounding the shore in a storm, but still he stood, transfixed. He started to make out a huge, snake-like head, easing its way around the last metal rung of the ladder. A creature with yellow eyes . . . he had seen them before . . . where was that? It was so quiet he could hear the scraping of scales against the rusted bars, the groan of metal. Terror wrapped around his bowels, his stomach.

I changed my mind! I don't want to die!

But he couldn't make the scream leave his mind and go to his mouth.

The eyes were right in front of his now; Izzy could see and

feel the yellow gaze as if it were heat, and he thought again of his father's ski jacket.

He was afraid.

So afraid.

Dad! I'm afraid!

He reached out, drawing closer to the yellow, wanting to catch his father, to grab his yellow jacket, pull him closer. He felt a tightening around his body. Was it his father? It was getting harder and harder to draw a breath in the deep cold of the New England air.

In the distance Izzy could hear the squealing of tires, the opening of car doors . . . pulling on his legs, pulling him down, back toward the ground, toward earth. None of that mattered anymore, because not only was the pull from above stronger, he found he wanted to go. He could almost touch his father's jacket, if he could just reach a bit farther. . . .

July 9, 1:16 A.M.

Lupe

LUPE WAS SITTING wedged between the cushions of the bamboo couch while a ridiculous variety show in Spanish featuring a filthy-minded clown blathered on TV. After Javier left there was no way she was going to fall back to sleep, so she had grabbed the remote, craving the noisy company of the idiot box. She'd been texting Izzy for hours, but midnight had come and gone with no response. Her aunt was asleep, her uncle had still not come home, and she had no vehicle.

She'd never felt more helpless.

Lupe was about to snap off the TV and head upstairs when the doorbell rang. The doorbell? At this hour? As she stood staring at the door wondering what to do, her aunt came racing down the stairs, tying her robe sash, her movements quick and jerky, her eyebrows knitted together.

This couldn't be good.

Was it Izzy?

Oh God, it was Izzy.

Lupe froze when she saw the uniformed man behind the door, her dinner pushing against the back of her throat.

The police wouldn't come here for Izzy. There would have been a phone call from Maria's sister. Right?

No.

Just, no.

She couldn't understand what they were saying; it was as if every Spanish word had left her brain. She heard the name "Isadore" but there was way too much mention of her uncle.

Then her aunt was yelling. "I need to see him. Now!" She was grabbing her purse and keys, still in her silky white robe.

"Vamos, Lupe!" she barked, pushing the officer out of the way as she made her way to the cruiser parked out front, its blue lights pulsating over the houses across the street.

Lupe ran, following her aunt down the pathway. She knew she should ask Maria what happened, but she was afraid she couldn't handle the response, afraid she would sit down on the sidewalk and never get up. The day had been a bad dream but she had a feeling the nightmare was just beginning. She was still worried about Izzy, but this was her uncle, her rock, the one sensible adult in her life.

As the police car pulled out, she heard the officer radioing in that they were heading to Doctors' Center Hospital with Chief Dávila's wife and niece.

The hospital.

Tío Esteban in the hospital.

Lupe couldn't imagine her broad-chested, 6'4" uncle as anything but invincible. The idea that he could be hurt—or, God forbid, killed—made her feel actual physical pain in her chest. Though she often thought of herself as an orphan, thanks to her mother's booking on her and her father's retreat into the bottom of a Bacardi bottle, without Esteban she truly would be orphaned. She tried not to projectile vomit all over the bulletproof plastic wall that separated them from the policeman in front.

The car jolted to a stop in front of the emergency room at

Doctors' Center Hospital, and her aunt was out the door before Lupe could even reach the handle. She hustled to follow Maria through the automatic glass doors. "Esteban Dávila?" her aunt barked at the first staff member she came to, who pointed down the hall, and Maria was off.

Lupe saw her aunt turn into a room just ahead, and Lupe paused for a moment. What if he was really hurt?

She doubled over, wrapped her arms around her stomach as the hospital hummed around her. Her breathing was coming in fast and shallow and the hallway started to spin around her.

No. Tío didn't need her to lose it. That was way too selfish and he was never selfish. She stood upright and sprinted to follow where her aunt had gone.

Tío's massive figure was perched on the edge of a hospital bed, bandages circling his neck and an IV running out of his arm. Lupe let go a breath she'd been holding since the doorbell rang. Okay. He was hurt, but sitting. He looked tired, but he looked like her uncle.

Tía was holding his hand in hers and when he saw Lupe he smiled, his mustache lifting with the corners of his mouth. All the tension left her body in a wave.

Maria gently pulled down the bandages and both women gasped at the angry red ring, blood drying in patches, the deep purple bruising blossoming around his neck like a collar.

"Ay, papi, you scared me to death!"

Lupe felt tears well in her own eyes as her aunt readjusted the bandages.

His eyes caught Lupe's in their special tractor-beam gaze. "And you, sobrina, were you worried about your old uncle?" He was smiling at her, but she could see something underneath. Something else was wrong.

Lupe's mouth pulled into a tight smile. "Nah, I knew you got this."

His smile faded. "It seems I should listen to you more often."

And then the other shoe dropped.

Her aunt looked into Esteban's eyes and asked a one-word question. "Isadore?"

Lupe saw him swallow and even before he shook his head, she knew. She dropped into the chair at the foot of the bed.

It had happened after all.

Izzy was gone.

Esteban held his wife as she sobbed for her nephew, his glassy gaze catching Lupe's, a silent nod as if to ask if she was okay.

Lupe swallowed and nodded back. She realized he was the only person with whom she communicated without words. The thought gave her some warmth despite the chill of the night.

Oh Izzy.

Oh God.

"He didn't even get to see eighteen years, mi amor! What will I say to my sister?"

Lupe's throat tightened at her aunt's pain.

Maria wiped away her tears, and pulled herself up. "Lo siento, mi amor. Enough selfishness, you're hurt."

Esteban took her face in his hands. "Querida, there isn't a selfish bone in your body." She kissed his hands then began clucking about his injuries, checking the bandages and trying to convince him to lie down. Lupe could see scrapes on his arms and more bruises on his ankles, calves.

Esteban was brushing off his wife's concerned hovering, forcing her fussing hands into his own. "I'm okay, really. I hurt most from the fall to the sidewalk."

Lupe couldn't stand it anymore, she had to know. "Were you there? What happened to Izzy? And what the hell happened to your neck?"

Maria gasped again. "Ay, Lupe! Give your tío a chance to breathe!"

Her uncle drew in a deep breath and let it out in a sigh, like he was resigned to something. "Ay, Maria, querida, can you get me some ice chips? My teeth cut through my lip when I fell and my mouth is on fire."

Lupe's aunt patted his hand. "Seguro, my love, of course." And she turned toward the door.

Then stopped.

She looked back at both of them with narrowed eyes, and noticed the half-full cup of ice chips on the table near the bed. She crossed her arms and stared at Esteban. "You two can discuss whatever you were going to discuss with me here." She pointed at the ground with her manicured index finger. "This is my family, too, and you will not exclude me. If you haven't figured it out yet, Esteban Dávila, I don't need protecting."

Esteban sighed, then gave his wife a heartbreaking smile.

Forget romance novels, sonnets, the smile they shared was the best representation of love Lupe had ever seen. He loved what made his wife strong. Maria sat down next to her husband and hugged him. Lupe sat down next to them on the bed, the springs' metallic creaking in response, and the three of them held one another.

Maria sat up, wiped her eyes, and said, "Bueno. What really happened?"

Lupe sat with her back bolt upright, ready to take the blow she instinctively knew was coming.

"It started the other day. I couldn't stop thinking about when you asked, 'What if the other two boys are in danger?' after we left the coffee shop. In my heart I knew you were right, that Isadore could be next and could be in trouble, so I grabbed Ramirez and we went to find him. When he wasn't at his house, we interviewed some of his less-than-savory friends. He'd been clean for a few months, he was telling the truth about that." He turned to Maria. "He was trying to turn his life around, they said, but there had been some commotion at The Factory in El Norte earlier in the evening."

Lupe stared at the floor. Were they responsible for Izzy getting hurt? If they hadn't gone to Ángel's apartment, would he still be alive? The one thing she was sure about was that now was not the time to admit to her aunt and uncle that she'd been there.

"Turns out the kid who was there when Guillermo was killed, Ángel Sanchez, it was his apartment and he'd talked to Izzy. We'd questioned him about the murders, but the kid was basically comatose, had been since he'd seen Guillermo killed. Witnesses say he said something to Izzy that upset him, something about being cursed. There was an argument, a fire broke out, and Izzy got a bag of heroin and works from a junkie at the party. I was praying he didn't use them. Even after all these years, I still hope that some of these kids will get out of the life." He patted Maria's hand. "And Izzy is . . . *was* familia."

Lupe pictured Izzy's face right after the alarm and sprinklers went off. He had looked resigned. She fought to keep her eyes from filling.

"Detective Ramirez and I jumped in the car and started to drive around the streets, hoping to find him, hoping it wasn't too late. We stopped by your sister's house, but she hadn't seen him. And then, a few blocks from his house, I saw . . ."

Lupe was breathless, waiting for her uncle's next words.

"What? What did you see?" Maria's voice was thin and tight.

"I'm not sure what I saw, but there was Isadore, hanging from a fire escape on the darkened street, his feet dangling. I yanked the car over onto the sidewalk, leapt out of the car, and grabbed on to his legs to pull him down."

Lupe shook her head. This didn't make sense. "Wait, he hanged himself?"

"No, no."

Maria pulled at his shirt. "What was he hanging by?"

Lupe's heart was banging like it wanted out.

"It was—ay, I don't know. It sounds completamente loco."

"What was it?" Both women were yelling now.

Her uncle rubbed his face from top to bottom as if to erase the memory, the clear tubes winding down his hairy arms. "It makes no sense. All I saw were shadows wrapping around him. It was night and hard to see clearly, but there something huge in the dark and it seemed to have hold of him. I could only see Isadore's feet, the rest of him was lost in darkness. Whatever it was, it seemed to be wrapped around his chest and was pulling him farther and farther up into the fire escape. I held on as best I could, but I couldn't budge him. My body kept rising along with Isadore's, until I could see Ramirez screaming down on the sidewalk, getting smaller and smaller. Then the thing wrapped something cold and strong around my neck." His hands clasped around his throat, the bruises with even edges like a shadow.

Maria held her hand over her mouth, silent sobs racking her body.

Lupe felt vomit rise at the back of her throat again. She knew that if she puked her uncle would stop talking. The feeling subsided but the image of Izzy dangling and her uncle being strangled was still behind her eyes. She didn't think it would ever leave.

"I let go of Isadore to pull the—whatever it was—off my neck. I had no choice, but it seemed to have no interest in me, because as soon as I let go of Izzy's legs, the piece uncoiled from my neck and then I was falling."

Lupe cleared her throat then asked in a quiet voice, "What are you saying? I mean, you're not saying this thing . . . it *was* a monster?"

He threw up his hands. "I still have no idea what it was.

How's that *posible*? And what are we going to tell Luisa? That her son was taken by a supernatural creature?" The three of them were searching one another's eyes, each desperate for an answer to the impossible.

Lupe sat there silently shaking her head back and forth. No, just no. Her uncle, he's the sensible one. He's the one she can depend on to always tell her the truth. But this? This was crazy. But he seemed coherent, and if he told her it was raining green Jell-O she would believe him. But she'd seen things in the last few days. Heard things. She thought about telling them everything, but she was afraid they would shut her out, or worse, send her home.

She realized her aunt was looking at her, watching her. Like she knew.

Lupe's phone buzzed in her pocket, saving her. She excused herself from her uncle's bedside, and found her way to a tree-filled atrium that was empty except for an old man reading by the windows. She yanked her cell phone from her pocket and looked at the screen. Five missed calls from Jessica, her friend from school. At this hour? Wait, and a text from a number she didn't recognize.

Ready to join your cousin?

What? Who the hell was this? Oh, they'd picked the wrong day to—

She jumped when the phone started ringing in her hand. Lupe was shaking so hard she almost dropped the phone as she pressed the button to answer.

"Lupe?" Jessica's voice was pulled tight like a string.

"Yeah." Honestly she didn't have any other words. Yeah.

Silence for a moment. "Lupe, what's wrong? Did someone already call you?"

Lupe dropped into an overstuffed chair nearby. How could Jessica know about Izzy in Vermont?

She couldn't.

"Did someone call me about *what*?"

"Oh. I. Oh."

"What's going on?"

"My mom just called from the hospital, she's working the night shift, and she woke me up to ask how to reach you. Lupe, your dad checked himself in to the hospital about fifteen minutes ago."

Checked *himself* in. That means they didn't find him in a ditch. She tried to breathe. "Checked himself in for what?" Her father never went to the doctor, like, ever.

"She wouldn't tell me, but I eavesdropped when she talked to my dad after, and I heard them say detox."

"Dad? Rehab?" Lupe's mind tried to grasp the two words that she never thought would be used in the same sentence.

"Yeah, but that's good, right?"

Lupe nodded, as if Jessica could see her through the phone. She started to feel as if the room was spinning around her.

"Lupe? You okay?"

She almost forgot that Jessica was on the other end of the line. "Don't worry about me. I'm fine," Lupe lied. "I should call my dad."

"You can't. Not for the first forty-eight hours, at least. No contact with anyone outside the hospital. Don't worry, Lupe, they'll take good care of him. My mom will look in on him, too."

Another call buzzed in, and Lupe jumped again, afraid it was whoever had sent the threatening text. No, it was Javier. Her heart took off like a horse out of the gate. Did he know about Izzy? He must if he was calling this late.

"Jess, I've got to get this. And . . . thanks."

Lupe switched calls. She didn't even get to say hello.

"Lupe?" Javier's voice was tense. "I just heard about your uncle—"

"Forget my uncle, Javier, Izzy—"

"I know."

Lupe didn't know two words could hold so much weight. But Javier changed the subject quickly.

"Are you all right? Where are you?"

"I'm at the hospital. My tío . . . he tried to save . . . he got hurt tonight." Her voice sounded braver than she felt.

"I know, I heard. Is he okay?"

"Yes, gracias a Dios." She answered absently, making the sign of the cross as she'd seen all the old ladies do.

Javier chuckled. Chuckled? WTF?

"Something funny?" Lupe's voice was icy.

"Sorry. I think I'm losing it. It's just, you sounded like a Puerto Rican."

Lupe bristled. "I *am* a Puerto Rican."

"Of course. I was just—" A sigh. "Look, Lupe. I wanted to say thank you. For everything. But after hearing about your uncle, about Izzy, I'm thinking that this fate is inevitable for me as well."

"No! No way. Not on my watch." She wasn't losing anyone else.

Lupe could hear the smile in his voice as he said again, "Thank you."

"For what?"

"For not giving up. You're stubborn, and I'm grateful."

A warmth like sunshine spread through her chest. "You can thank me when we get you past your birthday."

"Look, Izzy used. He gave in. I don't plan on scoring in the near future or again in this lifetime, for that matter."

Never say never. The phrase came back from Lupe's short

stint in Alateen. But she wasn't going to preach at the guy. "We don't really know if that's why Izzy and Memo were killed."

"No one knows. But I think our theory about addiction was right. Why Carlos is still alive and I'm . . ."

"But we need to find out for certain." She looked at the door. She didn't have much time before her aunt came looking for her. "What's our next step?"

"No, Lupe. You've done enough. Besides, I have to go to Old San Juan this morning. My mother wants me to take a casserole to Vico's grandmother in El Rubí. She'd made it for Izzy's birthday dinner, but . . ."

"Lupe!" Her aunt appeared in the atrium doorway.

Lupe talked quickly into the phone. "I'm coming with you."

"I'm not sure that's a good idea."

"Yeah, well, I am. See you at nine at the top of the stairs. Bye." She pressed End just as her aunt arrived and was staring at her with that look. The one that made Lupe feel like her skin, heart, and soul were suddenly transparent.

"Sobrina, is there something you're not telling us?"

Lupe looked at the floor, at the plants, but not into her aunt's probing eyes. "I'm just . . . freaked out about Izzy." That wasn't a lie. In the slightest.

Maria took Lupe's chin in her hand and she had no choice but to look at her. "I don't care if you tell me, but if you have something that will help your uncle figure out what's going on, share it with him. ¿Comprendes?"

Lupe nodded, tears blurring her vision.

Maria took her hand. "Bueno. Your uncle is insisting they release him. I need you to try to talk some sense into him. He'll listen to you."

Her. Talk sense into her uncle. Lupe was pretty sure it was

her sensible thinking that had kept her from seeing the truth. Now even her uncle had seen it.

It was too late for Izzy, but maybe not for Javier.

She was going to have to keep her mind open.

July 9, 8:58 A.M.

Javier

JAVIER SHIFTED HIS weight from one foot to the other, the crash of the waves on El Rubí's shore below providing a rhythm. It felt comforting to rock back and forth like he did when he was holding one of his baby cousins. Izzy was dead. Memo. Vico. If their birthday theory was correct, he was the last one left. For a minute he considered running in the other direction, away from Lupe Dávila, hopping in his car and heading east. He could sit on the beach in Luquillo and wait for the end to come, by himself so no one else would get hurt.

But he had to admit the idea scared him to death.

The clock was ticking.

Thirty-nine hours.

Was that all he had left? He was proud of all the work he'd done, kicking his habit. There were moments that were so clear from his past, moments seen through a filter of drugs, which were so damn painful. People he hurt, money he stole. After meeting Padre Sebastian he was surprised he got off so easy. Not that getting clean was a walk in the park, but he was surprised that there was no physical payment for his sins, no pound of flesh. He had thought the feeling of guilt was his punishment. But part of him wondered if he had been wrong and the true judgment was coming. Deep down he knew he wouldn't be allowed to ride it out alone on a beach.

If El Cuco really was coming for him, his end would not be peaceful.

To make things worse, he wasn't looking forward to going down the stairs. Javier rarely came to El Rubí since he stopped using. When he was fifteen it was like an adult carnival, the lights beacons in the night sky, and all he'd wanted was to have full admission. The first time he'd been there straight, he was shocked at how worn it looked, how poor. Even now as he looked down at the rooftops he could still identify where the best drugs could be purchased, the names of the dealers. If they were even still alive. Despite the reality of the morning sun washing over the streets, the barrio still held a pull for him.

And he didn't like it.

His eyes darted from left to right, wondering if the darkness was there even in the brightness of morning.

He heard someone running up from the direction of San Cristóbal and he turned to see Lupe jogging up the hill, ponytail bobbing on her back, her pale, muscled legs pumping as she ran. He liked the way her body was heavier on the bottom, like she was rooted to the earth. Lupe looked up then and smiled wide when she saw him. He realized in that moment he wanted to be in her company for as long as humanly possible.

Well, for the next thirty-eight hours and fifty minutes, at least.

Her face was glowing pink with the exercise and she was breathing hard. "Whose idea was it to meet at the absolute top of this city on a hill?"

He smiled back. "If you'll remember, Señorita Dávila, *you* were the one who wanted to accompany *me*."

She pointed to the stairs. "Are we going, or what?"

He grabbed the covered casserole dish that his mother had brought to him earlier that morning and headed for the stairs before Lupe could get there. No way was he letting her go first. When she got to the top of the stairs Lupe stopped, holding on to the handrails on either side, and stared at the barrio below.

He looked up at her, certain he saw fear in her eyes. "You can still change your mind. I can meet you at the Café Poético in twenty minutes."

"What? Why?"

"You look scared. It's okay, really—"

She gave him that look. "Scared? Excuse me, Señor Macho Pants?"

He put his hand up in surrender.

She smiled and he let out a breath. "I was just thinking how well they named it." She looked back over the neighborhood spread out below them. "The Ruby. It's so beautiful."

Surprised, Javier looked into her face then, really looked. Blanquitas from the states usually acted like they were above it all, that the island was a place to party and tan, no more, and boys like him were for flirting with, dancing with, or bringing them towels poolside. But Lupe seemed to really love the island.

He realized she had darted past him and started down the stairs. Independent or not, he was sticking to her like glue. Just before he took the first step, he froze. He had the feeling he was being watched. He spun around in a 360, looking at each tourist, jogger, and dog walker that was on the calle. No one seemed out of place. No shadows in his vision. *What's wrong with me?* He shook the feeling off and took the stairs two at a time to catch up with Lupe.

They reached the bottom together and he stopped and looked around, wondering if the stain of Vico was still on the pockmarked ground.

"You okay?" Lupe was looking at him with concern.

He nodded. "Just stay by my side, okay?"

"Why, you scared? Relax. I've been here before, you know."

He watched her as she looked at the life teeming around them. He knew she was taking in the shabby clothes of the children, the pounding music pouring from open windows. She kept walking in silence, but her eyes ran across everything, like a brush filling with paint. Javier began to see the streets through her eyes and, though he had come down there hundreds of times in his life, he began to notice things he hadn't before. The rich textures of the broken concrete buildings, the colors of the houses washed on in waves of patina, the children running in and out from between adults' legs like cat's cradle strings. It was as if even familiar places became new when he was with her.

Javier stopped in front of Vico's abuela's building, and pointed up the crooked staircase. "This is it." He led them up the stairs, stopped on the second floor and lifted his fist up to knock at a faded door, the black plastic number hanging upside down from one nail like some sort of dark talisman. Before his knuckles hit the wood, the door opened, leaving his hand in midair like an unfinished sentence. Vico's grandmother stood holding the inside knob, her tiny frame barely reaching halfway up the door, but her shoulders were up and strong like they had been at the funeral.

"Come in, come in." She brushed impatiently at them with her hands.

He handed her the still-warm casserole. "Doña Belasco, Mami sent you some arroz con pollo with her blessings. She is so sorry for your loss and that she couldn't make Vico's service."

The old lady patted Javier's cheek with a look of affection but no smile. She didn't have much to smile about these days. "Gracias, m'ijo. Please give your mother my thanks. She's always been so thoughtful, but I didn't expect her at the service. Things like that upset her. And lately we have too many young men's funerals to attend." She gestured to the love seat in the living room. "Sit, sit, children. Would you like some cake? My granddaughter made it. She brought it to me yesterday when she came to pick up some things of Vico's. Such a sweet girl."

Javier gave a tight smile. Marisol was many things, but sweet was not a word he would use to describe her. "No, gracias, Doña. We—this is my friend Lupe Dávila." He noticed Lupe had sat down on the love seat near the window and he realized he was going to have to sit close to her. Real close. "We don't want to impose." He concentrated on being nonchalant as he dropped down on the remaining cushion and the old woman settled in a chair opposite them. He looked down at Lupe's bare leg next to his and noticed the fine blond hair that shone on her thighs like gold dust.

Lupe spoke and pulled his attention up. "Actually, Doña Belasco, you and I met a couple of days ago a few blocks from here. The day after your grandson . . ."

"Yes, m'ija. I remember you. That was a difficult day. You did not find me at my best."

Lupe cleared her throat. "I was so sorry to hear of your grandson's death." She glanced over at Javier. "That day we met, you mentioned something about 'they' and their responsibility for Vico's death."

"Yes." She turned to Javier. "M'ijo, I'm sorry. Your mother and the others, they didn't know."

"Wait, what do our mothers have to do with what's going on?"

Tears started to fill her rheumy eyes, but didn't fall, just gathered against the dam of her eyelids. "They didn't know that he would come."

"That *who* would come?"

"El Cuco."

It was a whisper, but hearing those words for the second time, they reached for him with spidery fingers, wrapping around his neck like a noose. More memories broke through. "It was that night when my mother found us in the backyard, wasn't it? That last birthday party?"

She nodded. "You have to understand, your mothers were at the end of their ropes and nothing they said or did kept you away from those animales who were taking over the neighborhood with their guns and drugs. It used to be such a nice area, a family neighborhood, but it started to change when the economy failed. Jobs were lost, houses foreclosed. Your mothers tried to talk to you boys, but we couldn't fight the lure of their fast cars and easy money."

Javier remembered watching those tricked-out muscle cars drive by, the loud bass from the stereos rattling the windows, curvy girls with tight clothes in the passenger seats, and wanting nothing more than to be like them when he grew up. He'd blocked out what happened later that night, but the fog was starting to clear.

It was the first time they'd ever done coke, the five of them, thirteen-year-old cangrejos beneath the flamboyán tree. It was coming back to him now. It was his mother who'd found them, who'd seen the mirror covered with uneven white lines. Javier couldn't even remember where they'd gotten the drugs. Who had given them the drugs? They were children! It had to have been Vico. Then his mother was pulling him up by the arm, the other mothers spilling out the back door at the sound of her shrieks. When he'd looked back he'd seen the mirror was broken in half, cocaine sprinkled over the packed dirt like ashes.

He shivered despite the heat.

"That night we had all been in the kitchen cleaning up the last of the cake and ice cream, when your mother thought to check on you in the backyard. We were all so desperate, so scared to be losing you all. They didn't even know what they were going to do when they sat you down, but when they lined up in front of you boys, they grasped each other's hands for strength. And as they began to talk about El Cuco, it was as if some kind of power went from one to the next, like something from the Old Testament. I sat nearby holding Marisol. She was terrified, poor thing. She had nightmares about monsters every night after that, insisted she could see shadows everywhere. She and Vico fought a lot, but still, she was always protective of her brother, tu sabes? She was never the same again."

Javier remembered all of them, los cangrejos, squeezed side-by-side on the couch, hearts beating fast, while their mothers stood in front of them. He and his friends hadn't known what to expect, but they'd known it wouldn't be good.

Vico's mother had stood at the end of the line of women, pointing her finger at them. "If you don't stop this behavior, El Cuco is going to get you!" The boys had stared at them, mouths open.

"It was out of desperation that they turned to El Cuco. The threat of him had always made you behave before."

"We were thirteen, not seven." Javier could hear the shortness in his voice.

He remembered thinking: that's it? That was the punishment? He'd heard Vico snort, then cough, trying to cover his laughter. Javier had looked up at this line of women in front of him, adults who until that night had seemed so formidable, so in control, and it was as if he had been handed a pair of glasses and could finally see things as they were. He'd seen the powerlessness in their eyes, how frail they really were.

In retrospect, Javier realized this was the moment that turned him toward the neighborhood drug dealers, not away. If only he'd known just how much power those women had together, perhaps he would have more than thirty-seven-and-a-half hours left.

"*They* did it. Our mothers. They called him."

Doña Belasco nodded. "I haven't stopped thinking about it since Ludovico was taken from me. Then Guillermo and Isadore. Such a tragedy."

"But what does he want? El Cuco? How do I show him that I'm not bad?" Even his voice sounded thirteen again. The truth was, he hadn't ever been this frightened.

Her voice was tired. "I wish I knew, m'ijo."

Then Javier could feel anger spread through his veins like heat. The boys had trusted their mothers. They were their mothers, for God's sake. "They were supposed to take care of us, not have us killed."

Doña reached for Javier across the table, but he pulled his hands back.

No.

She didn't get off this easily. She could have stopped it. His mother should have stopped it. Doña Belasco folded her hands back in her lap, the papery skin almost clear over the blue of her veins. "They had no idea that he would come, Javier. We thought El Cuco was just a myth, something to get children to behave. Believe me, if I could take it back for them or call him off I would. I tried to talk to your mother about it, but she acted like that night never happened, kept changing the subject."

Javier snorted. "Typical." He wondered if it was after that night, after finding him and his friends, that she gave up and moved to Denial Land. Javier couldn't breathe. He stood up, knocking his knee against the glass coffee table, the pain almost welcome. "I have to get out of here." He bolted out the door and ran down the stairs, desperate to fling open the front door and grab a breath.

Javier paced up and down the cracked pavement in front of

the building. The morning sun felt like it was searing his eyes. There were so many feelings rattling around in his chest that he couldn't sort them out. Fury was the first, the easiest. Thinking about his mother often made him angry, but this was on another scale altogether. What were they thinking? What kind of parent sics a monster on their child?

He'd seen his share of monsters in his life, human and otherwise, but the main feeling, the one that pushed down on his shoulders as if he were being pressed into the ground like a stake, was guilt. If only he had been a better kid, this never would've happened. If only he'd stayed away from drugs like Carlos. But as Padre Sebastian often reminded him, you can't decide where you came from, but you can decide where you're going. Javier stopped pacing.

It wasn't helping.

"Javi, man! That you?"

A gravelly, smoke-roughened voice called from a nearby corner. Irritated, Javier turned and saw Flaco, a local character he hadn't seen since. . . . well, since. The cabrón had stayed true to his nickname, his skinny frame twitching, stained T-shirt draped over his shoulders as if on a hanger. Javier nodded but didn't move. Flaco peeled himself off the building's wall and strutted over, grabbing Javier's hand in a gang shake.

"What you been up to, jefe? Haven't seen you on these calles in a long-ass time!"

Javier looked toward the door, hoping Lupe would come through. And hoping she wouldn't. What would she think of him talking to someone like Flaco?

"Yeah, man. Been busy with Padre Sebastian, tu sabes?" That should do it. Nothing cuts short a conversation with a drug dealer faster than the mention of a priest . . . except maybe a cop . . . or the guy's grandmother.

"Oh right, the padre." Flaco was nodding his head. And not

leaving. Javier was about to bring out the big guns and ask after Flaco's grandmother when it happened.

Flaco looked around, reached into his jeans pocket, and pulled out a bag of white powder all in one practiced move.

Javier's stomach turned to ice.

"Man, pure Tigre Blanco H out of Asia. Guaranteed to take you for the ride of your life, pana."

Javier just stared, the clean white powder a soft pillow in the middle of Flaco's grimy hand. He was surprised to find he missed it, the going-home feeling only that little plastic bag could give him. The sounds of the street faded away and Javier felt the broken sidewalk spin. He felt some part of his mind blink off, and he could only stand and watch as his fingers reached out, sweat beading his forehead.

Black started spilling in from the side of his vision, but he didn't care.

The building door swung open and he yanked his hand away from Flaco's. Lupe came bursting through and onto the street, shading her eyes from the sun as she looked around for him. Her face lit up from inside when she saw him. Javier lurched toward her, grabbed her hand tightly, and started walking her fast toward the staircase up and out.

"I've been thinking about something Doña Belasco mentioned," she said as she was basically pulled along. She looked back at the barrio, at the skinny junkie yelling after them in the middle of the calle. She yanked her hand back from Javier. "Stop. What's going on? Who was that guy?"

Forgetting his commitment to stay by Lupe's side, Javier took off at a run and didn't stop until he was at the top of the stairs and safely on the sidewalk outside of the barrio, the pain in his lungs more from the brush with Flaco than from the stairs. Lupe appeared not long after, that look of fire in her eyes.

"Thanks for waiting for me."

He leaned against the wall and slowed his breathing. Lupe just watched him as his heart slowed, waiting, his vision returning to normal.

"You okay?"

"I am now."

She crossed her arms over her chest in a gesture he was realizing was a common one for her. "You gonna tell me what that was all about?" She pointed back toward the city. "Who was that sleazy guy back there and why the hell were we running from him?"

"Flaco is someone from my life before. Not a good part of my life. I wasn't really running from him."

"Really? 'Cause it sure looked like it."

"No." He looked out over the ocean. "I guess I was running from my past." He stood up and looked Lupe in the eyes. "I'm sorry I ran, but I'd rather not talk about this anymore."

Lupe stared at him for a moment. "Fine. Consider it dropped. For now. So I was thinking about what she said about calling him. And something you said to Izzy about talking to the mothers . . ." Her voice lost its energy on Izzy's name.

Javier kept forgetting that Izzy was gone . . . for both of them.

"It sounded like the mothers, that night when they called El Cu—him, when they got together and held hands it was like a ritual, almost like a religious one, and it was at a cangrejos birthday party, right?"

Javier nodded. Something was clearing as she talked, like they were heading up a mountain and were gradually hiking above the clouds.

"So Saturday, the night of your birthday, is Carlos's big party. What if we got them together again? What if we recreate the ritual five years to the day after he was called, to the minute."

"Five cangrejos, five years."

She nodded excitedly. "Five madres."

Javier stared at her. "Un momento. Are you saying you believe in El Cuco now? In monsters?"

"Yeah, why?"

He just grinned at her.

"Don't make me hurt you, Javier."

Lupe

💀

LUPE WAS TALKING faster and faster, her mind like a hamster on a wheel. "If we get the mothers together at the block party and make it a formal ritual, I think they might be able to reverse the curse, or whatever it is." She was shocked to hear how sure her voice sounded considering she didn't have a clue what she was talking about. "Remember what Doña Belasco said about the energy they created together? If they brought this on, maybe they can reverse it." The phone in Lupe's pocket buzzed; what she saw on the screen made her throat tighten.

your going to pay gringa

Lupe typed can I write u a check? then clicked off the phone and put it in her pocket with a shaking hand. She'd deal with who was sending the texts and why later.

Javier finally broke his silence. "But what about Vico's mother? She died a few years ago, que en paz descanse."

"Well, Doña Belasco was there and she's of the same

bloodline. As for El Cuco"—she still couldn't believe she was seriously talking about a monster—"I think I know why he comes before you turn eighteen—I mean, before your friends turned eighteen."

"Why?"

"Professor loco talked about El Cuco as something children are threatened with. When a guy turns eighteen he becomes a man. Voting, the military, legal drinking age." Lupe was talking still faster. "I reread that blowhard's article about El Cuco; the legend is always connected to kids, never adults."

Javier nodded slowly.

As they passed by Plaza Colón, a scent reached for Lupe through the stone balustrades that surrounded the small park. She stopped talking as her stomach rumbled. When was the last time she'd eaten? "What's that incredible smell?"

Javier smiled. "Don't tell me you've never had chicharrónes before?"

Lupe shook her head, afraid this was yet another PR test she would fail.

"Ah, you're in for a treat. My town is famous for chicharrón, but we'll have to settle for the San Juan version." He led her up to a van that was open on one side where a woman was serving up steaming plates of food. Javier ordered, paid, and held the heaping plate out in front of Lupe.

The scent really was intoxicating. She was not a picky eater by nature, but she had to ask. "What's in it?"

"Please, just taste it."

She warily took a piece and stared at Javier as she nibbled on the edge. As the crispy, salty taste hit her tongue, her eyes widened. It was as if that small piece of crispy meat encompassed her favorite tastes of Puerto Rican food, and it nestled in her stressed-out stomach like a warm blanket. She polished off the first piece and grabbed another as Javier chuckled.

"No one watching you eat that could ever doubt that island blood runs in your veins."

Lupe had to smile at that. They took a seat around the fountain in the Plaza Colón and she spoke over a mouthful, her fingertips shiny with grease. "Okay, so what am I eating, really?"

"Fried pork skin."

Somehow that wasn't surprising.

Her mouth full of pork, she said, "So I think we need to do some research into rituals to prepare for this event. I'd like to avoid going back to Professor Ass Hat, however."

Javier froze, food halfway to his mouth. "Rituals."

"What?"

"I have an idea!" He went to throw the plate in the garbage but Lupe snatched the final piece off with a cry before it launched. As she shoved it in her mouth, Javier laughed, took her hand, and headed in the direction of the car.

Javier

JAVIER TURNED THE car into the parish parking lot. There was a circle of yelling teenagers around the basketball hoop, the ball's rhythmic thud ringing off the stone buildings on either side. He pulled into a space and took a deep breath. Normal life, all around them. He could almost forget that the timer on his life might be running out.

Almost.

Javier took Lupe by the hand, and the crowd parted for them. Javier was pleased to see the looks of respect that came from the kids around them. They stood at the edge of the court and watched the game in mid-play, the priest smiling at his teenage opponent as he dribbled the ball, taunting him.

Javier pointed at the elder basketball player. "That's Sebastian."

Lupe gaped at the priest, his bare muscular chest glistening with sweat. "*That's* Padre Sebastian? *The* Padre Sebastian who helped you? The priest?"

"Yes, why?"

"I pictured some old white-haired dude, not Lenny Kravitz!"

Javier smiled. He was proud of his mentor, though the way Lupe was looking at Sebastian made his skin itch.

It was clear the priest was just toying with his young opponent, faking back and forth until he deftly snuck around him and dunked the ball into the net, the worn metal ring clanging like a bell as his sneakers reconnected with the asphalt. Judging from the crowd's cheers, this was the game-winning point and Javier applauded with them as Padre Sebastian put his arm around his opponent, wiping his face with his T-shirt as he beamed at the crowd. He saw Javier, left the losing boy with a fist bump, and walked over to Javier and Lupe.

Padre Sebastian shook his hand. "Hey, Javi! I thought I told you to take this week off. Were you drawn by my superior basketball skills?"

Javier grinned. "That's it, Padre. I could sense your game all the way across town."

"I thought so." He looked over at Lupe. "And who's this you have with you?"

"This is Lupe. Lupe, meet Padre Sebastian."

Lupe's smile threatened to split her face as she shook Sebastian's hand. His skin itched again, though he immediately felt stupid for it. The man was a priest, for God's sake, and over thirty years old. Ancient.

"Padre, could we talk to you? In private?"

Sebastian's face reflected the change in Javier's tone. "Of course, jóvenes. Vamos, let's make some coffee, hmm?" He pulled his sweaty T-shirt over his head and walked them into the cool parish basement. They sat down at the worn table in the priest's office and Padre Sebastian set dark, steaming mugs of Jamaican Blue Mountain Coffee in front of them. The sounds of kids' voices and the slap of basketballs floated in the windows.

Padre Sebastian put his mug down. "Now, I know it's the

best in San Juan, but I also know you young people didn't come here to have coffee with me. What's on your minds?"

Javier swallowed and looked at Lupe. She nodded slowly. "Padre, have you ever heard of El Cuco?"

"El Cuco? The Puerto Rican boogeyman?"

Lupe's voice came out in a rush. "Not just Puerto Rican. He appears in many different Latin countries around the world. In Mexico he's called 'El Cucuy.' His origins are—"

The priest cut Lupe off. "I know the legends well. What about El Cuco?"

Javier started talking fast. "We think our mothers—los cangrejos' mothers—called him by accident to keep us from getting into trouble, doing drugs. He's killing us one by one on our eighteenth birthdays."

Sebastian eyes widened. He took a deep breath. "Well, that's quite a lot to digest."

"I know it sounds crazy. I didn't believe it either, but with all I've seen these past few days . . . well, I changed my mind. About a lot of things."

"Where do you fit in this tale, Lupe? Is El Cuco after you, too?"

She shook her head. "No." But she looked at the ground and Javier wondered whether there was something she wasn't telling him.

"Izzy was her cousin," Javier said for her.

Sebastian put his hand on hers until she looked up at him. "I'm sorry for your loss, Lupe."

Her eyes teared up as she thanked him.

Sebastian sat back. "I don't know, jóvenes. I think you should focus more on where the drugs are coming from that killed your friends. Isn't that what their deaths came down to?"

"But it wasn't the drugs that killed them." Javier was confused.

"Oh sure it was, Javi." He sat forward in his seat. "Even in this crazy El Cuco theory of yours, it's when they give their lives over to the drugs that they die, right?"

Javier chewed on his lip. He and Lupe were silent. Hard to argue with that logic.

The padre continued. "I would like to see the source of the drugs cut off, perhaps starting with Las Calaveras."

Javier laughed. "Maybe Keno is El Cuco."

Sebastian seemed to think about that. "Maybe." Then he asked, "So, what do you need from me?"

"We're wondering about rituals. Like, how do we help the mothers call off El Cuco? I mean, hypothetically." Lupe smiled.

Sebastian thought for a moment. "Well, in the Catholic church we have the seven sacraments. We frown on heathen rituals."

Lupe sank in her chair. Javier shared her disappointment. Perhaps even Sebastian couldn't help them.

"But here in the Caribbean those rules are, shall we say, looser?" He smiled at them with that movie-star smile and Javier let out a breath. "I think what you're talking about is something much older." He turned to Lupe. "This legend was brought here from Portugal in the seventeenth century, a time of great unrest and revolt. I think it's no accident that it's coming up again now when the island is in such terrible shape. Legends like El Cuco reassure people that there are still consequences, that the laws of right and wrong are still upheld."

Lupe scoffed. "Yeah, but there seem to be differing concepts of right and wrong."

"Very true." Sebastian paused. "So, what's your plan?"

She outlined the idea of re-creating the events of that night in the hope of calling it off.

The padre listened and nodded. When she finished he said, "I think your instincts are correct. But what you're messing with is something not only very old, but also very dark. If we're talking hypothetically, as you suggested, Lupe, you would have to ensure that *all* the original parties are present."

"Yes, five cangrejos, five mothers. Well, except for the ones who have already . . . passed on," Lupe added.

Sebastian smiled at her. "Ay, joven, I might not believe in the supernatural, but I do believe that those who pass on are always with us. They're the one constant in this scenario. But I suggest you take a practical step since all this supernatural talk is highly unlikely. I think you should notify the police, particularly given the drug aspect of these events."

Javier and Lupe looked at each other. Lupe said, "Well, my uncle is with the police."

"I see. So, what does he think about your plan?"

Javier and Lupe just looked at each other.

"You haven't told him?"

Lupe looked at the floor. "No," she said, her voice small.

"Perhaps it's time to turn this over to a professional. This is a dangerous game someone is playing."

Lupe nodded and they stood. Javier guessed she had no intention of doing it, however.

"Wait, there's something you should understand. Though of course, as a member of the Roman Catholic Church I'm not acknowledging the existence of the supernatural"—he paused and winked at them—"as a Jamaican I want to ask you to keep in mind that in legends such as this, the monster always exacts a price."

Javier held his hands out. "But I have nothing to give."

"Not that kind of price. If he's not going to take you, he's going to need someone else."

Javier and Lupe protested at once. Then Javier said, "Well then forget it."

Sebastian put out his hands. "This is all hypothetical, of

course, but El Cuco would only want someone who truly deserved it."

Javier dismissed it. "Yeah, well, I'm still not giving anyone up. That's not who I am."

Sebastian put his hands on Javier's shoulders. "Javier, I've taken playing along with this too far. This whole supernatural interpretation is ridiculous, you realize that, don't you?"

Javier nodded, but he didn't really agree with his mentor.

Lupe had just left them to go to the ladies' room when the priest pulled Javier aside, speaking in his quiet, calm, in-church voice.

"Javier, what is your relationship with this girl?"

"Why? You don't like her?"

"No, no, she's perfectly lovely, but you know you're not supposed to get involved in romantic relationships at this point in your recovery. It's too early and you know it."

"We're not involved in *that* way."

"That's what they *all* say."

Javier pulled away, for the first time feeling angry with his mentor. "You don't understand. We're fighting this"—he gestured around wildly with his arms—"thing together." He could see the priest starting to protest. "I need her, and she needs me."

Sebastian's eyes softened. "Precisely why you should not develop feelings for this girl. You are in no condition to be taking care of anyone else yet. You have more work to do. And you can't really believe all this El Cuco stuff. You need prayer and respite, Javier. Too much has happened, too much loss."

Javier felt heat swirl from his belly and his spine straighten. It was a familiar feeling—he had it with his mother all the time—but he'd never felt disappointed with Sebastian before. He really didn't need lectures right now.

"You need to make sure her uncle is briefed on the situation. I know you like to fight your own fights, Javier, but this is serious. Someone could get hurt."

Someone could get more than hurt.

Lupe walked up right then, and Javier pulled Sebastian into a hug that felt more like a goodbye than it should have, took Lupe's hand, and walked out of the building without looking back.

Lupe's phone buzzed with a text. She pulled it out as she walked, but stopped when she read the screen. "I think Father Sebastian and my Aunt Maria might be right."

"About what?"

Lupe looked up at him, the darkening light shadowing half her face, and held her phone up to his face so he could read the text.

tomorrow u die 2

Javier's stomach fell.

"It's time we go talk to my uncle."

Lupe told him about the texts as they walked to the car.

"But why didn't you tell me before?"

"I didn't want to freak you out any more than you already were."

"Too late for that."

"Besides, I don't have a clue who's sending them, and I doubt El Cuco has a cell phone. And if he did I would imagine he'd have a toll-free number." She was trying to lighten the mood. Good luck with that.

"Your uncle can trace the number, verdad?"

She shook her head so hard her ponytail *fwapp*ed him in the face. "No! Let's just talk to him about the deadline, your birthday, even El Cuco. But not the threats."

"Or the blue car in Old San Juan?"

"Especially not the car in Old San Juan. I'll tell him, just not now. Okay?"

He thought of Padre Sebastian's urging. But it was their fight, not his. He nodded.

"I'll call tío and find out where he is.

"Tío? It's Lupe. Well, I guess you know that already since that's how it shows up on your phone—slow down? C'mon, keep up!" Javier loved the way the edges of her mouth lifted into a smile as she spoke. "Listen, we have to talk to you, like, now—who's we?" She looked at Javier and smiled bigger. "It's a long story. Where are you? Police headquarters. Six Oh One Franklin Delano. Wait, I have to type it into the GPS. . . ."

Javier nodded at her and gave her a thumbs-up to let her know he knew the address.

"Wait, he knows where it is—yes, he. I'll tell you when I get there. Don't worry, tío."

Her face was turning that beautiful rose color as she looked at him.

He maneuvered his way to the freeway. He must have stayed quiet a long time because he felt Lupe put her hand on his leg. He looked over into her bright eyes.

"We're going to stop this, I know it. My father says there's nobody more stubborn than yours truly." She pointed to her chest and smiled.

"You don't talk about your father much."

Lupe sighed. "No. I love my dad, but he's just not much of a father. I take care of most of the things around the house since Mom . . ." She looked out the window.

Javier nodded in understanding. "After my father left, he started a new family like we didn't exist. Mom and I didn't seem to fit his new plans." He found he didn't want to talk about this subject, either. Why was everything they had to talk about so dark? "But your tío, he seems important to you, no?"

"Yeah, tío is the best. He asked me to move in with him."

Javier felt his heart surge. The idea of her living on the

island so he could see her all the time was too good to be true. "Well? Are you going to move to Puerto Rico?"

"I don't know. At first I thought no way, but now . . . but I wouldn't want to leave my dad alone."

"He can't take care of himself?"

Lupe made a motion like she was drinking out of a bottle. "Nope. Though it seems he checked himself into rehab last night."

"You can't save him. Believe me, no one knows this better than me."

She shrugged. "I know, but he's my dad. I love it here, yet I love Vermont, too. It's almost like there should be some place in between, like exactly halfway between the two places, where I could really feel at home, you know?"

As they neared police headquarters, they saw news vans parked up and down the avenue. They pulled into the parking lot and had to drive slowly around a swarm of reporters who were buzzing around like insects, the lights from the cameras illuminating the entrance. Once they were out of the car, Lupe led the way through the crowd and the officer at the door noticed her, seemed to know her.

"Señorita Dávila! Let her through, make way!" he yelled at the reporters.

Lupe smiled despite the press of bodies behind her. "¡Gracias, Officer Ramirez!"

Ramirez opened the glass door for them and the reporters yelled through the opening into the lobby. The questions ranged from serious to ridiculous depending on the legitimacy of the publication.

"Is it true there's a serial killer loose on the island?"

"Are these murders part of a terrorist plot?"

"Is there a monster attacking boys in San Juan?"

Ironically, the sleaziest paper probably had it right, for once.

The doors closed behind them and muffled the din. Security in the building was tight and Javier struggled to put his keys and cell phone back in his pocket after going through the metal detector as Lupe asked at the desk if they could call her uncle. Javier arrived at her side just as her uncle came through the door to their left, almost having to duck to fit his tall frame through. Javier swallowed hard as Lupe grabbed his hand and pulled him toward the huge man. The bandages around the man's neck did little to diminish the intimidation of him. Chief Dávila's face softened the minute he saw Lupe. Then his laser-beam eyes fell on Javier, who wished he could crawl under a nearby desk.

"I know you. Javier Utierre." His eyes narrowed as he looked down.

Javier imagined the bright light they used in interrogations in old movies shining right in his eyes. "Y-yes, Señor. Officer. I mean, chief." Then Lupe was talking, fast.

"Tío, we have something important to talk to you about." She looked up at him with those eyes and the laser beam moved off and Javier breathed a sigh of relief. Couldn't he have fallen for a girl with an uncle who was a mechanic?

Chief Dávila narrowed his eyes at Lupe and Javier knew more questions were coming . . . later.

"Delgado! I'm using your office." And they were walking toward the nearest office; Delgado waved like there was no way he was going to argue. The chief sat down behind the desk, the wooden office chair groaning as he lowered his large frame into it.

Lupe and Javier sat in the two chairs in front of the desk.

"Well? First I want to know how you got here, Lupe." His eyes fell on Javier and the light was blinding again. Drops of sweat snaked their way down Javier's back.

"What? We drove, why? Tío, I have something important—"

"Oh no, Lupe, *this* is important. Did you drive in this young man's car?" When the man pointed to him, Javier felt he'd just been picked out in a lineup.

"What the hell does that have to do—"

"Do *not* use that language with me! I happen to know that this young man doesn't have the cleanest past."

Javier interjected, "Actually, sir, I've been in recovery over two years—" Neither of them seemed to hear him, or even know he was there. Javier sat back into his chair.

"No niece of mine will be driving around the island with strange teenage boys—"

Lupe looked as if she'd swallowed something that had gone bad. "No niece of yours? No one's ever told me who I can and can't hang with! My own father—"

"Yes, we both know that your father isn't doing much parenting these days. If you're going to stay down here, you have to obey—"

"Obey? Obey?? That word's not in my vocabulary and you know it!"

Javier's head was following the volleys back and forth like he was at a tennis match. Lupe stood and leaned with her palms flat on the desk, putting her face inches from her uncle's. Javier had seriously never met a girl as fiery as Lupe. Girls he'd dated in the past would never talk back to their uncle, let alone a man who just happens to be one of the most powerful men on the island. His mother would hate her. Javier smiled.

Lupe's voice lowered; he could see her working to stay calm. "I really don't get why this matters, but I met Javier at Papi Gringo's apartment—"

Uh-oh.

"You were at Papi Gringo's apartment?" The chief remained seated, but his face was starting to redden.

"Yeah. Nothing happened."

"I would hope not. For his sake."

Lupe took a huge breath. "Tío! I've been trying to talk to you since last night. Can't you just listen?"

"Well, I've been quite occupied with work."

"Yes! I know! And we're trying to help you!"

It was the chief's turn to sigh. "Okay, talk." He tented his fingers in front of his face and all of his body was turned toward them.

"It started five years ago. . . ."

Javier listened to Lupe tell his story, the story of five boys in a changing neighborhood, as if it were someone else. As if it hadn't happened to him. When she got to the murders, it started to sound like a horror movie.

Lupe stopped at that morning, at the conversation with Vico's abuela, and just watched her uncle. He noticed she didn't mention the car almost hitting her in Old San Juan, or the threatening texts. He certainly wasn't going to bring it up.

They sat and looked at the police chief, the silence in the room gathering like a storm. "I heard another theory. I just heard from Padre Sebastian, and he thinks the drug dealers are responsible for all this."

Lupe threw up her hands. "No! You yourself said you saw things! Weird things! I think it's time both of us consider that there's something else going on."

Her uncle stared at her. "Oh, so now you believe in monsters?"

Javier noticed the sarcastic tone underlying the man's words. He spoke up. "Sir, I think you should listen—"

Dávila pointed a large finger at him. "You stay out of this, Utierre."

"Don't take this out on him, tío. He's helping solve the murder case, and—"

The chief totally lost his cool then, his face red over the stark white of the bandage on his neck, his voice booming through the room and shaking the glass window behind him. He stood and bent down to face her so they stood nose to nose. "I should never have had you come to the crime scene. Good Lord, you've been here less than a week and you're already knee-deep in this damn case! This is nothing like the other ones we've talked about over the years. It's too dangerous for you—"

Lupe stood her ground, managing to overpower her uncle, despite the difference in their size. "Dangerous for *me*? For *me*? I'm not the one who almost got killed last night!"

"That's part of my job! I can't promise that I'll never—"

"I can't lose you, too, tío!" she yelled, her voice breaking. Everyone froze where they were for a minute, then Lupe dropped back into the chair, burying her face in her hands.

Silence fell over them all as the two men looked at her, as she seemed to become small and fragile before their eyes.

"I just can't." Tears were spilling down her cheeks and Javier had to restrain himself from reaching over and hugging her.

Everything about Chief Dávila seemed to deflate and he sat back down, and once again Javier envied the love between them.

Lupe's uncle sighed, clearly defeated. "Okay, sobrina, okay."

She took a long, deep breath, her eyes shiny with tears under the fluorescent lights.

"I should have known those shopping trips were a cover. You never did like shopping."

"I'm sorry I lied to you."

"Okay, okay, mi amor. But I expect it to never happen again, comprendes?"

She nodded.

The man folded his hands on the desk in front of him. "So, do you have some kind of a plan?"

Lupe sniffed. "Wait, I'm confused. You said you believed Padre Sebastian's theory."

He shook his head. "I never said that. I said I had *heard* another theory."

"Hold the teléfono! You get all flipped out about me driving here with Javier, but you have no problem believing me when I tell you a monster is running around the island?"

"Look, Lupe, I was pulled thirty feet off the ground by a massive shadowy creature. I'm not in the position to disbelieve anything. But my niece driving around with strange boys? Now that's nonsense." Then Chief Dávila smiled.

Lupe just shook her head, but she was smiling, too.

The chief asked them, "There's something that's been vexing me. Why were they all killed in such different ways?"

"I don't know. I'm thinking he can change shape. I don't have a clue what his real shape is. Did Abuela used to threaten you and Dad with El Cuco?"

Her uncle nodded.

"Did she ever say what he looked like?"

He shook his head. "That used to scare me more, not knowing what he was. Childhood imaginations are powerful things."

"Not as powerful as a mother's threat." Javier heard his voice like it was coming from someone else. He had planned to stay quiet. Now the light beam was on him again.

"Nothing is more powerful than that, son."

"Okay, here's our plan. We need to get everyone who was there the night of the thirteenth birthday together just before Javier turns eighteen. If they had all that power together to call El Cuco, why couldn't they call him off, too? We're thinking Carlos's concert is on the eve of Javier's birthday, it's in the neighborhood where it all started. It's the perfect opportunity to get everyone together, just like they did years ago, and try to turn this around. But we'd need your help."

He noticed she didn't mention the issue of the "cost" the padre had told them about. As she spoke, Javier held his breath. This was their Hail Mary pass, their only shot.

The chief didn't say anything for what seemed an eternity.

"You know, if this idea came from anyone but you, sobrina, I would think it was crazy. But something about it makes sense, not in here"—he tapped his head—"but in here"—and his chest. "Let's get in touch with the mothers of these boys—"

"Las Madres."

Chief Dávila smiled. "Las Madres, I like that. Sounds like some kind of superhero team." He pointed to Javier. "Young man, I expect you to take my niece straight home and you go home and stay there until one of my officers picks you up tomorrow night. It seems tomorrow is going to be a big day for all of us." He and Lupe just sat there as the chief picked up the phone and started dialing. "And, young lady, you're to call your father so he knows you're okay." When Lupe started to argue, he cut her off. "Now!" They jumped as if the chairs had been electrified.

Chief Dávila believed them.

This was good news, but it also meant that Javier had to try to talk to his mother again. He sighed and realized he'd rather hang out in the police station all night. Or get a sharp stick in the eye.

Still, there could be worse things coming for him tomorrow night.

Lupe

LUPE LOOKED UP the number for Copley Hospital in Morris-
ville, Vermont, and pressed Call.

When the overly cheery voice answered, she croaked out,
"Hi, um, my dad. . . . he's in, like, detox?" What the hell was
the name of the part of the hospital that did that kind of thing?
She could hear the fast, clean percussion of computer keys.

"Yes, Jorge Dávila. He's in Behavioral Medicine, I'll trans-
fer you—"

"Wait, how did you know my father's name? Does everyone know?" Anger rose like a wave. "I mean I know this town
is small and all, but damn—"

"No, Miss Dávila, I saw your caller ID and looked up the
last name."

"Oh, sorry."

"No need to apologize, I'll put you through."

While she waited, she imagined the conversation they'd have
if she could tell him what was *really* going on. *Hi, Daddy! I'm
so happy to hear you're in rehab! I was pretty damn close to
throttling you anyway. Am I embarrassed? Oh no! I mean,*

*everyone in our little town already knows you're a drunk and
your daughter's an angry outcast! Oh, and Dad? I'm hanging
with a recovering drug addict who might or might not have a
monster after him. I think you know him, El Cuco? Yeah, him.
And there's a small issue of someone saying they're going to kill
me. But everything's great here, don't worry! It's all beaches and
virgin piña coladas!*

The phone in her hand spoke: "Behavioral Medicine."

"May I have Jorge Dávila's room, please?" Her voice sounded
way calmer than she actually was.

"Mr. Dàvila's not able to receive outside calls at this time.
Can I ask who's calling?" The nurse's voice was clipped and of-
ficial.

"His daughter. Lupe."

A pause on the other end. The voice softer now. "I'm sorry,
Miss Dávila, but your father isn't supposed to take outside calls
or receive visitors for the first forty-eight hours of his treat-
ment."

Lupe was about to use this as an excuse: part of her wanted
to say, *Okay, thank you* and hang up. But she stopped herself.
She had pretty much written off her father, placed him in the
"yet another person who disappears on me" category, but then
all the things that had happened since she'd arrived on the island ran through her head in fast-forward. She was not the same
girl who'd left Vermont a few short days ago.

She put on her most mature voice, the one she used with the
guidance counselor and telemarketers. "I understand, but I'm
traveling with family and it's urgent that I speak to him. My
uncle, his brother, is a policeman and was injured in the line of
duty." Okay, so tío was just fine, but omission isn't lying and
the "in the line of duty" thing was sure to help. She needed to
speak to her father that night, not the next.

Who knew what was going to happen the next?

A pause. Then, "I see. Can you hold a minute, please?" The phone was muffled on the other side and Lupe pictured the nurse standing in a white-walled corridor, her hand over the phone as she spoke to the person in charge.

"I'm going to bring the phone into Mr. Dávila's room."

Lupe could hear the soft footsteps on the other line. "Mr. Dávila. You have a phone call." And then to Lupe, "Please limit your call to five minutes."

"Lupe?" Her dad's voice was stretched thin and tired across the line, but it was good to hear it.

"Dad! How're you doing?"

"I'm okay. Taking it one hour at a time at this point." A chuckle. "Lupe, I'm sorry I didn't tell you about this ahead of time. It was kind of a last-minute decision."

"Don't worry. I'm just glad you're taking care of yourself." No exaggeration there. Since she'd found out he'd checked himself in, she didn't have to worry about him driving himself into a river, or sleeping while the house burnt down around him.

"I was sitting at home, well into my fifth drink, when my cousin called about Esteban. I couldn't believe it. I always knew you'd be all right because you had Esteban to take care of you, just like he did me. After your mother left, he was a safety net, you know?"

Lupe just nodded into the phone. "Safety net" was a good way to describe her uncle.

"And then it hit me: I can't assume Esteban will always be there. I shouldn't have made him your default father. Your mother isn't coming back and it's time I stop feeling sorry for myself and step up."

Lupe's eyes filled as she pictured her dad lying in a hospital bed. It wasn't that she didn't fantasize about her father sobering up, about him being "normal," but she'd just kind of given up hope. The conversation had taken her by surprise, yet she was still cautious. Her father had broken too many promises for her to trust him outright.

She smiled into the phone. "I'm proud of you."

"Thank you, sweetheart." A sniffle. "How is Esteban doing? Is he still in the hospital?"

"Oh no, you know him. Anyone else would be there for a week with the trauma of it all, but not tío."

"Good. That's good. I never imagined him . . . well, never there."

"Yeah, I know what you mean." Then she thought of Javier and what awaited them tomorrow night. She wished she could tell him what was going on, but now was not the time. "Dad, did your mother ever threaten you with El Cuco?"

His laugh was warm and familiar. "You bet she did! Just about every day. Funny, I haven't thought about that for years. Why do you ask?"

"No reason. I just found out about him, is all. Did you believe in him?" Her father was the least superstitious person she knew. No God, no horoscopes, and no monsters. It's probably where she got it.

"Hell yes!"

"What?"

"I mean, back then I believed everything my mother told me. It was that time when you think your parents are all-powerful."

How would I know? But she kept that comment to herself.

"It's funny, now, as a parent, I realize that it's actually the children who have all the power. If I'd have known that as a child I would have been threatening *her* with El Cuco!"

They both chuckled, until Lupe heard murmurs of the nurse's voice. "Okay, wrapping up," he said, his mouth away from the mouthpiece. Then to Lupe: "How are *you* doing? Are you okay?"

She took a deep breath and pushed her head up as if making

herself taller, stronger. "I'm doing good, Dad." She looked around at the blazing flamboyán tree, a bright green lizard skittering across the short grass in the fading light. "I like it here."

"I'm glad. I do, too, m'ija. Maybe next summer I can come down and we'll fly back together. Like the old days, huh?"

Lupe smiled. "I'd like that."

The clipped voice was back. "Your father needs his rest."

Click. And he was gone.

Lupe stared at the phone in her hand for some time.

Vermont had never felt farther away.

July 9, 6:42 P.M.

Javier

💀

JAVIER PACED BACK and forth in front of the restaurant, looking for his mother among the foot traffic on Calle de Recinto.
Chief Dávila and his team were going to contact the mothers
of the other cangrejos. He thought it best if he asked his mother
directly. He was triple-guessing himself as the hour drew near.
Would she respond better to a policeman? He had almost called
and canceled a dozen times. What about Lupe? They still didn't
know who was threatening her.

As if he could keep her safe. Hell, he had a monster after him.
He was about to bolt when he saw his mother waiting to cross
the street from the parking garage. He actually wondered if he
could still run, if she hadn't seen him yet, but that time had passed.

He was done running.

Her face broke into a huge smile as she saw him in front of
Mojito's Restaurant. She was dressed in an immaculate pale blue
suit with her designer purse clutched tightly against her body.
She might act all sweet and gentle, but Javier pitied any thief who
tried to snatch that bag. She would probably beat them to death
with it without mussing a hair on her perfectly coiffed head.

When she reached him, Javier's mother gave him an air-kiss. God forbid she smear her lipstick. "Javier, what a lovely surprise this invitation was." She put her arm through his and led him into the restaurant.

As they were led to a table in the back, Javier's mother gushed to the hostess about how her thoughtful son made time to take her out to dinner. Javier bit the inside of his mouth.

He said nothing as they settled themselves in and perused the menu. He didn't really need to talk when having a "conversation" with his mother. Besides, his throat was so tight he didn't think he could squeeze any food through, so he let her order for him. Before the waiter left, his mother ordered them both champagne.

"You know I can't drink alcohol. I'm in recovery."

She dismissed him with a wave. "Nonsense, it's only champagne. You can toast with your dear madre to your birthday."

The waiter returned and placed two glasses on the table. Javier felt that familiar rage rising to the top like the bubbles in the champagne. He concentrated on pushing the anger down, through his legs, the floor. He'd turned to drugs in the first place because they took him out of his miserable existence with her and lifted him up in a kind of cyclone until he was up and over his small life.

She lifted her glass up for a toast. "To my baby boy: tomorrow at midnight you'll be eighteen. I can't believe it!"

Javier started to lift his water glass to meet her champagne, but changed his mind. Instead of clinking her glass, he put his back down on the table. "My birthday is what I wanted to talk to you about. I need your help—"

"Ooh, do you want me to help you plan a party?" She put her glass down. "I should have thought of that myself! Why should Carlos be the only one having a fête?" She was clapping like a toddler with a new toy. "Perhaps I can reserve a private dining room at the Caribe Hilton. I have the manager's card in here somewhere—" She started rifling through her large handbag, talking nonstop.

Javier reached over to put his hand on his mother's arm. "No, Mamá, I need your help with something else."

She stopped and looked up at him. "Seguro, my love. I would do anything for you, you know that."

There was so much Javier could have said in response, but there was no time for that. He took a deep breath. "Something might happen tomorrow night at Carlos's party and I'm going to need you."

"Yes . . ." She was clinking the large ring his father had given her against the glass-covered table, the almond-shaped yellow stone matching the gold of the champagne. He could see the wariness grow in her eyes, could hear it in the one-word response.

She sensed that his request was not the sunny kind.

There was nothing for it; he had to just get it out. "There's a chance that what happened to Vico, Izzy, and Memo—"

And she was up and going. "I should have known that was why you invited me tonight. I do *not* want to talk about those *incidents*!"

Javier was losing her. If he was going to get through to her, the gloves had to come off.

"I don't know why we can't just have a nice dinner without—"

He stood up and turned her around as she tried to walk away from the table. Was this going to be the last time he'd see her? No matter what, she was his mother. "Okay, Mamá, then I better say goodbye now. Just in case."

She started to pull away, then hesitated. "Don't be ridiculous." But she turned back. "In case of what?"

"In case I die tomorrow night. Izzy's dead now, too. I'm the last cangrejo to turn eighteen."

Her gaze settled on him then and he felt she was seeing him, really seeing him for the first time in a long while. He watched a huge wave of emotion crest and fall in her hazel eyes, her hands frozen around the straps of her purse. Then she just dropped back into the seat, as if the bones had suddenly abandoned her legs.

He crouched in front of her, putting his hands over hers. He felt that if he broke the connection she would take off like an untethered balloon.

She was looking off into nothing as she spoke. "We didn't mean for it to happen. I actually thought it was silly. I had no power over anything then, especially not you . . . or your father."

Her eyes landed on him and they had a desperate quality to them. "You don't know, Javier, you can't know what it's like to see your baby, your only baby slipping away. You have all these hopes when you hold this perfect swaddled creature in your arms, you imagine academic awards, nice little friends, Ivy League colleges, marriage to a girl from a good family, grandchildren. And then one day you realize you have no control, that any control you thought you had was an illusion. You realize you don't know how to save them as they teeter on the edge. We were all feeling that, all of the mothers. And then I found you all with those . . . drugs." She shuddered. "That night we would've tried anything to get you all back. I guess I shouldn't be surprised that he came. In order to save you I would've sold my soul to el diablo if he were there that night. I guess he was." She looked at the floor and started to cry. "We just wanted to scare you. He was a fairy-tale monster. Never, never in a million years did we expect him to come, for him to . . ."

He wrapped her hands with his own. "I'm sorry, Mamá."

She wiped her eyes as she looked up at him. "I am, too, mi amor." She put her palm against his cheek like she had when he was little. He put his hand over hers and closed his eyes, breathing in the familiar sandalwood scent of her Spanish soap. They held each other as the restaurant buzzed around them.

He knew it was time. It was time to ask. "I need your help."

She sat up in her chair, shoulders lifted, chin up. "I'll do whatever you ask of me."

He took a deep breath. "Bueno."

After walking his mother to her car, Javier wandered around the old city in a daze, wondering if it was the last time he would walk the cobblestone streets. He didn't have a destination in mind, but gravitated toward Fortaleza, the most populated avenue. He weaved in and out between the shopping tourists, comforted by their anonymous company, the ordinariness of it all. As he passed the small side street that connected Fortaleza to Calle San Francisco, he saw a large crowd of people straining to see into the Nuyorican Café. It was early in the evening for the salsa he heard blasting out of the club's front doors, so Javier was curious. He walked up the narrow street and fell in behind the crowd. He couldn't see what everyone was pressing toward, but camera flashes bounced off the surrounding buildings like lightning.

He turned to the guy next to him and nodded toward the building. "What's going on in there?"

"Papi Gringo's in the house!" His eyes were lit up as he tried to press forward to get a better look.

Javier chuckled. He never could get used to the idea that his childhood buddy was a star. He shoved his hands in his pockets and started up toward San Francisco, thinking about having his last sugary mallorca pastry at the bakery a few blocks up when he heard his name being called above the crowd.

"Yo! Javi!"

He looked back at the front of the club to see Carlos standing on the top step, waving him over.

Javier made his way back and the crowd parted before him like the Red Sea, onlookers gaping at him as if he were a celebrity, too.

Carlos pulled Javier into a tight hug. "Good to see you again so soon, hermano."

Javier pulled back, looked in Carlos's face, and grinned. God, he loved this guy. "You, too, man. You, too."

"Come inside with me." Carlos turned back to the crowd. "Good night, mi gente! And God bless!" They hooted and hollered as Javier was swept up in the wave of Papi Gringo's entourage. The owner escorted them to a table on a raised platform, beaming at Carlos as if the singer were giving him a gift. With all the press perched around the club, Javier supposed he was. Having Papi Gringo at your club was sure to get in the news.

They settled at the table and the beautiful girl Javier had seen at the apartment slid in next to Carlos while another girl slid in beside Javier. He nodded at her shyly.

"Javier, this is my girl, Carmela, and her friend Jeanine. Jeanine, this is the closest thing to a brother I've ever had." He thumped Javier on the shoulder and pulled him back into a hug. Ever since they were little they'd had a wrestling, tumbling friendship, warm and affectionate like puppies from the same litter.

Jeanine nodded coolly and didn't even glance at Javier. He looked at her under the club's low lighting. There were bumps all over her skin, probably from all the makeup. Her hair was a huge cascade of brown curls, but they moved as one mass and he imagined touching them would make a bell-like dong. She had four feet of legs tucked under the table and a short, tight skirt designed to show them off but she probably couldn't breathe much. Javier knew that, seeing her from a distance, most everyone would think this girl gorgeous, and close-up she was indeed beautiful, under it all, but she had to hide beneath the smoke and mirrors fame required.

"What're you doing in this part of town, Javi?"

"I had dinner with my mom. Had to talk to her about to-morrow night."

"She coming to the concert?"

"Yeah, man. Lupe and I—I mean, we have a plan and we need you and the cangrejo mothers."

"Lupe . . . that gringa reporter chick?"

Javier could feel his cheeks warm. "Yeah."

A smile snaked across Carlos's face. "You dog."

"It's not like that." But of course, just saying that made it seem as if it was *exactly* like that.

"What plan?"

A waitress arrived at the table and put a round of rum and Cokes in front of them, never taking her eyes from Carlos. Carlos called her back. "Amor, can you get my friend here a plain Coke? No rum. Thanks, sweetheart." A wink, and the girl swooned. In contrast to his mother, Carlos remembered and was supportive of Javier's sobriety.

"Well? What plan?"

Javier noticed that Carlos's date was listening and he felt un-comfortable talking about El Cuco. "You know, what we talked about at your apartment? With Vico and Memo? And now Izzy."

Carlos put his drink down at that, his carefully arranged face turned serious. "Yeah. I heard about Izzy. I tried to track him down, but I guess that cop even got there too late."

"Yeah, that's Lupe's uncle."

Carlos's eyes shot up at that. "You're doing the chief of police's niece?"

"I'm not *doing* her. I told you, it's not like that."

Carlos brought the drink to his lips and added in a low voice, "Still. Be careful, man."

Javier was suddenly aware that every eye in the club was on them. With all they were talking about, it made him uncomfortable. How did Carlos deal with this? "What a life you lead, pana." He nodded toward Carmela, who was talking with Jeanine across the table, both very aware of everything around them, their eyes scanning, their movements studied. It was as if everyone at the table was in a fishbowl. Except him. No one paid attention to his scruffy ass and he liked it that way. The girls seemed smart and were certainly beautiful: angelfish swimming in circles. He found himself feeling empathy for them. "Is this serious? You and Carmela?" Javier whispered.

Carlos scoffed. "No, man. This is what's expected." He made no effort to lower his voice so his date heard every word. "The only thing that's serious is my music and my family. En punto."

"I feel you."

"You and that gringa serious?"

"No, man. But I like her. A lot. In a different way than I've ever felt, you know?"

Carlos stared into Javier's eyes as if looking for something. He finally said, "I wish I knew. But that's why I can't get serious about no chicas, you feel me? It can only be about the music. It wouldn't be fair to put someone I really cared about through all this shit."

Javier looked around at the crowd of people entirely focused on Carlos and nodded. A man and a woman in expensive clothes leaned over the back of the booth as the owner introduced them to Carlos, and Javier thought about what his friend had said. If it wasn't fair to put a girl through Papi Gringo's stardom, it certainly wasn't fair to put Lupe through the supernatural probably fatal shit he was going through. In that moment he realized that if he really cared about her, he would end it, tell her not to come tomorrow. The thought made him feel slightly sick to his stomach and he considered downing the cocktail in front of him. She wouldn't listen to him anyway. He hated that about her. And loved it.

While Carlos posed for a photo with the grinning couple, Javier excused himself and made his way to the men's room. He was having trouble breathing in the club, the air felt so close. There was a guy at the far sink so Javier ducked into a stall to try to slow his heart rate. The whole wild day had left his head spinning. After a few minutes he started to feel better and figured he'd better get back to the table. He made his way to the sink to splash his face while the other guy messed with something on the marble countertop. As he grabbed a paper towel, Javier noticed lines of white powder the dude was snorting up one by one like it was his job. When the guy rose to standing and held his head back to ensure all the drugs made their way to his small brain, Javier dried his face and started to make his way to the door.

"Hey, bro." Gringo, probably Midwestern from the accent.

Javier stopped and paused before he turned around. It was as if everything were going in slow-motion.

"Wanna do the last line?"

Javier glanced down at the single line of coke pointing toward him like a finger. He stared at the rolled-up fifty in the guy's hand. He felt the sweat bead on his forehead and begin to roll into his eyes.

"No, man. And it's not cool to be doing that shit out here in the open." But his eyes still hadn't left that line of powder.

Javier rushed for the door and as it swung closed behind him he heard the cokehead say, "Fuck you, man. More for me."

The sound of snorting followed him like a shadow.

July 9, 9:15 P.M.

Sebastian

💀

PADRE SEBASTIAN TIED the last sneaker, and piled his clothes and clerical collar in a neat stack on the counter. He'd been looking forward to this run all day. His nerves had been tense since Javier and Lupe left.

The conversation with Esteban Dávila had put his mind somewhat at ease. He was worried about Javier, that the boy was more willing to put the blame on the supernatural instead of the real monster here. He'd given Dávila Keno's name, knowing all too well what the dealer was capable of. Three young boys who had grown up playing in the church rec center had been arrested for dealing Keno's junk. One twelve-year-old overdosed. Twelve! Sebastian would never forget the look on the parents' faces when he'd told them about their son's death. Well, now all that was in the hands of the proper authorities, gracias a Dios.

He switched off the lights, then realized he didn't have a water bottle. He opened the old, humming refrigerator, its yellow light spilling out on the dusty floor, and grabbed a frosty bottle of water.

As he closed the fridge and darkness returned to the room, the outside door swung open. The figure was silhouetted by the glow of the parking lot streetlamp behind them, their front totally in shadow.

"Padre." A girl's voice, calm and clear in the quiet room.

"Yes, who's there?"

"Why did you have to go and call the police, padre?" The figure stepped forward and, in the pool of dark yellow fading sunlight coming through the high windows, he saw Marisol. "Marisol, joven, you scared me." He put his hand to his chest. "I was just going for a run—"

Marisol sighed and stepped forward into the shadows again. "I wanted to keep you out of it. It's not your fault, after all. I came to warn you."

"Warn me? What are you talking about? Wait, how did you know I called the police?"

Marisol shook her head gravely. "And did you have to call Dávila? Him and his niece, that gringa, they're the reason my mother's house was taken away, they're the real reason Vico's dead."

Sebastian shook his head, but worked to keep his voice calm. "M'ija, Lupe's a teenager like you. She didn't buy your mother's house, or kill Vico."

"You're wrong, padre. The gringos are the reason this island is in the situation it's in, the reason my mother couldn't pay for her house."

"I can't argue with that, but—"

"And that girl had the nerve to show up at Vico's funeral? To disrespect my brother?"

"Javier said she wasn't even at the funeral, only there—"

Marisol cackled, the sound unwieldy, like a needle being pulled across a vinyl record. "Javier? Javier thinks he's above it all, that he's better than me, than Vico. It's his fault Vico is dead."

"What? No, no, Vico did that to himself. Izzy, Memo, they made choices that—"

It was as if a switch was flipped. She started to shriek, the sound bouncing around the empty room. "Choices? They had no choices! I have no choice! I can't let that gringa get away with this! She's going to pay for what happened to my brother!" Spittle hung off her lips, her eyes huge and all black pupils. She put her hand to her head as if in great pain.

He imagined she was.

It was as if Padre Sebastian's legs had turned to stone. His stare locked on her. It was his job to read people, to listen and hear what they were really saying beneath their words. Could he have totally missed this? He'd known Marisol since she was a child, visited her mother in the hospital, organized a failed intervention for Vico. He knew she was damaged, but he'd thought she was more of a wounded bird, not a rabid dog. "Marisol, let's sit down and talk. Let me just—"

"It's too late for talking, padre."

July 9, 10:15 P.M.

Javier

💀

JAVIER PACED HIS apartment, wondering how he was going to make it through the night. It could be his last full night on earth and he was stuck staring at the four walls of his sad rented room like a dog in a kennel.

He couldn't breathe.

He grabbed his car keys and bolted out the door.

He didn't have a destination in mind but, as usual, the car found its way to the parish. He knew Padre Sebastian was probably at home sound asleep, but when he was stressed it comforted him just to see the building. His headlights swept the half-shadowed parking lot; they caught the metal trim of a car at the far end.

Sebastian was still there!

He parked and walked to the door. The building was dark, but the knob turned easily and Javier closed the door behind him. He smiled in the darkness. Padre was so bad about locking the doors, as if the neighborhood weren't rough. Not that there was much to steal, and besides, even the sketchy guys respected Sebastian. Javier decided to stretch out on the tattered couch in the rec room in case his mentor returned. He flipped the switches near the door and the fluorescent lights blinked and filled the room with sickly blue-white light.

Then he saw the priest.

He froze for a second, trying to understand what he was seeing. The dark red pool spread in a circle around the body on the floor.

Javier pitched forward, a sob catching in his throat.

"No!"

He dropped to his knees and touched the blood, as if he didn't believe it was real. Sebastian was dressed in his running clothes, a stain spreading on his vintage Chicago Bulls T-shirt. Javier felt like he was being strangled; no breath could get through his constricting throat. It was a nightmare, but worse than any he'd ever had, and his dreams were bad. He covered his head with his hands and started to rock back and forth, his thoughts clouding black instead of his vision.

Vico, Memo, Izzy, and now Sebastian?

No.

He couldn't make it without Sebastian, he just couldn't.

What would he do?

He grabbed his mentor's hand, pulling its dead weight into his own. He closed his eyes and held the hand against his face, his hot tears dripping onto the priest's knuckles.

I give up.

The thought was loud in his head.

He was done fighting.

This was more than he could take.

He stood, went over to the desk, dialed 911 on the phone, and placed the receiver on the desk. At least they would find his mentor soon.

But they wouldn't find him. Until after.

He closed his eyes, but he could still see Padre Sebastian's body in a pool of blood.

The scream came all the way from the base of his spine, the sound filling the room and rattling the closed windows. He ran out the door, leaving it open. He got into his car and turned it on. Javier beat his hands on the steering wheel, wanting his own blood to mix with the priest's that had darkened his fingertips. The car roared out of the parking lot and toward the highway as if it were driving itself. The lights along the thruway rushed by in a long, white blur.

He yanked the car to the right as the exit to El Norte appeared, careening around the concrete-walled corner on two wheels. It felt as if hot lava were coursing through his veins, hatred boiling up into his head, pouring out his eyes, his nose, his ears. He didn't wonder who killed the other cangrejos and Padre Sebastian. He already knew.

It was him.

He was the kiss of death to anyone he cared about and he would not add Lupe to that list.

He'd rather die and rob El Cuco of the honor.

Javier's car roared through the streets, running red lights. He slammed on the brakes in front of the dilapidated two-story building, stopping at an angle under the broken streetlamp, smashing into a metal garbage can on the sidewalk's edge. It was as if he had been there the day before instead of two years ago.

He had arrived at Omar's.

His dealer.

July 10, 12:15 A.M.

Marisol

💀

MARISOL WALKED ALONG the Malecón, the low sea wall that ran along the very bottom street in El Rubí. She walked and stared out at the glittering sea. The wind was blowing off the ocean in blustery gusts, the almost full moon's light struggling through a gauze of clouds. She loved the waterfront in the dark, the way the reflection of the lights skittered across the surface of the black water, the crashing of the waves not needing to compete with children's voices.

She'd gone to her abuela's after she left the priest. She'd tried to get Sebastian to understand, tried to warn him, but he wouldn't listen. But she left there and was able to have a relaxed dinner with her grandmother. Marisol had done what she could with Sebastian. Her conscience was clear.

Her abuela had tried to convince her to stay over—she didn't like Marisol driving to Isla Verde at this hour—but in the end the old woman was too tired to argue. She wanted to get sleep because there was a plan in place that required the cangrejo mothers to all be together, and she was standing in for Marisol's mother.

El Cuco. Marisol couldn't help laughing.

Not about the monster, no, she had no doubt he existed, but at the idea that the group of old women could have any control over a force such as El Cuco. They couldn't even stop Marisol's house being repossessed. Didn't even care.

The worst thing?

This whole ritual to call off the monster? Was Lupe Dávila's idea. Marisol's own abuela was in cahoots with the enemy. So disappointing.

The best thing?

Now she knew where to find Lupe Dávila.

And when.

July 10, 10:55 P.M.

Lupe

💀

LUPE GNAWED THE edge of her fingernail as she looked out the cruiser's passenger side window. Almost eleven P.M. and Javier was nowhere to be found. His phone went right to voice mail, and he wasn't at his apartment or his mother's house. Esteban left an officer waiting in front of their house, just in case he went there. She hadn't heard from him since he'd dropped her off at the house more than twenty-four hours ago, and the entire police force had been looking for him since they found Padre Sebastian. Who had stabbed the priest, and did they get Javier, too? And the question she really didn't want to face: What would happen tonight if they weren't able to stop El Cuco?

Lupe felt her uncle's gaze and she looked over.

"Javier is fine, he'll be there." He took his hand from the steering wheel and put it on top of hers. "I've learned a lot about people in my years of policing, and if anyone can beat this thing, Javier can. With all he's overcome, he's one hell of a fighter."

She loved him for trying, but she still felt a pressure on her chest. "What if whoever attacked Padre Sebastian followed Javier and . . ." Lupe felt disloyal speaking it aloud, like saying her worst fears would conjure them, make them true.

"I have cars looking for him all over the area and at the hospital where they took Sebastian."

"Any news on the padre?"

He shook his head. "He's in surgery, listed in critical condition. The good padre is in God's hands now."

That was what her family always said when they had no answer, when the outlook was bleak. Except her father. She suspected he had stopped believing in God long ago, but the rest of his family used those words like a poultice. It felt like a Band-Aid over a gushing wound.

She had almost forgotten about the two madres in the backseat behind the cruiser's bulletproof divider sitting on either side of her aunt. Maria held her sister's hand; Izzy's mother Luisa's eyes were red-rimmed and haunted. The women were silent and in the rearview mirror Lupe could see their eyes glued straight ahead, or out the windows, but none looked like they were really seeing. They had picked up Javier's mother last. She sat near the window, her hands prim and tight in her lap, tension coming out of her pores. Just before Lupe looked away from the rearview mirror, Mrs. Utierre's gaze caught hers and for just a moment they stared into each other's eyes.

Traffic was at a standstill, so Esteban flipped on the flashing lights and snaked the cruiser around the other vehicles. They were still several blocks away, but the music was already so loud that the closed car windows throbbed with the beat. They were waved through the police barricades and turned the corner onto Calle Amarillo, inching their way through the sea of people. Pulsing floodlights were sweeping the crowd from the far end of the street, and Lupe could see two guys strutting across the stage with wireless mics pressed to their lips, their dark sunglasses reflecting the lights that lit the stage. Even from a block away she could tell that neither of them was Carlos. Papi Gringo had a certain quality that electrified the air around him, leaving no doubt that you were in the presence of a star.

They parked last in a line of police vehicles. Keeping close to the car and away from the press of the crowd, Lupe climbed out and looked around.

The night was warm but not oppressive, the black sky crystal clear, the full moon like another spotlight shining down on them. The entire block was a sea of bodies, all moving to the music in waves. Lupe was always shocked at how dressed up people got on the island. Vermont was a very casual place, concerts especially. She loved the colors and fabrics, the skin showing on shoulders, the click of heels on the pavement. The air held scents of rum, beer, and fried pork. The energy that hummed over the entire event was like a tangible thing, something she wanted to touch.

She turned back to the car and saw her uncle helping the three women from the cruiser. Another pair of officers approached them with Carlos's and Memo's moms and Vico's abuela between them. Most of the mothers looked around with wide and horrified eyes, except for Vico's grandmother. She looked unhappy but resigned. The driving pulse and obscenity of the music was a language she understood from living in El Rubí.

Luisa approached Lupe since they hadn't yet said hello. Izzy's mother pulled her close. "Gracias, Lupe," she whispered. Lupe pulled back. She had been so certain Izzy's mom would blame Lupe for her part in his death. "For what?" Her voice cracked.

Luisa smiled sadly and rubbed her fingers over Lupe's cheek. "You tried, m'ija. You tried to save my Isadore. You knew him, he was attracted to danger like most kids are to a new bike. We all did what we could."

Lupe wasn't sure that was true, didn't feel it in her belly, but she smiled back.

Carlos's mother was serious, but totally at ease, clearly accustomed to her son's world. She was just as attractive and dynamic as her son, and Lupe noticed she was even wearing low-waisted skinny jeans; she was under the impression those were illegal for moms.

Las madres hugged one another and then joined hands like kindergartners on a field trip. Javier's mother looked emboldened by having her friends around her and began to yell over the throbbing music.

"Chief Dávila, are you certain it's necessary for us to be in this unruly crowd? Until my son gets here it seems futile. I mean I—"

With one look from the chief, Mrs. Utierre's mouth snapped shut and she shrank back in line with the other ladies.

"Lupe, do you think we should move them closer to the stage?"

It took her a minute to realize her uncle was talking to her. Asking her advice. The other officers and the women were looking at her as if awaiting pearls of wisdom from her lips. In that moment her tío's spotlight of attention spread, like suddenly her input wasn't just a game they played on the phone or in his backyard. Like her words held weight and meaning.

Lupe swallowed hard and nodded. "Yes, I think the key is to keep Carlos, las madres, and Javier, when he gets here"—she smiled reassuringly at Mrs. Utierre—"in the same vicinity, to try to reproduce what they did that night when they called him." Her voice sounded stronger, more sure with each word.

Her uncle shouted, "You heard the lady, let's move out!"

Javier, 11:35 P.M.

Javier pressed through the people, making his way toward the stage inch by inch. He felt strong, but out of his body, like he was watching this happen to someone else. He pushed by the smiling faces, mouths echoing each word of the artist singing onstage, and wondered if he'd stumbled into a carnival funhouse. He wanted to scream at everyone *How can you just go on like this?* These might be the last few minutes of his life and all around him it was apparent that everyone was just going to keep going no matter how many people were dead. Vico, Memo, Izzy, Sebastian.

He was ready to face El Cuco.

He had a few things to say to him.

The anger built in his chest like the fire under a grill. He imagined orange flicks of flame licking his internal organs, turning them darker little by little. . . .

Focus! He struggled to rein in his thoughts. His trip to the mission when he found Padre Sebastian had been in stark relief. The edges clear and crisp, the colors overly bright. But after that, well, after that the night was buried beneath a thick haze. He remembered weaving up the stairs to his dealer's, stepping around the people draped all over like discarded clothes, loud music blaring from inside the apartment. It was a scene from a dream, or a nightmare. He squeezed his way through the doorway and looked around for his dealer, Omar. When he blinked he could see flashes of Padre Sebastian on the back of his lids as if burned there, the blood seeping from the priest's body in slow-motion.

He remembered Omar appearing, slapping him on the back. "Hey, man! I knew you'd be back. Everybody comes back to Omar."

A woman, all big hair and breasts rising from her low-cut top like bread dough, pressed her messy red lips to his, the smell of cigarettes and alcohol overpowering him until he thought he would retch. He saw everything through a distorted lens, each face more monstrous and mocking than the next.

Then Omar was pressing a clear plastic bag with a vial, spoon, and fresh needle into his hands.

"First one's on me, pana."

Javier stared at the bag in his palm. The sight was so familiar, so comforting.

Five minutes was all it would take.

Five minutes and he could escape.

Five minutes and he wouldn't care if El Cuco was coming for him or not, wouldn't care that most everyone he loved was dead.

Then the darkness appeared at the corners of the room, only it wasn't just in his head this time. It was in the physical room, in the world, bleeding toward him like smoke. Panic tightened his muscles, pressed against his lungs. Javier dropped the bag to the floor in a rustle of plastic and an echoing *thunk*, and lurched toward the door. He had to get out before the darkness ate everyone, everything.

He could hear Omar's voice behind him. "What the hell?"

He gasped for breath. The door was moving farther and farther away.

When he finally caught up with it, he burst through the door, and when he got to the stairs they began to melt, the railing lashing before he could grab it, like a snake pulling back to strike. Each wooden stair seemed to disintegrate before he could step on it, and the voices around him started closing in. When he got outside, he leaned against his car and dragged in ragged breaths.

He hadn't given in.

He hadn't used.

But it held little comfort since reality had become darker than the worst trip he'd ever had.

He drove around through the night, into the next day. He realized that using was no way to honor the death of the man who'd saved him from drugs. Sebastian had taught him to face his fears, his addiction.

So to honor him, he would face El Cuco.

He rolled his head around, shook his shoulders like an MMA fighter, and headed toward Amapola.

One way or another, it ends tonight.

Lupe, 11:40 P.M.

💀

Lupe spoke to las madres, making sure her voice was strong enough to be heard over the din of the concert. She had to go ahead as if Javier was on his way, as if this was all going to work. "How were you standing when you spoke to the boys five years ago?"

Carlos's mother spoke up. "We held hands as we talked to them. It gave us strength."

Memo's mother cleared her throat. "Yes, it felt like we were supporting each other, mother to mother. I remember that feeling well. I was standing over here. . . ." And the women shifted into place, Vico's abuela standing in for her daughter.

Lupe tried to sound encouraging, though without Javier she was certain the ritual was futile. Hell, even *with* him who knew whether it would work? A week ago she hadn't thought monsters existed. But they had to try something. "Good, good. Hold hands, stand like you did that night. We need to bring this whole thing full circle."

As the women shifted, Lupe's gaze swept the crowd, hoping to catch a glimpse of Javier's curly head, to see his smiling eyes. Her aunt Maria came up behind her and put her arm around Lupe's shoulders.

"You know, when you said you wanted to see the real Puerto Rico, I didn't imagine this was what you had in mind."

Lupe laughed.

"So, sobrina, do you have a better idea of what makes you Puerto Rican? What part is Dávila?"

"I'm starting to. But I think by the end of the night I'll have a full answer."

Maria patted her cheek and stepped toward Esteban.

"Oh! Tía?"

Maria turned around. "Yes?"

"Is it too late to go to the caves?"

Maria smiled back at her.

The police officers stepped back, still behind las madres but giving them room to take one another's hands. As the last hand was grasped, the line of women was complete. They looked so incongruous among the crowd, like a line of sparrows in the middle of a sea of crows, but the people around them started to move back, giving them space.

Lupe stepped in front of them. "Great! That's great. Now all we need"—she glanced over at Javier's mother and saw pain in her eyes and imagined she had the same look in her own—"are the two remaining cangrejos."

Javier, 11:45 P.M.

☠

Javier saw Chief Dávila above the crowd, to the left of the stage. He didn't want to see the chief: he'd only try to stop him, and Javier wouldn't let anything do that now. He kept pushing but the crowd continued to shift and he ended up off course. He began to feel as if he would never get through.

Javier finally made it to the front of the crowd, his belly

against the stage. He stopped to catch his breath when a voice bellowed from the massive speakers.

"Ladies and gentlemen! I'm proud to introduce Amapola's favorite son, el jefe, Papi Gringo!"

The applause rose like a massive flock of birds until Javier could feel it shake his internal organs. All faces turned as the spotlights brushed back and forth across the stage. Javier looked up to see his friend, the only other living cangrejo, Carlos Colón, strut his way across the stage. When he reached the center, Carlos thrust his arm into the air with the beat, the crowd jumping up and down until it was as if the audience had a single heartbeat. Javier swore he could feel the asphalt pulsing beneath them.

While the DJ scratched, Carlos caught Javier's eye and his lip lifted in that grin that hadn't changed since they were five years old. The crowd pushed forward as Carlos moved to the front and Javier was shoved hard against the stage, the metal edge digging into his belly, the pulse of the music beating faster and faster.

He wondered if he would be cut in half and save El Cuco the trouble. He looked at his watch: 11:53. Seven minutes left.

Javier turned around, putting his back to the stage so he could lift himself up, and his eyes scanned the crowd. He saw Lupe just a few feet away, the circle of mothers right beyond her. She was talking to his mother. Las madres were there. He felt a warmth spread over his skin for this group of women who'd come here just to help him, to join in his fight. But there was no way he was going to risk their safety, too. Look how that had served Sebastian.

Someone was calling his name.

Lupe. She'd seen him. He looked up to see her reaching for him across the shoulders between them. He reached toward her, but she was being pulled farther into the crowd. No! He had to reach her. And how could she be pulled *against* the wave of people? How was she being pulled back when the crowd was pushing forward? "Lupe!" He shouted her name over the heads between them, and in that one instant he could see so many things in her eyes: relief, fear, confusion. She reached her hand out toward him, screaming his name.

Just then Javier's feet left the ground, the asphalt falling away beneath him. No! He still had a few minutes!

So this is it, he thought, his heart thrumming in his chest. In that instant he locked eyes with Lupe and he caught her panicked gaze. She was struggling against someone.

"No!" They were both screaming at once.

He heard his name booming off the buildings and knew that El Cuco had really come for him; despite all his hard work, his abstinence, he was calling Javier out in front of all of these people, in front of his mother, in front of Lupe. At least Padre Sebastian would not have to see his end, would not know that he had failed with Javier. He could feel hands around his upper arms and he looked up to see Carlos's bodyguards lifting him onto the stage, placing him next to the singer as if he were a chess piece.

Javier took a deep breath, grateful to feel the solid wood beneath his feet, to see all the people spread out in front of him.

He realized Carlos was talking about him into the mic. "This is my hermano, my fellow cangrejo, Javier Utierre! Give it up, mi gente!" The obedient crowd roared in response. Javier blinked and looked down at the mob pressing in toward the stage, the line of madres an eye in the hurricane of people.

He could no longer see Lupe.

"At midnight, in four minutes, this pendejo turns eighteen." Again a roar from the crowd. "So this next one's for you, man."

The instant the first notes of the synthesizer hit the heavy night air, the noise from the crowd reached a crescendo, a level that Javier didn't think was possible, then Carlos yelled the song's title into the mic next to Javier's ear.

"El Cuco!" The bass and drums built up as the lyrics began to pour out of Carlos's mouth, his scantily clad backup singers echoing the chorus and the monster's name as if they were in church.

Retribution, El Cuco will find you

Carlos's voice was echoing throughout the street.

Javier's head was buzzing. The audience was frenzied, pushing forward, and the space between the women and the crowd narrowed.

Retribution, it begins inside you

The police were having trouble holding the multitude back, away from las madres. He could see his mother and the others mouthing the Hail Mary in Spanish. He didn't even need to hear them; he could feel each word in his chest. The energy coming off his mother and the others was like the electricity that runs through the air before a storm. He'd underestimated them.

Retribution, he sees all you do

The crowd was singing along with Carlos, as if it were a hymn.

Javier looked at his watch as the glowing yellow numbers switched from 11:59 to 12:00, the date counter to July 11, a date that used to fill him with joy, images of new video games and bikes, birthday cake and a party with los cangrejos.

Every night I pray for you

He didn't feel any different. Maybe nothing was going to happen. Maybe he was safe.

Javier tried to take a step forward, hoping to find Lupe in the crowd, but when he looked down at his sneakers he realized he was no longer standing on the stage; his feet were off the floor just a bit, hovering. He spun around, expecting to see stagehands or someone holding him up, but there was no one.

El Cuco doesn't prey on you

As he looked at the shadow of his body on the stage, it felt like hot embers were catching across his skin. In that instant he thought of all those times in his childhood he'd dreamt he was flying, up and out of his too tidy house, away from Amapola. But this time he was being taken.

He whipped his head over to look at Carlos, who was still next to him.

Your fate is under your control

His friend was looking down at Javier's feet, his brown eyes wide, but he didn't stumble at all with the lyrics, he just put his arm around Javier's shoulders to hold him down, but then they were both rising, slowly, higher and higher above the stage.

Don't let him find and bind your soul

Javier could feel a pull from las madres, but something stronger was pulling him and Carlos from above. Javier looked up and saw a tunnel of darkness, the type he saw at the edges of his vision, in the room at his dealer's, but this was different, stronger. Tendrils of shadow reached down for him, flicking their thin, skeletal fingers.

Carlos was still singing beside him, but Javier could see fear in his friend's eyes.

Conscience is growing evil

Carlos was hanging there, the words to his hit song spilling from his lips into the metal mesh of the microphone, then spreading over the heads of the crowd like vapor.

Life's pumping through a needle
Your mother's words fade to black
El Cuco's cure will conjure that

Carlos. Javier pulled at his friend's hands. "You have to let go!" Javier yelled over the driving beat from the speakers and the screaming from the crowd. Javier could hear his words amplified over the street, like a voice from God. Was that how it felt to be Carlos?

The song was driving on and Carlos responded. "No way, man! You go, I go. We're in this shit together!" At that, a deafening roar came from the crowd in response and the wind picked up, the crescendo of the driving music, the screaming of the crowd, the pop of fireworks overhead, the garbage from the street pulled up in the shadow that cycloned around them both as they were slowly lifted into the dark night. Carlos was pointing his microphone toward the barely visible crowd as if this were just part of the show, as if it were their turn to sing.

Retribution, El Cuco will find you
Retribution, it begins inside you

Javier wondered when it had gotten so cold; he almost imagined snow among the swirling winds.

He heard Sebastian's voice in his head. *The monster always exacts a price.*

No.

Carlos didn't deserve this.

Javier pried his friend's fingers loose and watched Carlos drop to the stage. The singer landed on his feet as the crowd went absolutely wild. The last thing Javier saw before being fully engulfed in the shadow cyclone were the worried eyes of his childhood friend as Javier was pulled up and away from him.

Lupe

As Lupe watched Javier being pulled up, there was someone pulling her back by the neck of her shirt, yanking her through the flood of people to the darkened sidewalk, far away from her uncle and the safety of his police force. Javier had made it! But something had him, was dragging him into the building storm.

El Cuco was a black hole/tornado forming in the middle of a suburban street in a San Juan suburb? She had to get back, had to make sure nothing kept las madres from the plan. But who—or what—the hell was pulling her?

She reached back and grasped at the sleeves of whoever had her, her arms flailing against the press of people. Wildly she strained to see Esteban's men trying to subdue the crowd, las madres trying to keep their hands together. Lupe watched as Memo's mother's hand slipped from Mrs. Utierre's and instantly the energy retreated. It was like a vacuum had been shut off, and as she looked back at the stage she saw Javier rising faster, Carlos dropping to the stage, the cyclone pulling Javier farther and farther away. She was jerked to the ground away from the crowd, behind the sawhorses that lined the sidewalk. Lupe felt the concrete scrape skin off her palms, her knees, and she struggled to get to her feet, looking up at the shadowed face above her.

Then a knife was against her throat. The glint of the blade contrasted against the deep black handle, the yellow skulls glowing in the moonlight. Lupe froze, her chest heaving as she tried to catch her breath. Was this it? Was it her turn to die?

"Now, gringa. Now you pay for what you did to my brother."

A girl.

It was a girl's voice.

Lupe squinted in the darkness, trying to make sense of the features. Then she looked into her captor's wild eyes, and it was as if the last piece of the puzzle had just snapped into place. The blue car in Old San Juan. The texts. It was all Marisol.

"I never even met your brother!" Her voice was raspy over the music; it was hard to speak with the edge of the blade across her throat.

"It's gringos like you that stole our house from under us, idiotas like Javier"—she gestured wildly toward the stage—"who got my brother hooked on drugs! And killed my mother!"

Lupe laughed. Not the best response when a lunatic was holding a knife to your throat, but scared as she was, she couldn't help it. "So I'm to answer for an entire continent of people?"

Lupe felt Marisol's body tighten again and Marisol's face grew red. "You don't get it, gringa! Someone has to pay for what happened to Vico! To my mother!"

"Yeah, right. Look, let me up." Lupe made a move to stand. Before she got halfway up, Marisol drew back her arm and bashed Lupe across her jaw, knocking her head back against a garbage can behind her and back on her butt on the sidewalk. It felt as if Lupe's jaw had exploded, her teeth shifted. The taste of metal filled her mouth and she was having trouble focusing her eyes.

But at least her throat wasn't slit.

Why wasn't it?

Marisol shrieked in Lupe's face. "You think you're above it all? That you can take over the island, poke the bear? I tried to warn Padre Sebastian. But did he listen? No!"

Through a haze of pain, realization slowly dawned on Lupe. It wasn't bad enough that los cangrejos had El Cuco hunting them down. Since she'd arrived on the island Marisol had been threatening her, trying to kill her. And she'd stabbed the priest. El Cuco wasn't the only monster in this scenario. Lupe's eyes narrowed, fury foaming behind her eyes.

The music rose in a crescendo, the crowd throbbing with the beat.

Retribution, he sees all you do
Retribution

Lupe roared and threw her body forward at Marisol, both of them tumbling to the sidewalk. They rolled back and forth, stones and glass pieces from the sidewalk cutting through Lupe's thin cotton shirt, blood gluing the fabric to her back. Marisol was trying to go for her eyes, but Lupe managed to keep her just far enough away that she couldn't reach. The peaks of the concrete scraped the skin off the backs of her arms and she wasn't sure she could hold Marisol back much longer.

Why wasn't Marisol using the knife?

Lupe managed to push Marisol away enough that she could lift her leg between them, shoehorning in more space, until she pulled her whole leg back, aimed, and brought it up full force just as Marisol's bent down. There was a sickening crunch as her knee connected with Marisol's chest. Marisol let out a howl, hands flying to her chest. Lupe took the opportunity to scuttle backward on her butt, until she was just out of reach. She ran her finger over her teeth. They were all there, but her jaw felt like a cement truck had hit it. When she pulled her hand away from her mouth it was dark with blood and dirt.

They both sat back, breathing hard. This was never going to end, and her odds were only getting worse with exhaustion. She had to get Marisol to talk, to distract her so that she could get to Javier, that was the priority. "Javier was a victim, too. That night—"

"Don't talk to *me* about that night! I was there! Would they let me into their stupid little cangrejo club? No! But I got to share in the monster's curse!"

Lupe froze. "What?"

"You think I don't feel the same things they do? The dark shadows following me everywhere, the feeling that something's just ahead, waiting to get me? No, I didn't get to share in the brotherhood but I could feel their monster." Her whole body seemed to sag. "I just want it to be over."

So Marisol felt it all. It was like she was haunted. That didn't excuse what she had done to Sebastian. But Lupe had to get her to understand that tonight was different. "But Javier is clean; he worked hard to get there. El Cuco won't have to take him."

Marisol shook her head back and forth, a smile snaking across her face. "Such a gullible little gringa. I followed him last night, figuring he would eventually hook up with you. He went to his dealer's."

Lupe shook her head, but suddenly she wasn't so sure. "You're wrong. He must have been there looking for . . . doing something else." *Don't be an idiot, Lupe,* she thought. *If ever there were an excuse for a relapse . . . but he couldn't have . . . could he?*

Marisol shrieked again. "There's only one reason he would go there! He's just as weak as the rest of them." She glanced back at the stage. "And he deserves whatever he gets tonight. And he's the last one, so it will finally be over. I'll be free."

"You're lying." Lupe could hear the uncertainty in her own voice, the panic. If she wasn't convincing herself, she sure wasn't getting through to Marisol.

Another shriek and Marisol stamped her foot on the ground like an angry toddler. "Javier is bad, just like the other three cangrejos! I tried to warn them! I knew from that night that those drugs would destroy us all. When I sat there on that couch with my abuela I knew it in my bones those boys were going to ruin everything with their bad behavior. And look! My brother and mother! Gone! They took everything from me." She took a ragged breath and the mania decreased in her eyes, just a bit. "Now, it's midnight. Time for you *and* Javier to pay."

Lupe turned around, looking for a bottle, something to use as a weapon.

Marisol jumped her from behind, the duo staggering until Lupe was pinned to the garbage can, knife again to her throat. As the grip tightened, Lupe breathed deep, trying to pull away. It was no use. Marisol was way stronger than her, and so much savvier. *Who am I fooling?* she thought. Every one of her sixteen years had been uphill; it was only fitting that she should die on a street on her father's island, in over her head once again. She was tired of fighting, so tired. But she had to get to Javier; she had to try.

Marisol put her cheek close to Lupe's. "You should have stayed in Canada where you belong, hermana."

Lupe relaxed. "I'm from Vermont, bitch." She pulled her elbow up and jammed it back into Marisol's nose, blood flying out in an arc.

Marisol dropped to the sidewalk, the switchblade clattering to the ground between them. Lupe jumped to her feet and kicked the blade into the sewer grate, the metal clanging down into the bowels of the street below them.

Lupe cut through the edge of the crowd, her eyes searching for las madres. She needed to make sure the plan was in place. She had to find a way to get Javier away from El Cuco. As she neared she saw the women stretching their arms toward one another, the line broken, the cyclone onstage blowing out toward the crowd. She had to get closer to try to close the break. She pulled herself onto the stage, turned, and leapt out onto the crowd. People cheered and held her up over their heads and started to pass her backward, closer to las madres, whose frightened faces were getting swallowed by the crowd. As she held her arms out from her sides, it was almost as if she was finally flying.

"Tío!" she screamed over the heads around her. Her uncle was trying to push the edges of the crowd back. "Esteban Dávila!"

His head rose and she caught his eye. She pointed down at the broken line of women and then Esteban was pushing his way inward like a linebacker, cutting through the crowd. Just as Lupe reached las madres she tried to put her feet down, but the crowd was pulling her away, farther into the sea of people. She flailed her limbs, kicking people as they moved her along, and she started to shake. She had no control over her body, no control over where she was going, and the panic spread through her like flames. She began to sob like she was five years old again, and her mother was gone. She put her arms over her eyes, her voice now nothing more than a whimper, when she felt arms around her waist, pulling her upright. When her feet hit the ground she started to crumple, but her aunt Maria was holding her up, while a new group of police officers surrounded the mothers. Lupe watched the women reclasp hands, the air electrifying again, the crowd giving them space once more.

Lupe whipped around toward the stage again.

Was it too late?

It's retribution that rules the night
La madre's fateful words were right

Javier

☠

Javier noticed he had picked up speed and looked up, the tunnel of wind and refuse buffeting him from all sides, the dark void behind it all, deepening to the black of space above him. He shored up his shoulders to prepare for whatever awaited him, but he was terrified. Beyond terrified.

Then all sound stopped and Javier was suspended in the air, a sensation of being pulled from below reversing his rise. It made more sense to him in the middle of all the madness that he was being pulled down, not up.

Hell was down.

He looked toward his feet, expecting to see claws dragging him down, but as he squinted at his ankles he saw hands. Human hands, women's hands pulling on his ankles, digging into his jeans. And then he saw the glint of the yellow stone of his mother's ring. Were they on the stage with Carlos? Or were they in the crowd? That was the plan. He didn't want to put any of them in danger: that was *not* part of the plan.

He was about five feet off the stage now, his head even with a stand of large lights that were off, their glass reflecting the nightmare on the stage. As the wind brought him closer, he looked over and saw his face reflected in the clear glass of a light. He started to turn and just caught the sight of his eyes in the mirrored surface.

They were yellow with black reptilian lines for pupils.

A scream caught in his throat as the pull from above increased. For a moment Javier thought he would be torn in half, las madres pulling from beneath and El Cuco from above.

Lupe

Las madres' pull was working! Lupe hooted as she saw Javier's ascent slow, then reverse.

"He's going down!" she yelled back at the line of mothers in the crowd. But their eyes were closed in concentration, and the energy that was coming off them was so strong that Lupe's hair was blowing back as if from a breeze.

But when Lupe looked back toward the stage, she saw Javier moving upward, the grasp of the mothers slipping.

"No!"

It wasn't working.

Las madres' pull wasn't strong enough.

And there was no plan B.

Javier

When it was clear that las madres' hands below him were losing their grip, Javier looked up into the swirling cylinder of shadow above him, and in the darkness he saw two yellow glowing orbs like cats' eyes, the same as he'd seen in his own. As they got closer, a face was forming around the eyes, human-shaped but covered in scales, the nostrils nothing but two slits. His stomach froze as his stare locked with the creature's and it was as if all hope and joy were being sucked out of him.

He was ready. He had gotten clean, redeemed himself. Turned his life around. Damn it, his conscience was clean. He was ready to face El Cuco.

Retribution, it begins inside you

As he stared into El Cuco's face, the noises got farther away. Time stopped. It could have been a second or a year. The air around him was shifting, reorganizing itself into a different setting, the stage lights fading, darkness and silence buffering him.

He was standing in the middle of a street.

Huh? He spun around.

Wait, it was the block he grew up on, a few doors down from his house. The concert was only half a kilometer away, but there was no throbbing music, just the hum of traffic in the distance.

"Javi, I'm not sure about this."

He started at the whispered sound of his nickname, and noticed two thin boys walking toward him.

"Hey, hermanitos?" he called to them as they passed by, but they didn't seem to hear him.

"Man, Vico, for once in your life, don't be such a chicken."

Vico?

Wait.

Javier pulled ahead of the boys and looked at their faces.

Holy shit. It was him. A younger version of him and . . . Vico. Javier grabbed his head as if to stop it from spinning.

Vico stopped. "Nah, I think we should give it back. My moms will kill me dead, bro."

"You always do what your mom tells you to do?" Javier hated the taunting music of his childhood voice. He could see his younger self staring at Vico and realizing his friend was not going to budge. His tone changed. "Look, man, don't you want a fancy car like Keno? And money to buy whatever you want?"

Vico shrugged. "Yeah, but—"

"This is the only way we can get it, hermano!"

Javier's throat tightened as the glow of the streetlamp caught the shimmer of the bag of white powder in the center of his younger self's palm. He was holding it out just like Flaco had that afternoon in El Rubí, just like Omar had earlier that night.

"Look. Tonight's our thirteenth birthday party. Thir*teen*! We're practically men. So it's time to start acting like men."

"I don't know. . . ."

Javier watched the thoughts spin behind his younger face, and he wanted to shake him. To take the kid version of himself and scream, "Stop!" But he could do nothing but watch as he manipulated Vico.

"Look, you can even have this!" He put the cocaine away and pulled something from the back pocket of his jeans.

Javier felt his stomach lurch as he saw the black knife, the yellow skulls glowing in the lamplight.

"Really?" Vico stepped forward hesitantly and touched the knife. "I can really have it?"

Young Javier handed it over while a smile spread across his face. He knew Vico was hooked. "Of course. Keno gave it to me, but I want you to have it." He watched Vico press the button, the shiny blade flicking out like a snake's tongue.

"Whoa! It's so cool! Thanks!"

"You can be my lieutenant."

Eighteen-year-old Javier watched the thirteen-year-old version of himself and his now dead friend walk away, strutting with their new, dangerous toys, and his legs gave out. He dropped to his knees on the cracked asphalt.

It was him.

He had started los cangrejos on the path to El Cuco. Had he blocked that memory with a haze of drugs, or had he known all along?

It didn't matter. It was his fault his friends were dead.

An explosion started in his chest and roiled its way up his neck until it escaped from his mouth in a primal scream that echoed off the line of houses on either side. He looked up and saw the two boys disappear around the side of his house, heads bent together in excitement. He threw his head back and screamed to the night sky. "But I was just a kid!"

In an instant the wind swirled around him, lifting up his hair, his jacket. He had to close his eyes from the street's dust churning in the air around him.

Then it was still. Silence fell over him like a cloak. He opened his eyes and found himself in his mother's darkened living room.

"What now?" he whispered, as if he and El Cuco were in the middle of a conversation.

He stood at the sound of galloping steps coming down the stairs. Once again he was face-to-face with a younger version of himself, judging from the hair and the clothing about fifteen years old. As he watched his younger self put on a jacket with shaking hands, his movements jerky with impatience, he recognized the signs of withdrawal.

"Javier! Javier, stop!"

Cue his mother from upstairs. Javier braced himself for his mother's passive-aggressive abuse. This was a scene that replayed itself pretty much nightly when he'd lived at home. He crossed his arms and glared at his mother as she clutched at her robe with her thin fingers.

"Please, stay home, just for tonight. I worry about you."

Javier dropped his arms to his sides as he heard the concern in his mother's voice. The surrender.

His younger self whipped around as he swung open the front door. "Well stop worrying about me, Madre. Why don't you worry about yourself? Get out of this fucking house and live your own life for a change instead of trying to live mine! I can take care of myself."

Javier flinched at the language, the revulsion in his younger voice. The door slammed and both he and his mother stared at the back of the door. The sound of sneakered footsteps thumped down the front steps, down the walk. A car door opened, a rush of loud, thrumming music, a car door slammed, then the roar of engines and squealing of tires receded down the street and onto the avenida.

"Wow. What an asshole." His voice sounded loud in the quiet house. Then he noticed another sound. He looked over and saw that his mother had put her face in her hands, her whole body shaking.

"You've got to be kidding me." He padded over to the foot of the stairs, staring at his mother. She was sobbing. He'd never seen his mother cry other than conjuring a few crocodile tears for dramatic effect. But there hadn't been anyone watching that night. She lifted her face, her skin all splotchy, her makeup-free eyes red rimmed.

"Oh, Javier. I'm so sorry," she whispered.

Javier's throat tightened. It was as if she could see him, as if she were talking right to him.

He had an overwhelming desire to move up the stairs, to wrap his arms around her and comfort her. To tell her it was he who was sorry. But he couldn't make his legs move.

What difference would it make? She couldn't feel it anyway. He looked up, willing his eyes not to fill just as darkness swirled around him. He was relieved to feel it this time.

When the wind stopped, the light was blinding, and he whipped around to try to get his bearings. The scent of pizza, burnt coffee, and sweat was overwhelming. The echo of hundreds of voices, babies crying, toddlers whining.

A food court. He was at Plaza Las Americas, the island's biggest mall, in the food court. Why the hell would El Cuco bring him there? In that moment, a kid at the bright yellow table in front of him knocked over his Coca-Cola, the dark brown liquid spreading across the table and onto his mother's white jeans. She screeched, jumped up, and rushed over to get some napkins, leaving the now crying kid and her baby in the stroller with her purse hanging over the back.

Javier watched a skinny kid pass by, slip the purse off the handle in one swift movement, and lose himself in the crowd before the woman came back to the table dabbing at her stained jeans.

Javier yelled after him. "Hey! Hey you, kid!" He weaved in and out of the sea of people, keeping the kid's curly, overgrown head in sight. He ducked out a side exit and Javier caught up with him just as the kid pressed himself against a column, shadowed from the sun and traffic going in and out of the mall.

Javier approached as the kid was pulling the cash out of the woman's coral-colored wallet, the bright leather contrasting against the dirty, scabby hand. He slipped the credit cards out with practiced fingers, and threw the now-empty wallet into the manicured bushes that framed the entrance. When the boy whipped his head around to make sure he wasn't being watched, Javier's hand flew to his mouth.

It was him. But he'd known that, hadn't he? This version was painfully thin, dirty, and stealing from young mothers with babies in the mall. It was Javier right before Padre Sebastian found him, helped him clean up.

Javier screamed in the face of his younger self. "What's wrong with you?" Then again, toward the sky, "I cleaned up! I did the work!" But it was half-hearted. When he left Amapola he had turned his back on who he was, on his role in the life that had killed his friends.

As he was thinking and the younger version prepared to bolt, he heard a whizzing sound and felt a sharp pain on the side of his head.

He reached up to his ear and when he took his hand away he saw blood. "What the hell?" He whipped around—purse snatching was not exactly worthy of being shot at—but then he realized if it had been aimed at the kid, it couldn't have hurt him since he wasn't really there. A *pop* and another whistling sound, then the mall scene evaporated as if made of smoke, the pounding beat of Carlos's music rushing in to take its place.

Javier was once again suspended in the cyclone, but he could see straight ahead to the scaffolding behind the stage. Through the swirling refuse he saw someone hanging from the metal beams, pointing a gun directly at Javier's head.

Keno.

Javier was still in El Cuco's grasp, but this was no memory. This was happening. "Keno?"

Keno moved the gun away from his line of sight, and a smile snaked across his face. "Who you expecting, Javi? The boogeyman?"

Javier's mind scrambled to figure out what was happening. It wasn't enough that he was suspended in a supernatural hurricane, now he had this gangsta trying to shoot him? But words weren't coming easily. "Why?"

The smile dissolved. "You kidding me? I have the chief of police climbing up my culo because of you!"

"It's not my fault you're a thug!"

"Don't bother. Because of you my business is dead. Dead, man! With all the heat I've had to pull back. Other players are trying to move in."

Javier put up his hands. "Look, the life isn't worth it." He gestured down to his shoes, suspended twenty-five feet off the stage. "I know what I'm talking about. You'll have to pay at some point."

"Yeah, well, Carlos's efectos especiales don't impress me."

"They're not special effects! You see any wires here?" He moved his feet back and forth, waved his arms.

"Whatever, man. I got work to do and you're in my way." He pointed the gun again and squinted to take aim.

Javier braced himself for the bullet. Ironic to go out this way before El Cuco could take him. He closed his eyes and pictured los cangrejos before their lives went off the track. Swimming beneath the waves at Luquillo Beach. In the background he heard the cocking of the pistol, a crash of glass breaking, the crack of a shot.

He felt nothing.

Javier opened his eyes to see Keno leaning back and looking toward the ground. His gaze followed and there was Lupe at the base of the stage tower, pitching bottles up at Keno.

"Cut it out, you gringa bitch!"

Lupe took aim and launched another bottle up at Keno like a softball, hitting him squarely on the thigh. "That's *Ms*. Gringa Bitch to you!"

Javier laughed and Keno growled at him.

"You need a little white girl to fight your fights for you now, Javier?" Then he switched the aim of the gun down toward Lupe. "We'll see how you feel when I take out your little snowflake girlfriend."

Javier watched Keno's thumb move to cock the gun. All that was going through his head in that split second was: no. He was not going to be responsible for another death, even if it meant his own. And with that thought, he launched himself toward the tower and at Keno. He was able to throw his body at Keno's, and grasped for the gun. Keno swiped and kicked at him, all while hanging with one arm from the metal bars. Javier had Keno's arm under his, and had his fingers wrapped around the barrel when Keno lifted his knee and kicked Javier in the stomach, hard. Javier lost his grip on the weapon and it left both their hands in slow-motion, falling to the ground in a clatter.

Keno was pissed then. He started punching at Javier's head, but with the movement of his arms he lost his grip on the bar and started to fall backward. Javier lurched forward and caught Keno by the sleeve. Keno dangled, looked up into Javier's eyes, and said, "Don't you drop me, pendejo!"

Pendejo? The guy was insulting him while he saved his ass? *I should just let him drop,* Javier thought. But really, how close had he come to being Keno? Who was he kidding? If Sebastian hadn't found him he would totally be Keno.

Or dead.

He'd be dead.

Keno looked at the unforgiving asphalt below him and back at Javier, his eyes panicked and pleading. Suddenly he didn't look like an evil drug dealer. He looked like a scared kid, not all that much older than Javier.

Javier reached down and pulled Keno up until he could once again wrap an arm around the crossbar.

"Thanks, man." Keno was breathing heavy, but then an oily smile spread across his face. In one swift move he bashed his free fist onto Javier's fingers that were wrapped around the metal bar, and Javier struggled to hold on.

"See? I don't even need the gun. I should have just stabbed you like I did that idiot Jamaican priest." Keno was yelling over the background of wind and music.

Javier's blood froze in his veins. "*You* stabbed Sebastian?"

"What the hell?" Lupe's voice came from the ground beneath them.

"Yeah, he wouldn't tell me where you were. Vico's crazy

sister tried to warn him. Disloyal bitch. But enough talk, time to die." Keno lifted his fist to bash Javier one final time.

Something black whizzed by Javier's head, he heard a thud, and then Keno was falling.

Lupe

💀

Lupe watched a combat boot whack Keno on the side of the head, and he fell two stories down to the pavement. She looked down but she had both of her shoes. She looked over and saw Marisol standing there with one sock-covered foot. Lupe gaped at her.

Marisol shrugged. "What? No one stabs a priest on my island."

"Nice boots."

Marisol nodded. "Well, they're for combat." She gestured to her bleeding nose. "Nice move."

"Yeah, you know. Combat."

They smiled at each other.

"This is sweet and all, but I won't forget you tried to kill me."

"I never tried to kill you, I was just gonna scare you, to make you go back to Canada—"

"Vermont!"

"Whatever."

"You didn't need to try to run me over with your car. Or send me threatening texts!"

Marisol tilted her head. "What?"

"In Old San Juan."

"That was Keno! He borrowed my car. I was surprised since it's way too ghetto for him. And I didn't send you any texts!"

Javier

After Keno fell, Javier hung there for a moment with his eyes closed, grateful. Then, the air began to move again, the tower shaking with the growing wind, and Javier screamed in total animal rage.

After all that, El Cuco was still going to take him.

As the cyclone rebuilt around him, the pain began. He felt as if his skin was being ripped from his body in sheets, the water in his eyes boiling from the heat. But worst of all was that with the darkness came a feeling of overwhelming solitude. For most of his life, all he'd wanted was to be left alone, to not have to rely on anybody else's help. Particularly in the last two years. But in that moment, he saw his solitude as dark and empty, here at the precipice of a black hole that was sucking any memory of love or friendship from his soul.

Everyone dies alone, he thought. But here, at the moment of his death, all he wanted was to *not* be alone.

For the first time since his father left, he prayed for help.

Lupe

Lupe stared up at the cyclone rebuilding above the stage. She could no longer see Javier through the swirling darkness.

She looked over at Marisol, her mind buzzing.

There had to be something. She managed to keep her father

alive on a daily basis, but getting her friend back from the grips of a mythical monster might be beyond her skill set.

Wait. What had her father said during their phone conversation?

"'It's actually the children who have all the power.'" She said it out loud as it came back to her. "'If I'd known that as a child I would have been threatening her with El Cuco!'"

"What are you going on about, gringa?"

"It's something my father said. 'Children have all the power.' Los cangrejos were kids back then for sure. But there are only two left and they don't seem to have any power in this situation." She gestured back up to the stage.

"Yeah, but they weren't the only children there that night El Cuco was called."

"You! There weren't five, there were six!"

Marisol's eyes widened with memory. "That was the night I knew the drugs were going to ruin my family."

Lupe nodded, following.

"And when my mother and the others threatened the boys with El Cuco, I secretly hoped he would come, that he would punish those boys." She looked back at Lupe. "I—I was just a kid."

"But between you and las madres, maybe El Cuco was listening." She pointed over to where las madres still held hands, their faces etched with exhaustion, their mouths moving in prayer.

Marisol grabbed Lupe by the arms. "I have to call him off, too! The ritual isn't complete without me!" Then she stopped. "Wait, why should I? Javier earned his place up there."

Lupe stared into the other girl's eyes, as if she could climb into them and change her mind. "He did. He absolutely did. But what about second chances? Don't you believe in them?"

Marisol paused. "I do, but I'm just not sure Javier deserves one. Carlos is an asshole, but he never used, never broke a law in all the years I've known him. Why do you think he's still alive? El Cuco wouldn't take *him*!"

"True, but look at Carlos!" She pointed up at the star. "He hasn't taken his eyes from Javier, he's staying right there even though his life is in danger just standing near the storm from hell. Doesn't that say something about Javier's worth?"

Marisol looked into Lupe's eyes and for the first time there was no sign of contempt or anger in them. "You're his friend, too, that says even more. One small problem, though. I don't know how to call him off!"

The girls looked around as if the answer lay on the sidewalk around them. Then Marisol stopped and grabbed Lupe's hands into her own. "Help me! Hold my hands, close your eyes, and we'll ask him to leave Javier be! Ask him to just leave!"

Lupe closed her eyes and concentrated on the places where Marisol's cool, smooth skin touched her own. She imagined giving all her power, what little power she had, to Marisol and las madres. She thought of her father, of Esteban, of the people who meant so much to her, and imagined their power going into Marisol as well. Nothing. She felt nothing. There had to be something else they could—

Her hair.

It was blowing back, as if she were standing in front of a fan.

She opened her eyes and saw that Marisol was emitting power like las madres. Her clothes, her hair, all were pulled away from her body as if the wind were coming out of her pores, but it was even stronger. Marisol seemed unaware, her eyelids moving as if her eyes beneath were watching a private performance.

Lupe held tight, but looked above the stage to see the cyclone hover, just above the tops of the streetlights. Then a powerful blast came from the mothers and from Marisol and the tornado's outside wall started to break up like a windshield shattering, the dust and garbage floating for a split second, then all fell to the stage.

Including Javier.

Javier

Javier closed his eyes, certain he was heading for the very bowels of hell as he fell.

But then his feet hit the ground as if he had only jumped a fence or a wall.

He opened his eyes and spun around as he stood up, his bearings seemingly lost forever. His feet were on the ground, but the darkness of El Cuco was still swirling above him, as if waiting for something; at least it had stopped pulling him. For now.

He saw Lupe climbing over the edge of the stage. He grabbed her hand and pulled her up, and as soon as her feet hit, she wrapped herself around him, her whole body shaking. He kissed her hair and whispered soothing things.

Marisol walked up the stairs behind them, and Javier whispered, "Thanks."

Lupe pointed up to the swirling darkness above them. "Why is that still here, though?"

"That's what I'm worrying about. *The monster exacts a price.*"

"But what's the price?"

"Um, guys? I think I know."

Javier and Lupe whipped around to see Marisol standing at

the top of the stairs, Keno, blood streaming from his temple, holding his recovered gun to her head.

Lupe actually started to lurch toward them when Javier pulled her back against him. "Even you can't win against a gun, amor," he whispered into her ear.

Javier could see the police gathering at the base of the stairs, guns drawn, but they didn't dare make a move while Keno held a gun at Marisol's temple.

Despite the threat, Marisol's voice was cool and clear. "I only dated you because hanging out with your little gang was better than going home to my cousin's house. But only slightly."

Keno snickered. "Well, I put up with you because I figured you were so crazy I could get you to do shit, like kill this guy. But for all your talk, your conscience got in the way."

"That's because Marisol is a human, and you're the real monster, Keno. Sebastian was right." Javier spat at him.

"Ah, yes. The good padre did quite a bit of threatening at the end. He shouldn't have called the police and given them my name. God rest his soul."

Lupe held up her hand. "But Sebastian's not dead."

"What?" Javier and Keno said at once.

Marisol snorted. "Guess you failed yet again, Keno."

Javier must have heard wrong. He could still see the padre's body on the floor. It was etched behind his eyes. "Are you serious, Lupe? He's not dead?" She nodded, never taking her eyes from Keno, and Javier felt as if he were lifting off the stage again, with joy and relief this time.

"Well, maybe now I'll really kill someone you care about." He slowly moved the gun from Marisol's head, keeping his arm around her neck. "Like the Canadian bitch, for instance." He slowly lowered the gun to point it at Lupe, clearly enjoying the drama.

"She's from Vermont," Marisol said and then, before he was

able to aim, she brought her elbow back and up, catching Keno right in his nose, blood flying onto the stage.

Marisol pulled away and ran to stand with Lupe and Javier as the police rushed up the stairs toward Keno. In that moment the darkness from above began to turn fast, the pull like a vacuum above them. The police weren't able to get closer to Keno, it was like they were walking into a wind tunnel. Javier and the girls held on to one another, hovering closer to the stage so they wouldn't get pulled in.

Javier looked back and saw that Keno was lifting, his body leaving the stage, holding his bleeding nose, his eyes frantic. "Wait! What's going on?" He looked all around as the stage dropped farther and farther below him.

Javier, Lupe, and Marisol watched as Keno rose up in the sky, his screams piercing the air until he was swallowed into the black hole and the cyclone disappeared.

Lupe

Lupe could feel Javier's heartbeat against her own, and she didn't want to ever let go. With her eyes squeezed shut she could almost forget the sight of Keno being lifted up into the void, the sound of his screams getting farther and farther away.

She opened her eyes to find that Javier was looking at her, their faces almost touching. "Javier, what happened up there? Did you see El Cuco?"

"Oh, I saw him all right."

Marisol asked, "Well? What did he look like?"

Javier chuckled. "That's hard to say. I think he looks different to everyone."

Lupe wasn't satisfied with that answer. "What did he do to you up there? I mean, before Keno showed up?"

Javier smiled down at her. "I think he took me to the Narcotics Anonymous meeting from hell."

Lupe cocked her head. "What does that mean?"

Javier was silent for a moment. "It means that I had more of a role in all this than I ever imagined." He shook his head. "I don't know what it all means. All I know is that I have another chance to make amends."

"Let's give it up for my hermano Javier!" Carlos's amplified voice bellowed around them. Javier put his arm around Lupe's shoulders and steered her toward the stage. Lupe reached back and grabbed Marisol's hand, and dragged her with them. At first Marisol made to pull her hand back, but Lupe knew it was an act. Carlos gave Javier a huge hug and, when he pulled away, looked deep into his friend's eyes. They were two of only a handful of people who knew what had really happened there that night. The two cangrejos who survived. And then Carlos pulled away and gestured to Javier's left.

"And let's not forget my sister in the good fight, badass Lupe Dávila!"

Lupe stared at Carlos. Did Papi Gringo just call her sister? And a badass? She'd always fantasized about having a brother, a normal, bickering family. Well, normal was a relative term. In her daze she looked over the crowd, which was yelling for her. For her, an attitudinal Gringa-Rican from Vermont. She saw las madres in the middle of the crowd with their arms linked, looks of exhausted relief on their faces. The whole thing felt so surreal, like it was happening to someone else. It was like . . . having a family. This handsome boy with his arm around her, a new friend beside her who had as much attitude as she did, a rock star calling out her name, a monster thwarted. Her eyes fell on her tío in the crowd. His face was above everyone around him as he stood over to the side, not wanting attention as was his fashion. But his smile was all Lupe's. He smiled at her all the way to his eyes in a way that said all was real. That all was good.

That he was proud.

The thumping in her head.

It was gone, truly gone!

And there was no feeling of a darkness behind her, next to her.

Nope, the only thing next to her was the crazy gringa who had saved her life and whose life she'd saved.

For the first time in five years, Marisol felt hope.

Carlos took Marisol's hand and smiled at her and she could remember why she had such a crush on him when they were younger. Lupe held on to her other hand, and Carlos pulled the line of friends into a bow across the stage, the crowd screaming in one joyous wave.

As she stood up, Marisol saw her abuela in the crowd in front of the stage waving. Her abuela smiled and blew her a kiss. She looked like she was ten years younger than she had been yesterday. Maybe they could get an apartment together back in Amapola. Start to work to bring the old neighborhood back.

Marisol squeezed her friends' hands, dropped them, and headed toward the front of the stage. She might have been set free, but this was still way too much attention for an introvert. Several people from the crowd helped her off the stage, and she made her way to her abuela and hugged the tiny woman tightly.

Javier

Carlos's stage manager was slapping the star on the back. "Man, I wish you'd tell me when you plan surprises like that, but that was dope, pana!"

Javier smiled at Carlos as all the stagehands congratulated the singer on the special effects. As the crowd called for an encore, Javier and Lupe made their way backstage. In the shadow of the massive speakers, they turned back to watch Carlos fire up another of his hits.

Javier kept thinking about how unreal it all seemed. What an insane night. Would he have been killed if Marisol hadn't joined las madres to call him off? Javier stood there, his arm around his girl, most everyone he loved in the world with him on this Amapola street on his eighteenth birthday. No way he was going to take any of it for granted.

"So, Miss Lupe. Does this mean you're going to take your uncle up on his offer and come live in Puerto Rico?"

She shrugged. "I don't know. But I'm looking forward to the summer more than I ever have before. And for now, right now, I feel at home."

Lupe put her arm around him and held her cell up, and images of their two smiling faces with Carlos strutting on the stage in the background popped up on the phone's screen. She typed for a minute, then put it away. "Had to post it. No one back in Vermont is going to believe me."

After a few bars of the song, Lupe yelled into his ear over the music throbbing from the speakers, "My Spanish might be rusty, but is this song really entirely about a girl's butt?"

Javier smiled. "Yes. Does this offend you, Miss Lupe?"

"I'm just glad it's not about yet another monster waiting in the dark."

He gently tugged her chin up to his. "I'm not worried. We'll fight it off together." He leaned in, thinking only about pressing his lips against hers, but as he neared she pulled back. Javier felt his heart fall as if he were dropping to the stage again.

"Lupe, I—"

"No, wait." She put the tips of her fingers against his lips. Her smell of sun and apples made his head spin.

"I need to know that you're not going to use again."

He took her fingers from his lips and gently kissed them. "You know a promise like that from an addict is worthless."

She nodded and pulled farther away. "I know." He could almost see the fear tumbling around in her mind.

Javier stared into the blue of her eyes. "But I *will* promise that I never want to go back to that place." He pointed up into the memory of the cyclone, of El Cuco above them. "And I'll work every single day to make certain that I don't. Not for you." He pointed to his own chest. "But for me."

Lupe was looking into his eyes as if she were searching for something. He watched a series of emotions pass over her face. Then a small, sad smile pulled up the edges of her soft, pink lips.

That was it. She was done with him and he would accept that. He'd done all he could do, and though it made him sad, he didn't blame her.

"Well, I should get you to your uncle—"

He didn't get a chance to finish his sentence. Lupe grabbed the front of his shirt, pulled him against her, and kissed him.

Acknowledgments

There are so many wonderful humans who provided support in this endeavor it is hard to include them all without another fifty pages!

Overpowering thanks to my agent, friend, and fellow Boricua, Linda Camacho, who saw the potential in this story from day one and helped me bring it to fruition. My brilliant editor, Ali Fisher, who loved Lupe as much as I did and helped make this a stronger, cleaner, and fleshier novel. My fabulous publisher, Kathleen Doherty, and the Tor Teen team, including production editor Melanie Sanders, art director Peter Lutjen, designer Heather Saunders, interns extraordinaire Sarah Yung and Anna Parsons, the Macmillan sales force, and the Tor/Forge marketing and publicity team. Thank you all for your support and belief in this project.

Huge gratitude for my brother, George Hagman, who read the manuscript more times than was his sibling duty, gave me great feedback, and shares my love of good horror. My Vermont College of Fine Arts (VCFA) family, specifically the MFA in Writing for Children and Young Adults program. I cannot adequately express the support and love this community has given me. Especially our president, Thomas Christopher Greene, who has been a mentor in my writing and professional life from the very beginning. And, at VCFA, Sharon Darrow, Dana Walrath, and Daphne Kalmar, my power writing group whose early feedback was invaluable. Gary Miller and Gary Moore, a pair of talented writers and friends who read and gifted ideas to me. Sarah Madru, Rene Lauzon, and Sabrina Fadial, who read early versions and gave me emotional and psychological support and friendship throughout. Domenic Stansberry, who, on a balcony in Puerto Rico, taught me all about minions and human threats (Marisol wouldn't have come into being without Domenic). To fellow speculative writer, Vermont Latinx, and dear friend and author William Alexander, who gave me friendship and lunches where we talked about monsters, and a fabulous blurb! To writers I idolize and respect who were willing to do a blurb read of my little ol' manuscript: Julianna Baggott, Nova Ren Suma, and Cynthia Leitich Smith. Generous and lovely literary citizens all. A special thank-you to Mary Cronin and Jim Hill, fabulous writers and friends and my submissions support group. I would have given up on it all if not for you.

Thanks to my sensitivity readers, Fernando Betancourt and Bianca Vinas: gracias, lovelies! Mi prima Tere Dávila, who not only did a sensitivity read, but took me around the island for research, talking it through and making invaluable suggestions (though I ignored her repeated urging to "Kill the priest! You've got to kill the priest!"). And my cousin Carlos Dávila, who would get bizarre messages from me about local expressions or the geography of the island and would reply quickly and with enthusiasm. And my beloved tío Esteban, who got texts like, "What kind of gun would a heroin dealer have?" and answered with no question as to why the hell I was asking. Ed Baker, MSW, for his professional input on narcotics addiction and addict behavior (any mistakes were totally mine and not his). Sheryl Scarborough and Nicole Griffin, dear friends, brilliant writers, and amazing beta readers who brought this to another level. My mentors who are young enough to be my children but smart enough to be my betters, Cori McCarthy and Amy Rose Capetta (AKA the Queer YA Power Couple), for their unrelenting advice, support, and enthusiasm. Miciah Bay Gault, my friend and partner through this incredible publishing journey . . . we did it, girl!

And as always, to my beloved husband, Doug Cardinal, who read through the book and was my rock and go-to person through the entire process. I'm so grateful for our long conversations on the porch about addiction and plot. My lovely and talented son, Carlos Cardinal, who not only supported me emotionally throughout, but wrote the El Cuco reggaeton song for his namesake, Carlos "Papi Gringo" Colón.

I am grateful to you all!

Turn the page for a sneak peek at
the next novel from Ann Dávila Cardinal

Available June 2020

Chapter One

Bio Bay, Vieques Island, Puerto Rico

RIGOBERTO SIGHED. ONCE again the trio of gringo college students devolved into a splashing fight, using their kayak paddles to fling arcs of glowing water at each other in the velvety dark. The miracle of bioluminescence, organisms that lit up the water like microscopic fairies, was totally lost on them. Not to mention they clearly weren't taking classes in maturity at their pretentious Ivy League university. Rigo had only just finished high school, but he was about three decades more evolved than these douchey frat boys.

He glanced over the dark bay, the stars of the moonless night reflected in the black surface of the water as if there were heavens above and below. After Hurricane Maria the mangrove trees were practically stripped clean, but now, nine months later, though they weren't yet tall, they were proud, their roots digging deep beneath the salty water, holding strong. It would take a lot more than a category five hurricane to destroy those trees.

Not that these a-holes would appreciate the magic of the place.

He breathed deep and prepared his "guide voice."

"Gentlemen, if we could get back to the tour . . ." *so I can dump your asses downtown and head to Bananas for a cold beer and an intelligent conversation with my friends.* But he left the second half of his thought unspoken. Insulting tourists didn't go over well. He'd tried it more than once.

"Yeah, cut it out, you apes!" The leader, Jason, chastised the others with a smirk even though he was the one who had started it.

Rigoberto had met many versions of this kid during his various summer jobs on the island. They always came with an entourage, since, he figured, bullying was no fun alone. He glanced at his watch: 8:15 p.m. Only forty-five minutes more. That's all Rigo was contracted for. He could survive that long. He sat up straight and returned to tour guide mode. "The tiny island of Vieques was inhabited by indigenous peoples, the Taínos, fifteen hundred years before Columbus set foot in the Caribbean."

"Indigenous, huh?" the smallest one said, then patted his mouth and did a racist hoot, laughing. But even his Neanderthal friends seemed to recognize how offensive that was and no one laughed with him.

Actually, no. That was giving them too much credit. They just seemed to ignore everything that one said.

No one would blame me if I strangled them all and left them here. Seriously.

He twisted in his seat to look back at the group, taking a head count without even thinking. It was something you had to do when running tours. Four. He faced forward.

Wait, what?

He spun his head around and looked over the group. One, two, three. Phew! That was weird, he could have sworn he saw a fourth head. A chill passed over his skin despite the warmth of the evening. This whole trip had him on edge. To top it off, that night the bay looked . . . darker somehow. He was used to giving these tours in pitch blackness since it was the best way to see the dinoflagellates light up, but there was something . . . menacing about the dark. Another shudder ran through him as he felt something brush across the back of his neck. He just needed to finish this tour so he could go back to civilization and shake this creepy vibe. He turned around and continued in a monotone voice since they weren't listening anyway, and they clearly weren't capable of actual learning. "Then, it was taken over by the Spanish, and eventually in 1941, the United States military took over two thirds of the land, displacing residents and, some say, taking advantage of the island when they were struggling to recover from many tragedies."

"Hey, watch it, ah-mee-go. My dad was military," Jason said.

"Of course he was." Rigoberto gave him his best and biggest patronizing smile. "So was my father, actually."

"What, like, in the Puerto Rican army?" The hairy imbecile named Steve asked.

Rigo winced. "No, the same military. You do understand that Puerto Ricans are U.S. citizens, don't you?" Okay, so *the tone* was in his voice, the tone his boss had warned him about. *They're assholes, but they come from very important families, so don't give them that superior tone of yours,* he had warned Rigoberto. But sometimes he just couldn't help it.

"Hey, I don't like your tone."

Great, now Jason was channeling his boss. He bit his tongue: he had to deescalate things. He needed this job. High school was over, and it was time to save for college. His family's restaurant had closed in the spring. Winter tourism was nonexistent since they hadn't had power and the palm trees looked like they'd been gnawed on. "I intended no disrespect, of course."

The guy grinned at him. "Of course." Then he went back to lazily running his paddle through the water.

But Rigo knew he wouldn't get off that easily.

Jason proved that by adding, "You do understand that our parents could buy this island out from under you, right?"

Don't take the bait, Rigo told himself. *Don't do it.* He kept paddling.

Jason followed with "Oh wait, we already did!" and the group dissolved into uproarious laughter and a round of fist pumping.

As he pushed his kayak through the glistening water, Rigoberto fantasized about hitting them all over the head with his paddle. "Let's continue with the tour, shall we?" Wasn't it enough that the kid Jason's father had helped buy a huge chunk of land out from under the locals to build a monstrosity of a hotel? Now he had to take this abuse? He clenched his teeth tight, the tension spidering up from his jaw into the sides of his skull.

"Why does the water glow like this again?" The one named Steve asked, as if they hadn't already gone over it several times.

Rigo took a deep breath. "As I was saying, the overly salty water of the bay is the perfect environment for the dinoflagellates, the plankton who light up the water when it's agitated—"

"Hey, like you, Steve!" The little whiny one in the last kayak interrupted.

Steve turned around. "Wattya mean?"

"Dino-flatulence! Get it?"

Steve gripped his paddle with his overly hairy hands, his knuckles whitening, and Rigo had this weird feeling things were about to get out of hand. Was Steve going to beat the kid? Was that where the dark feelings were coming from? Rigo watched him carefully—with no plan to intervene, he wasn't stupid.

But then a smile spread on Steve's face and he used his paddle to splash the other guy.

Rigoberto took a deep breath. Lord, his thoughts were dark tonight. But as the group sprayed one another, he realized this could go on all night. "Okay, okay, why don't we paddle our way across the bay to the other side where I can show you examples of red, white, and black mangroves." They moved a few yards, the only sound the dripping of water off their wooden paddles. A rustling sound came from among the greenery that ran along the shore.

"What was that?" Steve whispered, and they all froze, their heads turning nervously, staring into the darkness.

One by one they looked into each other's eyes and Rigo saw they were all scared. So, it wasn't just him. But he didn't hear anything unusual in the quiet night. "It's probably one of the stray dogs that roam the area," he whispered. The trio was silent for a few more minutes, listening as they looked around with big eyes. *Just enjoy the quiet,* Rigo thought, his heart rate slowly returning to normal. But the quiet was short-lived.

"Man, this is boring as shit." Jason threw his paddle down into the water and it hit with a blue glowing splash. Rigo watched it begin to float away and thought there was no way in hell he was going to chase that paddle down. Jason swayed in the kayak, holding his arms across his chest like a petulant toddler. A lot like a petulant toddler. He was certainly compensating for his fear the moment before. He was peacocking, chest out, bravado back in place. But Rigo could see from the dart of his eyes that he was still nervous. "Why do we have to stay in the boats? It's not like we can't swim."

"Except for Kevin," Steve added.

"I can too swim!" So, the little one's name was Kevin.

Now the toddlers were arguing. Rigo wasn't paid enough to babysit entitled spoiled rich white kids, and he really was anxious to put the bay in the van's rearview mirror. So weird—he was usually more comfortable out here than in town. The edges of his voice got sharper with his impatience. "You can't swim here because the organisms in the water are very sensitive."

He ignored the exaggerated whispers mocking his slight accent "Ooh! Very 'sen-sa-teev'!"

"The chemicals on your bodies—deodorant, sunblock, insect repellent—kill them. We need to protect the delicate ecological balance of the system—"

Jason cut him off. "Ah, I see now. You're one of those liberal tree-hugging types. Wanna save the planet, and shit."

Don't engage, don't engage, the voice in Rigoberto's head warned. But he'd had enough, so he ignored it. "Don't you?"

"Don't I what?"

"Want to save the planet?"

"Nah, man! You can take my Hummer over my dead body!" Fist-pumping again.

"Hopefully that could be arranged." Rigo said under his breath.

Obviously not quietly enough.

"What did you say?" It was said low, but challenging, like a growl.

But Rigo's mouth didn't seem to be under his control anymore. "Actually, it's narcissistic, entitled attitudes like yours that got us in this—"

He was midsentence when Jason stood in his kayak, trying to reach for Rigo. He stood swaying back and forth as he balanced in the narrow boat as if surprised it were on water. He seemed as if he was distracted by the movement and was using it to forget about beating Rigo to a pulp. "Oh, screw you and your dino-shit!" Then he raised his arms over his head and dove headfirst into the water, the blue glow surrounding him as his arms and legs scissored beneath the surface.

Yeah, Rigo was about at the end of his patience.

"I'm afraid I'm going to have to insist we return to the van if this behavior continues." Great. Now he sounded like his third-grade teacher, Mr. Rodriguez. He hated Mr. Rodriguez. He looked around for Jason to surface.

But it was quiet. Too quiet. The water calm and glass-like. Where did Jason go?

"Hey, do you guys see that? Those shapes under the water?" Kevin whispered as he leaned over the side of his canoe and peered into the dark water.

Rigo looked where Kevin was pointing. Did he see something too? "It's probably just Jason," he said quietly, though he wasn't at all sure it was Jason.

Steve chuckled nervously. "You're afraid of the freaking wind blowing, Kevin!"

Kevin's voice was shrill. "No, there's two! Look! They were around here somewhe—"

A pale hand reached up from beneath the surface, the water dripping from it in black rivulets like blood. Its fingers stretched and coiled and pulled the edge of Steve's kayak over, dumping the large guy into the water in a pinwheeling mass of limbs.

Oh good, maybe something will eat him, Rigo thought, until it hit him that perhaps he was in danger, too.

Kevin screamed in a high-pitched voice, desperately paddling to turn his boat around. "See? See? I told you there were shapes in the water! Human shapes!"

Rigoberto looked at the two abandoned kayaks and began to wonder how long Jason had been under. Was it too long? Was there really something else in the water?

In that moment, two figures broke the surface and pulled Kevin into the water.

And suddenly, Rigo was sitting there alone in the middle of the bay. His heart was pounding as his kayak rocked gently from side to side. Was he next? He grabbed his paddle and, without a sound, placed it just above the water. He could make it to shore if he really booked it, then go get help.

Just then two forms breached the surface with a huge gasp

of air and Rigo screamed . . . then recognized Jason and Steve as they shook the water off like large dogs, laughing and sputtering. Rigo was horrified he had actually been nervous for a second there. The splash and *thunk* of the kayak was followed by the cackling of the two other men as Kevin sputtered and shrieked to the surface, all three of them in the water now, probably killing the dinoflagellates with their entitled negativity alone.

Rigoberto felt heat rise beneath his face.

Basta. Enough.

He efficiently turned the kayak around and started for the shore, the welcome silhouette of the van calling to him. For the first time that night, he felt good. He'd leave these assholes to get back to town themselves. He'd retrieve the kayaks in the morning. He'd catch shit from the institute's director, but it would be worth it.

He got out in the ankle-high water, yanked his kayak onto the sand, and secured it, dripping wet, onto the trailer behind the van. He climbed into the driver's seat and smiled big as he turned the key and the engine came to life. "Have a good walk back, assholes!" he yelled out the driver's side window as the van's headlights lit up the road sandwiched between dense foliage. He could still hear the sounds of roughhousing coming from the water as he pulled away. The idiots hadn't even noticed he'd left. "Serves them right." He fiddled with the radio and found a station playing reggaeton. He tapped the wheel along with the beat of Papi Gringo's latest hit, "Tormenta." Perhaps his night could be salvaged.

He was out of earshot when the screaming began.

Chapter Two

Marisol

WHEN SHE ARRIVED in Yabucoa, Marisol parked her 2001 Toyota Corolla under the only available shade, a caimito tree that was still able to protect her car from the sun even as it worked hard at pushing through the sidewalk with its tangle of roots. Not that she was worried about the paint job; no, the once-steel-gray finish had been beaten to jellyfish translucence by the Caribbean sun. It was more about the broken air-conditioning and a long-ass drive back to San Juan on Friday.

Not that it was sunny. There had been threatening dark clouds hovering on the edges of the overcast sky for days now, like actors waiting for their cue. But hadn't they had enough storms for several lifetimes? The drive along the east coast was beautiful despite the weather. You could see the scars from the hurricane, sure, but all the new growth was neon green and it made her happy to see life going on.

Life going on.

She was trying to figure out what that looked like. Life had been anything but smooth for her thus far, but after Maria . . . well, any kind of complaining felt frivolous. So, this summer she was determined to make a difference. To that end, she grabbed the petition she'd created at 2:00 a.m. that morning when she couldn't sleep. This kind of protest seemed to make the most sense until the island was back on its feet again. So many people were busy trying to meet basic needs, she wanted to help give them a voice.

Marisol took a swig from her bottle of water and walked through the center of town toward the church that had become the operations hub for all the volunteers and organizations doing repair work in the area. Pablo, an ancient man who set up his folding chair near the town's barber shop every day, waved at her and smiled his warm, toothless smile. She waved as usual and started toward the church.

No.

She stopped, convinced herself to turn around, and made her way toward him. Deep breath. "Señor, I have a petition to stop the purchasing of land by companies attempting to profit from the devastation of the hurricane." Here it comes, the ask. Best to practice on this mild old man first. "Would you be willing to sign it?" She thrust the clipboard toward him. "You'd be my first," she added, somewhat pathetically. He peered at the paper, and then looked up at her. She gave him the broadest do-gooder smile she could muster, but, truthfully, she worried it just looked like she was in pain. But he smiled back, took the proffered pen, and signed the first blank line with a shaking hand. When he gave it back to her with a nod, she let out a breath, smiled, sincerely grateful, and stepped away.

One down. She looked at the shaky scrawl on the first page, then held it to her chest in a hug. She could get used to this.

She'd been coming to this town and staying during the week since school let out for the summer, and she was getting to know the locals and the other volunteers from the island and beyond. She was usually more of a loner, an introvert who preferred a good book to human interaction, but there was something about being here for a shared purpose. And having to talk to hundreds of strangers for the petition was a perfect demonstration that she was not the same person she'd been a year ago.

But who was?

There was a nice breeze on the east coast, and she loved how she would occasionally catch the scent of flor de maga blooms riding on the air. Then it would disappear so quickly she would wonder if she'd imagined it, if it was a ghost scent of a bush destroyed by the storm. But then she would see a splash of bright red peeking out from among the damaged foliage like hope. As usual, she planned to stop at the church's senior center before heading to the worksite to check in. She stepped into the dark, cool building, with no lights on to save generator fuel and stave off the morning heat. The smell was so familiar—antiseptic, medicinal, with an undertone of urine and talcum powder. Okay, it wasn't flor de maga, but it still comforted her. For most of her childhood her great-grandmother Giga was stationed in a back room of their house, occasionally yelling out to the Virgin or her long dead husband, and Marisol would spend hours playing dolls on the old woman's chenille bedspread or applying blush and lipstick on her wrinkled, thin lips. On the island old age wasn't something you hid in a nursing home; it was right there in the next room.

"Mari!"

As her eyes adjusted to the dark interior, Marisol saw Camille, the stylish Haitian nurse who helped out with the elderly patients, walking toward her. Camille was a pro, had volunteered as a nurse in war-torn countries all over the globe, and it had taken Marisol awhile to earn the woman's trust. But sometime over the last few weeks, she'd broken through. A smile here, a hand pat there. Now, Camille pulled her in tight for a hug, the Magi's-gifts smell of her naturopath oils bringing a smile to Marisol's face. Her graying hair was cut stylish and short, and her clothes were crisp linen, practical but elegant, the mango color of the shirt a warm companion to her dark brown skin. In other words, she was a total badass.

The nurse pulled her out of the hug and held her at arm's length and then did her "staring into her soul" type thing. Did all nurses have that skill?

"Are you sleeping, Mari?"

And she was a mind reader, too. She laughed it off. "Too much to do to sleep!" Camille had no idea. Since the nightmares of the previous year had faded, she slept so much better. Just probably not long enough.

Camille did that cheek-pinching thing older women tended to do with teenagers. The woman's skinny strong fingers had a pincer-type feel. But it also felt like family.

"You have to take better care of yourself, niña! Don't make me drive out to Isla Verde and force chamomile tea on you!"

Family always includes just a dash of guilt and reprimand.

"I'm fine, Camille! Worry about your patients, not me."

Her lips pulled into a reluctant smile. "Someone has to take care of you. You're too busy taking care of everyone else!"

"Look who's talking."

Camille did that dismissive wave thing again.

"How's Abuelita today?"

Camille turned to look at the tiny old lady in the wheelchair nodding off in the corner, her frail body wrapped in a thick cotton blanket despite the heat. Her real name was Ofelia Gutiérrez, but everyone just called her "Abuelita" because she was like everyone's grandmother.

"Ay bendito, bless her, she's doing well today, gracias a Dios. I think she'll enjoy a visit from you." Camille glided off to reprimand one of her charges for shuffling toward the exit in his old-man slippers. Every hour or so he would insist he was going to walk back to Rincón, the town on the far west coast of the island he came from, and she would convince him to wait until after lunch, or a nap, or dinner.

Marisol pulled a folding chair next to Abuelita and took her cool, dry hand with its papery skin into hers. The woman didn't move, her chin on her chest, rising slightly with every breath. Mari's phone dinged with a text. She pulled it out with her free hand.

Hey! I'm here! Heading 2 Vieques w/ Tio. When can I c u?

"Vieques?" Marisol said out loud, smiling at the message from Lupe. She was so glad her friend was there for the summer, but why was she going straight to Vieques? At least it wasn't far from Yabucoa.

"Vieques?" Abuelita echoed. She tended to repeat pieces of conversation that happened around her like a gray-haired parrot.

"Hola, Abuelita! Es Marisol. ¿Como se encuentra?"

"My grandmother is in Vieques. She's . . ." She appeared to lose her train of thought. Another frequent occurrence.

Marisol smiled. Abuelita was eighty-eight. She doubted her grandmother was in Vieques or anywhere at this point. Besides, Abuelita was from St. Croix, not Vieques. But Marisol hated how most people talked to the elderly as if they were children, so she always responded to their questions and comments, no patting of hand and patronizing, *Sure, honey, whatever you say.*

"Why would your abuela be in Vieques?"

Abuelita didn't seem to hear; she was nodding her head up and down in that way she did when she was lost in her own thoughts. Marisol decided she would sit with her for a few more minutes, then head over to the worksite. She was already focusing on what lay ahead on the repairs to the Vazquez's house when Abuelita spoke again.

"She's angry."

"Who? Your abuela?"

"Yes. She's so angry. . . ."

"At you? No, Abuelita, who could be angry at you?" She stroked the woman's thinning hair, trying to comfort her. Mari often wondered where the woman's thoughts went, or when. She would have to do some research into cognitive functions of the elderly.

"Not at me, at them. They made us leave . . . left her there alone," Abuelita said again, then looked up at Marisol and with tears welling in her cloudy eyes.

"Oh no! Don't cry! It's okay!" Marisol's throat tightened and she thought she would cry too. How had she upset the woman?

And then Camille was there, all comforting hushes, and lifted Abuelita to her feet gently, as if she were a bird, and walked her over to her room. Abuelita was snoring before the nurse had finished tucking in the white blankets.

Then Camille came back and looked over at Marisol and noticed the tears in her eyes. "Oh no, sweetheart, it's nothing you said! The old ones, they get sad sometimes. So much loss . . ."

"She was talking about her grandmother being angry. And on Vieques. Isn't she from St. Croix?" Camille handed her a tissue and she blew her nose.

"She is, but maybe she had family from there. Don't worry, amor, she's just confused."

Marisol shivered, though the room was quite warm. No wonder the poor old woman was anxious. She'd lost her home to a hurricane. Marisol swallowed so she wouldn't start crying again. She hugged Camille and left quickly, anxious to get to work.

The last ten months had been like something from a post-apocalyptic nightmare. Volunteering was something, but Marisol had to do more. She looked at the clipboard in her hand

and considered tossing it in the car but decided she would bring it to the worksite and gather some more names. But what good was the petition if she couldn't get it to the right people? The people in power.

Marisol vowed right then that she would do whatever it took to help get the island past this, whatever she could do to help people like Abuelita recover from Maria.

She just didn't know how yet.